Chris Cander

THE WEIGHT
OF A PIANO

Europa
editions

Europa Editions
8 Blackstock Mews
London N4 2BT
www.europaeditions.co.uk

A catalogue record for this title is available from the British Library
ISBN 978-1-78770-210-3

Cander, Chris
The Weight of a Piano

Book design and cover illustration by Emanuele Ragnisco
www.mekkanografici.com

Prepress by Grafica Punto Print – Rome

Printed and bound in Great Britain by Clays Ltd, Elcograf S.p.A.

For my lovely Sasha

THE WEIGHT OF A PIANO

Hidden in dense forests high in the Romanian mountains, where the winters were especially cold and long, were spruce trees that would be made into pianos: exquisite instruments famous for the warmth of their tone and beloved by the likes of Schumann and Liszt. One man alone knew how to choose them.

Once the leaves had fallen and snow blanketed the ground, Julius Blüthner made the trip from Leipzig by train and walked through the forest alone. Because of the elevation and the brutal cold, trees there grew very slowly. They stood straight and thick against the elements, their grain dense with rosin. Blüthner nodded to the young trees as he passed, occasionally brushing their bark in greeting. He sought the older ones, whose branches he couldn't reach, whose diameters were so great he couldn't see if a bear were standing behind the trunk. He knocked them with his walking stick, and pressed his ear against them as his intuition dictated, listening for the music hidden inside. He heard it more clearly than any other piano maker, better even than Ignaz Bösendorfer and Carl Bechstein and Henry Steinway. When he found what he was listening for, he marked the tree with a scrap of red wool, which stood out bright against the snow.

Then the lumberjacks he'd hired cut down the trees he'd chosen. Watching closely, Blüthner could tell which were the finest specimens by how they fell. Only those with a minimum of seven annular rings per centimeter, all evenly spaced, would be carried out of the forest on sleds, then shipped back to Germany. And the finest among these would become the soundboards that beat like hearts inside his famous pianos.

As protection against splitting, the logs were kept wet until they reached the sawmill. There they were quarter-sawn to unlock the purest tones, then sawn and planed into uniform planks. The wood chips went into the furnaces to heat the mill and power the steam engines. Because of knots and other imperfections revealed in the cutting, many of the precious tonewood planks also ended up in the furnaces. What was kept was nearly perfect: white in color; light and flexible; the faint traces of the rings densely spaced and running parallel across the faces of the soundboard planks. These raw boards were stored for at least two years, covered and uncovered until their humidity dwindled to about fourteen percent.

When it was ready, the wood was transported by horse cart to the enormous Blüthner factory in the western quarter of Leipzig and laid out on racks near the ceiling in hot rooms for many months. But even then it wasn't ready to become an instrument. To ensure that the soundboard would someday conduct Blüthner's peerless golden tone, the wood had to dry out for another few years in the open air.

It was with reverence, then, in 1905, that an assistant *Klavierbaumeister* selected a number of those carefully seasoned planks and glued them edge to edge to form a single board. He cut it to the proper shape and planed it to the proper thickness, flexible enough to vibrate but strong enough to push back against the pressure of more than two hundred strings. Once crafted, it was returned to those warmer rooms to dry further before thin ribs could be applied to its underside, perpendicular to the grain lines. Then the soundboard took on a small amount of moisture, enough to allow its top to swell into a gentle curve, upon which the bass and treble bridges would sit, their downward pressure meeting the apex of the opposing curve as if around a great barrel. The *Klavierbaumeister* admired his work: the impeccably matched parallels of the grain, the precise curvature of the crown. This particular soundboard would provide the heart for the factory's 66,825th piano.

The frame of the case was built by other craftsmen, its five back posts sturdy enough to bear the weight of the soundboard and the iron plate. The pinblock was cut and fitted. The agraffes were seated into the plate at a height that would determine the speaking length of the strings, which were then strung; tuning pins were hammered in, and the action set and fitted. Cold-pressed felt was layered thick onto the wooden hammers, thinning appropriately toward the delicate treble side. Dampers were installed next, along with the trapwork of pedals and levers, dowels and springs. The case was ebonized after the guts were in, requiring countless coats. The finishers' arm muscles bulged above their rolled-up shirtsleeves.

Next the instrument, nearly complete, was tuned, the tension of each of the 220 strings adjusted to the correct pitch. Then it was regulated, the touch and responsiveness of the action attended to until the motion of the fingers on the keys would be properly transferred to the hammers that struck the strings.

At last, after many years of effort by many expert hands, the piano was delivered to its final station for voicing. The *Meister* there lifted the linen blanket covering it and passed a hand over the shiny black top. Why should this piano be special? Each one was special, with its own soul and distinct personality. This one was substantial but unassuming, mysterious but sincere. He let the linen drop onto the factory floor.

"What will you say to this world?" he asked the instrument. He shaped the hammers one by one, listening to every string, shaving and minutely aerating the felt again and again. He was like a diagnostician, knocking the nerves below a patient's kneecap, measuring the response. The piano called out each time in compliant reply. *Hello, hello.*

"*Fertig*," he said when the work was done. He wiped the sweat off his forehead with his sleeve, pushed the wisps of white hair away from his face. Standing back from the piano, he regarded this complete and brand-new entity that would be—after being played in properly—capable of incredible feats. The first few years were unpredictable, but over time it would open up and gather into itself a unique history. For now it was a perfect instrument, characterized only by its potential. The *Meister* fluffed his apron as he sat down on the barrel he'd borrowed for a seat and, flexing his fingers, considered which piece to christen the piano with. Schubert, his favorite composer. He would play the rondo of his penultimate sonata, the big A Major; the opening melody was pretty, with a feeling of hopefulness and joy that preceded its more pensive, agitated development. This would be the perfect inauguration of the glistening black Blüthner No. 66,825.

"Listen!" he called out, but nobody could hear him above the factory's ambient noise. "Here she is born!"

And he pressed his finger down on C-sharp, the first note of the rondo, listening hard, and it rang out to meet him with the innocence and power of a child's first cry. Finding it as pure as he'd hoped, he began to play the rest of the sonata. He would send off this shining new piano with as much optimism as he could gather, knowing it would no longer be as vestal once it was touched by its future owners' desperately human hands.

C lara lundy kicked a step stool against the front tire of an old 1996 Chevrolet Blazer and leaned over the engine, tossing her dark blond ponytail over her shoulder. She unscrewed the cap of the relief fitting and put a shop towel over it to catch the gas that leaked out when she pressed the valve. When the lines were bled, she stuffed the towel into her back pocket and went to her toolbox to grab the 16mm and 19mm wrenches and the quick-disconnect tool. Then, with an athletic jump, she disappeared into the yellow-framed pit so she could work from underneath. She removed the bracket, released the snaplock fitting, and pulled the rubber hose off the outlet side of the filter first to keep the fuel from dripping in her eyes. She'd learned that lesson long ago in her uncle's garage and had never forgotten it.

"Hey, Clara?" Peter Kappas, one of the shop owners' three sons, peered down at her. A halo of late afternoon sunlight outlined his bulky silhouette. "That guy with the rack-and-pinion job's back again. He says it's still making noise."

"Same noise or new?"

"Popping. Bolts, probably."

"Can you do it? I'm not done with this filter."

"I promised the Corvette would be done by five."

Clara slipped the new filter into the bracket. "Okay, give me fifteen. I'll get it up in the air and see what's going on. But if it's the mounting bolts, then you'll have to do the alignment again. You got time?"

"For you?"

"Stop."

He raised his arms. "Kidding. Yeah, I can do it."

After she tightened all the bolts and checked the lines, she went back up to prime the system. She turned the key to On, waited for the fuel pump to kick on and off, then switched the key to Off. She did that a few more times, and sitting there, she glimpsed herself in the rearview mirror and was startled to see that she looked older than her twenty-six years, like she'd aged a decade overnight. Her eyelids, in spite of the little bit of makeup she'd put on, were still vaguely puffy from her crying jag the night before. Her mouth was set so hard that tiny lines radiated from her lips; she'd been clenching her teeth. When she relaxed her jaw, her pale cheeks seemed to sag, and her mouth turned down at the corners. There was a smudge of grease across her forehead—probably from having pushed her bangs out of her eyes—that resembled her late father's birth-mark. She looked at herself, at his light brown eyes and pale eyelashes, their matching high cheekbones, and felt a gut punch at this unanticipated image of his face in the mirror. An old grief added to the new.

She turned the key all the way, and the Blazer's engine fired up perfectly.

"Clara! Phone for you!" someone called above the noises in the shop: the hydraulic torque wrench and the air compressor, the glide and slam of toolkit drawers, the relentless clinking of metal, the ever-present *laïko* music coming from a grease-covered boom box in the corner, the shouts in Greek and English.

She wiped the stain from her forehead with the dirty towel as she walked over to the phone that hung on the wall. Peter's brother Teddy stopped her with a hand on her forearm.

"It's Ryan," he said. "You might want to take it in the office." Who knew what they'd been saying about her and Ryan. Peter's mother, Anna, could read her face as though

Clara were her own daughter and turn an opinion—*I don't think this Ryan is good for you*—into a topic for general discussion. Clara usually found herself offering supporting information without even meaning to, and the entire Kappas family soon knew all her personal business. She didn't mind, though; they were the closest thing to a real family she'd had in a long time.

Clara nodded. The office was little more than a desk against the wall in the waiting area, between the water cooler and the coffeemaker. It was hardly private, but there weren't any customers inside at the moment, and Anna, who was behind the counter writing an order for parts, winked at her and said, in her thick accent, "I'll give you a minute."

Clara sat down and tried not to look at the flashing caller-on-hold light on the phone. She gazed instead at the framed photos on the wall of the Sporades Islands: the family's whitewashed villa, the curved rock beach, the impossible turquoise water.

When she could avoid it no longer, she took a deep breath and picked up the line. "Hey," she said.

"You're not answering your cell."

"I'm working."

"Whatever, Clara. Listen, I'm taking off for a few days so you can pack up your stuff. I really want you to be out by the weekend, okay?"

"Wait, what? Seriously? I thought we were still talking about everything."

"Clara, did you not hear me last night? I'm tired of waiting for you to make up your mind. You just don't want what I do."

"I never said I didn't want the same thing, I just asked for time." She turned her body toward the wall. "Ryan, please."

"I know you needed time, and I've tried to give it to you. But I can't keep putting your needs ahead of mine. I'm ready to move forward. I want a family. I'd like it to be with you, but if it can't be . . . well, what choice do I have?"

"Look, I love you, Ryan, you know I do. But marriage is a big step. Why can't we just be together? Why's everything such a rush?"

"What is it about making this permanent that freaks you out so much? I know you love me. Why can't you just say yes?"

Clara sighed. She could change this conversation, change her entire life, with just one word. But she couldn't do it. "I don't know. I'm sorry."

"Then we're done. I need you out. I need to move on."

"So you're really going to kick me out? After two years you're giving me, what, four days to move? How do you expect me to do that? And where am I supposed to get the money for it?"

"You know I wouldn't leave you on the street. I found you an apartment in East Bakersfield. I already put down the first and last month's rent. I figured this would make things easier."

"Jesus, Ryan. Couldn't we have talked about it first? *East Bakersfield?*"

He made a huffing sound. "Do you really care where you live? It seems like all you really care about is that damn garage."

She balled the spiral phone cord into her fist, fighting the urge to cry again. Was she crying over losing him? Losing her home? Her own indecision?

"The lease and key are on the kitchen table," he said. "When you're out, you can drop your old key through the slot."

Clara rested her forehead against the wall and exhaled. "So that's it?"

"Yeah, that's it."

He paused, they both did, and she wondered if he'd say what he always did at the end of a phone call. *You're my girl— you know that, right?* She couldn't speak. She couldn't let go. She leaned forward in anticipation, waiting, yearning, yet reluctant to give in.

"Good luck, Clara. I hope you figure out whatever it is you want, I really do. I'm just sorry it wasn't me." Then he hung up. She held the phone against her ear, listening to her heartbeat until the busy signal began beeping. When she turned around, Peter was standing at the door.

"You okay?" he asked.

She didn't answer right away. Maybe she hadn't really loved Ryan after all, certainly not how he wanted her to. But she was used to being with him, to having someone to go home to, and life with him had been easy. "Will you help me move?" she asked Peter.

He pulled off his ball cap—*Havoline, Protect What Matters*—and raked his fingers through his thick black hair. "Of course," he said, and put the cap back on. "You know I will."

Clara refused both Anna's suggestion that she leave early to take care of herself and Teddy's invitation to stop by the Early Ford V-8 Club swap meet to help him pick out some flathead engine parts for a restoration project. Instead, she splashed water on her face and went back to work. She'd told Peter she'd handle the rack-and-pinion job, and she would, even though she knew that under the circumstances he'd gladly do it himself.

When she was finished, she returned her tools to their places in the chests that lined the wall beneath a shelf of Chilton service manuals, gathered up the dirty towels and threw them into the rag bucket, and told everyone good night.

Peter stepped across the open pit and the greasy cement floor and met her at the open bay door. "We're going for a beer later," he said. "Want to come?"

"Thanks, but I have to start packing."

"Want some help?" Peter asked. She could've mouthed the words as he said them. At least once or twice a day, whenever he'd finished whatever he was doing, he'd wander over to wherever she was to see if he could lend a hand. When Ryan was out of town, as he often was, Peter would show up with cling-wrapped plates of his mother's cooking or tickets to a game or a DVD to watch. During the most recent forest fire, he'd defied evacuation orders and driven to her house and convinced her to go south with him to the coast. Clara had always prided herself on maintaining her composure, something her mother would've admired as stoicism. Even if she was sick or lonely or worried, she was always "fine" to anyone who asked. Yet Peter could always tell when she wasn't, and there he'd be, loyal as a dog, never asking for anything in return. It grated on her, how much she relied on him. She allowed herself to like certain people, but that didn't extend to needing them. Especially him.

"No, you guys go," she said with a small wave. "I'm good. I'll see you tomorrow."

Outside, though the sun was low, there was no relief from the stagnant heat in the air, no westerly breeze to blow away the visible heat rising off the cars' quivering engines or to move the thin, dust-covered palm trees that lined the chainlink fence by the road. Clara stood next to a stack of old tires that separated the Kappas Xpress Lube entrance from the trailer park next to it, looking out between passing trucks at the empty dirt lot across the street. The soot and ozone that always hung in the air in Bakersfield seemed especially thick and yellow today, like the sky was infected with something.

She played a game with herself: if she turned around and someone was standing there watching her, Peter or even one of his brothers, she'd go back inside and say yes, let's go get a beer. She would postpone the inevitable return to the rental house she had shared with Ryan, where a different key to some unknown place awaited her. She could have a beer or two or maybe three and forget that she was about to start over, alone, again. She looked back just as Teddy was pulling down the rolling door on the last open bay from the inside, and she took that as a sign. When there was a break in the traffic, she jogged across the street to her car.

She stopped at the Mexican grocery store where she and Ryan had met and subsequently shopped, and immediately regretted it. The piñatas hanging from the ceiling and *banda* playing over the loudspeaker seemed too festive for her errand. She asked someone stacking produce if they had any empty boxes, and while he went to find some she browsed the liquor department for beer. Ryan had been fussy about alcohol, especially beer, talking importantly about bitterness, notes, and finishes. He never drank straight from a bottle, insisting that it diminished things like creaminess and mouthfeel. Clara strode past the displays of craft brews and imports, picked up a sixpack of Pabst, then went to the checkout to pay and collect the stack of collapsed boxes the worker had left for her there.

Katya, come. I have something to show you."

Ekaterina Dmitrievna looked from her father to her mother, who was kneading dough for their dinner—again there would be no meat or butter. Her mother smiled and nodded. Katya put down her doll, took her father's extended hand, and they walked down the hall of the four-story prewar apartment building, through the scent of cabbage and the sound of babies crying, past the tattered propaganda posters. EXPLOITS ARE WAITING FOR THE BRAVE! BREAD—TO THE MOTHERLAND! POWER TO SOVIETS—KHRUSHCHEV! She was tired—they all were tired—but for her it was because she'd lain awake all night in her small bed listening for the music that had stopped three nights ago.

"Where are we going, Papa?"

"*Chi-chi-chi.* You will see. A surprise."

Katya grew anxious, though, as they approached the apartment belonging to the old blind German. He'd been her father's acquaintance, a client. Her father visited him more often than he did his other customers, because his piano went out of tune so frequently. "He plays too hard," Dmitri told his daughter. "He puts all his sadness into his songs. Bad for the piano but good for me, eh?"

The German had been banging on his piano for as long as Katya could remember. Mostly he played at night, when the children in the building were trying to sleep. The music made them restless and their mothers angry, but they feared speaking up. They imagined they knew what he would say in his gruff, bellowing voice: *It is always night to me!* He rarely left his rooms, and whenever he did he groused loudly in German as he shuffled his too-large body down the halls, knocking into the walls with his cane, his empty blue eyes roving over everything. He grew monstrous in their imaginations, and the neighbors whispered rumors about him that might or might not have been true: Wilm Kretschmann was not his real name. He had volunteered with the Waffen-SS. He was half Jewish, not one of Hitler's Aryan *Herrenvolk,* but still had killed hundreds of Jews and partisans. He'd defected from his SS division, *Das Reich,* in 1941, before his ethnicity could be discovered, slipping away from his unit in Naro-Fominsk during the Battle of Moscow; Hitler would've had him executed otherwise, because no "subhumans" were allowed membership in the Waffen-SS, even if they were willing murderers. He'd hidden in a textile factory, listed as missing, until the Wehrmacht had been pushed back by Soviet forces. He'd been blinded by either shrapnel or guilt. Who knew how he'd made it to Zagorsk? He had made his money as a building contractor or a thief. He still carried his Mauser HSc in his jacket pocket. The music was proof of his torment. He was a monster, a demon, an ogre.

Katya loved him.

The first time she followed her father to the German's apartment, she was six. The door had been left ajar. She slipped inside and crouched down against the wall, her back pressed against the peeling wallpaper, ready to run if she had to. Her father didn't see her; he was bent inside the case. The German sat straight in an old chair like a soldier, looking at nothing, his ear cocked toward the piano. Katya worried that he could hear her heart beating, it was going so fast, like one of his musical pieces, so she hugged her knees to quiet the sound. After sitting unnoticed for several minutes, she grew bold. She stuck her tongue out at him. Nothing. She did it again, then pulled a silly face. The German was impassive. Only when Katya stifled a giggle did he turn toward her. She was silent after that and directed her attention to the shiny black piano that had swallowed her father's head.

In the months to come, she went repeatedly, stealing inside to watch the German as he listened to her father tune his piano. What she wanted most was to watch him make the music she heard at night. Unlike others in the building, she liked the strange and complicated lullabies that came from his apartment. She wanted to know how it was done.

"Please will you play," she finally said one afternoon, emboldened by this desire, the words lisping from the gap where her two front teeth had fallen out. She had just celebrated her seventh birthday. Her father turned and spoke her name sharply. "What are you doing here?" But the German only lifted his hand, as in blessing, and beckoned her from where she stood in the doorway. "I wondered if that was what you were here for," he said in a voice not at all like an ogre's.

He paid her father, asked him to sit down, and guided Katya to the near end of the piano, his giant hand warm and slightly trembling on her shoulder, and told her to stand there. He maneuvered himself onto the bench, sitting heavily, and rested his hands in his lap. Katya held her breath. After a moment, his hands floated up elegantly to the keyboard for a beat, a moment of silence, then drifted down to touch them: careful, slow, gentle. Katya thought of how her mother stroked her hair when she was upset or had difficulty sleeping.

But what was this music? It wasn't the wild, pounding music he played at night; it was more like soft rain, or clouds passing overhead, or the dance of snow fairies. It unfolded like a story she'd never heard before. Secretly, she pressed her hand against the shining wood. She watched the old German's fingers moving over the keys, barely touching them, and felt the music enter her entire body through her ears, her eyes, her feet, her hand. When he finished, her smock was wet with tears, and when he stood up—his movements gruff again, shaking from age and blindness—there were tears on his face, too.

"A Russian composition for you," he said in his strange accent. "Piano Sonata no. 2 in G-sharp Minor by Alexander Scriabin. First movement. You know him?"

She shook her head, forgetting that he couldn't see her.

He put his thumb against her cheek and felt the tears.

"*Blagodaryu,*" he said. "Thank you."

Her father understood his statement as a dismissal, so he took Katya by the hand and led her away. "Thank you," she said over her shoulder. "Thank you."

She had hoped he would invite her back and teach her something, but he never did, and she was too awestruck to sneak in on her own.

For the past three nights, she hadn't heard him playing, and when she and her father entered the old German's apartment, it was empty except for his big, glossy piano. "Where is he, Papa?" she asked. "Where is his chair? His bed?"

"*Chi-chi-chi,* calm down, Katen'ka. He is gone. But there is something. He left you his piano."

"Gone where?"

"He is dead. Someday I will explain. He left us a letter."

Katya hadn't noticed that he was holding something in his hand. "What does it say?"

"Only that he wanted you to have the Blüthner. He bid me to take care of it for you, and that you should learn to play. He said even a blind man could see the music beating in your heart."

Katya's father and three neighbors pushed the piano down the hall and into the tiny living room. Two new families moved into the old German's apartment and began complaining of ghosts. He blew his brains out with that Mauser HSc, the whispers went. He's gone home to the land of ogres and fiends. We're glad to be rid of him!

But without the German and his music, Katya could fall asleep only if she lay down with her head beneath his piano. With her hair tangled in the pedals, she dreamed of snow fairies dancing, and gentle rain, and clouds blithely passing by overhead. In the mornings she tried to copy the sounds, picking the notes out one by one, learning their order. Her father encouraged her, taught her what he knew. He said the German's gift was proof of the goodness in mankind's heart. To her, this meant there was magic to be discovered in such a special piano.

And she did.

It was the first great love of her life.

Until shortly before her twelfth birthday, Clara and her parents lived in a Santa Monica neighborhood that was within walking distance of both her elementary school and the beach and only seven miles from UCLA, where Alice and Bruce both taught. From the outside, their house was picturesque: a Craftsman-style cottage, just big enough, painted a pale yellow and surrounded by an actual white picket fence. It was filled with books and art and sunlight and an industrious sort of silence they ignored by keeping the vintage Marantz stereo system in the living room on much of the time—NPR for her mother, the classical music station for her father. They worked a lot, even at home, while Clara read or watched TV or made up gymnastic routines.

The stereo hid other silences, too. Those that came before and after her parents' fights. Or seeped out from their separate studies, where they spent hours after dinner. Her mother usually kept the door to her study closed; Clara could smell her Virginia Slims smoke through the jamb. Her father left his door ajar, and sometimes he let her do her homework on the red Kazakh rug while he read aloud in languages she didn't understand. His silences, though, were the loudest. *Hush,* they said. *I'm busy* or *Maybe later* or *I forgot.*

Yet Clara was certain it hadn't always been like that. There were flashes of memory, faint proof of happier times: the three of them walking to the beach with cardboard buckets of fried chicken for a sunset picnic, or sitting outside playing cards on the small back patio. After they died, these were the moments Clara recalled most vividly. The greasy chicken, the creaky wicker patio furniture, the crisp, salt-flavored air, the warmth of holding hands with both of them at the same time, walking between them.

Her only remaining family was her father's sister, Ila, and Ila's husband, Jack. She and her parents had visited them at their home in Bakersfield a few times—holidays and her grandparents' funerals—and it was obvious that these trips were obligations, not adventures. Whenever they entered the city limits, her mother would shake her head at the pall outside the car window and say, "I still can't imagine how you grew up in this wasteland, Bruce." He would look at her sideways and reply, "Go easy, Alice."

Ila had what her father called a nervous condition, often exacerbated by Alice's aloofness. Ila pointed out flaws in her own cooking or housekeeping or reading habits, overfilling conversational gaps with twaddle. Once, during a meal there, she knocked over a water glass, looked like she might cry, and kept apologizing for ruining the tablecloth, even after Alice assured her coolly several times that it was only water, it would be fine. Jack, on the other hand, with his old jeans and soft, worn shirts, his kind blue eyes and southern drawl, didn't seem to mind being either underdressed or undereducated. Adjacent to the house, he had a garage and body shop that he'd built into a steady business. He had a curious nature and liked to hear what Alice had to say about politics, and he often asked Bruce for book recommendations, though he didn't follow up on them. He always asked Clara about school, and when it came time to leave he would shake her hand and say, "It was a real pleasure to see you again, young lady," and she could tell he meant it.

After her parents' memorial service—there were no remains to bury; the fire had taken almost everything—Ila and

Jack drove her from Santa Monica to Bakersfield, her aunt crying and repeating how awful it all was, how terrible to lose everything like she had. Clara didn't speak. She watched out the rear window as the sky darkened and everything she knew receded until her eyes were dry from not blinking, not crying, and her knees ached from kneeling on the seat. She curled up in her stiff new black dress, the patent leather shoes pinching her toes, and for the rest of that seemingly endless two-hour drive thought only about how badly she wanted to go home. But home as she knew it was gone.

It was in her uncle's garage that she learned how to live with her losses. While her aunt tried to soothe her with soft, idle chatter and constant expressions of grief, Jack understood Clara's need for quiet. He made a comfortable place for her under an old desk in the corner of the shop's office where she could rest or hide, but where they could keep an eye on each other. Eventually, as she emerged from her shock, he showed her how to check tire pressure, refill windshield-washing fluid, jump-start a dead battery. She was enrolled in a new school where she made some acquaintances and then a few friends, but she was always drawn to the safety and comfort of the shop. Over the years, she learned how to fix tires, change oil, do minor engine tune-ups, handle auto inspections and, later, to troubleshoot breakdowns and repair electrical systems. She worked as many as twenty hours a week throughout high school, even though her uncle encouraged her to spend more time with her friends, to start thinking about college and her future. He brought home a brochure from CSU Bakersfield, but when she looked at the endless list of majors offered, she panicked.

"Clarabell," he said. "Listen here. You're the little girl your aunt and me never had. I'm glad for it, you know that. But this wasn't supposed to be your life." He swept his arm through the air, indicating the house, the shop, even the city. "You don't have to stay here. You can do anything you want." The only problem was that she didn't know if there was anything else she wanted to do.

Then, shortly after she turned twenty, she met Bobby, a UCLA philosophy student who was driving through Bakersfield to visit friends up in Fresno. His Jetta had been misfiring as he drove up 99, and when his engine light came on, Jack's shop was the first one he could find. Clara adjusted his throttle and smiled as she handed him back his keys. He smiled in turn, and their dinner that night was the start of a year-long relationship. He was a few years older, and talked with gravitas about his ideas for several start-ups, and said that, after graduation, he wanted to found his own company. She liked that Bobby opened doors for her, and held her hand when they were in a movie or walking anywhere, and gazed at her when she was speaking. It turned out that he lived not far from where she'd grown up in Santa Monica. At her request, they spent a Saturday on the beach she'd once considered her own, and then he drove her up the street she'd lived on with her parents. "Drive slow," she said, and he did, making no clumsy attempt to cheer her as she suffered that intensely difficult experience.

After a few months, though, he began campaigning for her to enroll at UCLA. "You're too smart not to," he told her. "You like cars, so study mechanical engineering. We could spend more time together." She shrugged and said she was happy being a mechanic, that she liked it and was good at it, her uncle having trained her well. Soon frustrated by her continued lack of interest, Bobby said hurtful, pointed things like "Don't you think your parents would've wanted you to go to college?" Eventually, he told her he didn't want to be with someone who wasn't going to do something more significant with her life than changing oil, and that was that. Her first real heartbreak after the original.

She met Frank at a bar a few weeks after her twenty-second birthday. Jack had been diagnosed with late-stage throat cancer, and she needed to escape Ila's desperate hand-wringing. She'd always been more likely to cry on Clara's shoulder than to offer the comfort of her own. Frank was a bartender and fly fisherman with tattoos that began at his wrists, disappeared into his rolled-up shirtsleeves, and emerged again at his collar. Clara, approaching him drunkenly that first night, asked where she should go to get inked, something like a socket wrench and a heart in her uncle's honor. Frank told her she'd regret a tattoo, swapped her whiskey for hot tea, and defended her from jeering patrons while she slept it off, head down on folded arms at the bar. She woke up when the lights came on, and once he'd finished cleaning up, Frank took her home and put her to bed on his couch.

Ila died of cardiac arrest early in their relationship; then Jack was transitioned into a nursing home. Clara had to sell Jack's shop, along with the house that had been her home since she was twelve, in order to pay all the bills, and Frank made room for her in his small apartment. She needed a job, and he introduced her to his friend Peter Kappas, who gave her one in his parents' garage. When her uncle died, Frank helped out with the funeral arrangements, stood with his arm around her as the preacher delivered the eulogy, let her cry in the bedroom undisturbed. He was a sweet and decent guy, so much more laidback than Bobby, so much less demanding, and she thought maybe he was the kind who wouldn't break her heart—until he brought a girl named Willow home and told Clara how hot it would make him if he could watch them get together.

She didn't have many friends, so she asked Peter and his brothers to help her move into a new apartment. Afterward, Peter asked her to dinner, and she said she'd go, but only as a friend. She tipped her head far back, looked him in the eyes, and told him, "I like you. Let's don't fuck it up."

She had a handful of casual dates, though never with anyone she wanted to see again. She had a policy against socializing with customers, and since she didn't like to hang out in bars or coffee shops, meeting new people was hard. When she wasn't working, she spent most of her time either alone or with Peter.

Then she met Ryan, who was pushing his cart down the grocery aisles with cool aplomb, smiling at shoppers and workers alike. With a high, domed forehead, a hooked nose, and a slight paunch, he wasn't especially handsome, yet Clara noticed that people were turning to watch him. He nodded at Clara as he passed by, and she understood: that brief and beatific glance felt like a blessing. When he walked away with his back to her, she became aware of the simultaneous sensations of loneliness and longing. He stopped at a display to accept a sample of *agua fresca,* and she wheeled her cart next to his. The employee handed her a small paper cup, and Ryan turned to her and said, "Cheers" in what she soon learned was a South African accent.

They loitered next to the juice bar, their carts touching. He was a freelance pilot who flew King Airs for an air-ambulance service, delivering harvested organs to recipients or flying patients to hospitals for transplants. He loved being able to help the children especially, he said. While he talked, she noticed and developed an immediate affection for the crookedness of his teeth, the deep blue-brown of his eyes. When she told him she was a mechanic, she worried that he might lose what seemed to be a mutual interest, but he slapped his thigh and said, "That's so cool!" Then, uncharacteristically forward, she asked if he would take her flying.

She moved into his two-bedroom rental house five months later. Now, almost two years later, she was moving back out again.

She dropped the stack of boxes by the front door and looked around the twilit room. The overhead lights were too bright for her task, too normal, so she cracked open a beer and let her eyes adjust. There on the table, as promised, was a lease agreement and a shiny gold key. Next to it was a note that said simply, *I wish you the best.—Ryan. P.S. Don't forget to leave your key.* She crumpled it up and tossed it in the trash.

There wasn't much to pack, just her clothes and books and CDs, a few things from the kitchen. The hibachi she'd given him for a birthday present and he'd never set up. A couple of lamps. Her uncle's favorite tools and the one family photo album her aunt had put together. She could fit most of her stuff into the Corolla; after starting over as an orphan fourteen years before, she'd never gotten into the habit of collecting things. But she would need help, and a truck, for the futon couch that would become a bed again, a small table and chairs, her bike, the piano.

She opened a second beer and wandered into the spare bedroom. Her old Blüthner upright was against the wall, unplayed and mostly ignored, as it had been since she'd moved in. In the beginning, Ryan didn't complain about the space it took up, didn't urge her to try lessons again. He accepted it as one does any relic of a lover's history—generously at first and then, when the inevitable discords arose, with increasing degrees of irritation until, finally, it came to symbolize the worst failures between them.

"Why don't you just get rid of that thing?" he'd snapped in the middle of a recent fight. His thirty-fifth birthday was a few months away, and he wanted to turn the room into a nursery. "You don't even know how to play it," he added, with unforgivable disgust in his voice.

"Fly to hell," she told him. He marched into their bedroom and slammed the door so hard that she could feel it in her teeth. That was two weeks ago.

Now she sat down on the bench, took another swig. She mashed a pedal with her bare foot and listened to the faint sound of nothing, of dampers lifting from strings without sustaining any notes. It was like pressing the accelerator and wanting to take off—but where?—in a car that wouldn't run.

The trolleybus squealed to a stop, the triangle ropes swinging in lazy arcs above the passengers' heads. "*Извините*," Katya said, rushing, and brushed by the stockinged knees of old women, the bored gazes of tired men. Due at the Theater for Young People in fifteen minutes, she would almost certainly be late.

She walked as fast as she could, occasionally breaking into brief sprints until her feet pinched inside the leather heels she'd borrowed from her roommate. She fanned away her perspiration with the thin portfolio of sheet music—at least the weather hadn't turned too hot yet—and hurried past the statue of the diplomat Griboyedov, the neat rectangle of grass down the center of Pionerskaya Square, the mothers pushing prams along the tree-lined walkway, the young *stilyagi* pretending to be fancy Americans in their narrow pants and bright shirts, smoking cigarettes and laughing too loud at one another's jokes.

"Katya!" called her friend from the Leningrad Conservatory, Boris Abramovich, as he jogged up and took her hand. "I thought you'd changed your mind, I was so worried."

"No, of course not. It was the trolley's fault. Late again."

"Soviet timetables aren't so precise after all," Boris said, practically pulling her along, his dancer's stride longer than hers by half.

"Don't talk like that, Borya. The walls have ears."

He gestured gracefully toward the cloudy sky. "In the middle of the promenade! You shouldn't be so serious all the time, you know. Loosen up a little bit." He slowed down and tried to undo the top button on her blouse, but she slapped his hand—mildly, though, as if shooing away a housefly. He laughed. "Besides, now Gerald Ford will save us with *разрядка*."

She liked Boris, but he was too fanciful. He was studying choreography at the conservatory, where she was three years into her specialist degree in the art of instrumental performance. Piano students were sometimes invited to accompany the ballet dancers during practices and performances, and even to compose scores for their choreography. This was how they'd met, and while she admired his dancing and his intellect and enjoyed his company, his enthusiasm for seemingly everything exhausted her. He tended to break into dance if provoked by a sunny day or traffic around Theater Square, by news good or bad. Once, when they were waiting for the subway, he'd performed pirouettes down the entire length of the Sadovaya station.

The previous winter he'd invited her to go with him to a party at the apartment of another student whose parents were away. She was reluctant to go—having heard stories about those student parties, how wild and loud they got—but he convinced her that she spent too much time alone, practicing. "You'll turn into a mushroom," he said. At the party, there were black-market jazz records and raucous laughter, cheap cigarettes and even cheaper vodka, dancing and kissing among strangers, a steady parade of couples taking turns to gain a few minutes of privacy in the closet. After losing the one drinking game Boris had dragged her into, she found her coat in the pile by the door and snuck out into the relative quiet of the night, so relieved to be alone that she didn't bother to worry whether any of the citizens walking along the Fontanka River were KGB.

"Did you invite anyone to the performance?" Boris asked as they approached the rear of the building and peered around the corner at the small crowd gathered in front of the low steps. He'd arranged for a grand piano to be moved from inside the theater to the concrete deck that would also serve as his stage. The show was Boris's idea. A professor had asked him to reinterpret a classical ballet, and he'd chosen *The Little Humpbacked Horse,* which was based on the familiar old fairy tale about a foolish boy named Ivan and the magical horse who helped him win the love of the beautiful Tsar Maiden. Traditionally, the ballet was staged with large casts, grandscale scenes, and sentimental music that followed Ivan on his adventures underwater and to the edge of the world. But Boris had wanted something dramatically different—one dancer, one instrument, outside in the open air—and had also wanted Katya to compose the score.

"No. This is your performance," she told him now. "I'm only helping."

He glanced at her, pretending to be hurt. "What, you don't want to show me off to your friends?"

She rolled her eyes at him.

"I'm just teasing you!" he said. "But you should've extended an invitation. Your music is magnificent. The whole orchestra translated into a single instrument. You made it better than I could ever have imagined, Katya."

She blushed and turned slightly away. "It's only one scene."

"Yes, but it's the best one." He winked at her and unzipped his trousers. "It's time. Let's go."

He nudged her forward, and she walked carefully to the piano. There was no applause, because nobody knew what to expect when she sat down. Then she played a chord and Boris swept out onto the stage wearing flesh-colored tights, slippers, and a pointed felt hat, carrying a large orange feather and a stick horse. There were a few laughs, mostly from the children. He took a bow, nodded to Katya, and they began.

Alone on the improvised stage, Boris became Ivan, ordered to a mountain to find the mythical firebirds and the imagined

Tsarevna. As he folded and unfolded, winding and twisting, dancing solo among the building's columns but conveying all the necessary roles, bringing the drama to life, Katya felt the stage begin to recede. The audience, swelling with passersby, was pushed away from the concrete steps and into the distance. Beyond them, the trolleybuses and cars stopped on their tracks, the murky river paused its flow into the Baltic Sea. Leningrad and maybe the entire USSR grew still; there were no sounds except for the music. It was better on her Blüthner, she thought, but it still felt like magic.

Katya was lifted off the piano bench, her shoes no longer pinching, off the paving stones. Only her fingers on the keys tethered her to the physical world as she floated on the notes into the overcast sky. Now the clouds were parting, the gray smog burning away, the urban smell of sadness and decay gone. Katya closed her eyes. Had she ever seen such colors as those that swirled around her when she soared with the firebirds up to the top of the Tsarevna's mountain? Bursting flowers everywhere, a sparkling sky. Then there was the princess, swishing her skirt and fan out on the bright balcony above the world, on the edge of newfound love. And here the fool was, discovering her, convincing her to return with him to the capital. It nearly blinded her, it was so beautiful.

She only ever felt like this when she played.

The dance went on for seven minutes, over in a flash. Katya's soul was still lingering above the stage, covered in music, when Boris put his hand on her back, urging her to stand and bow. She moved as though awoken from a deep sleep. The audience clapped for nearly a minute, calling *Браво! Браво!* before dispersing. Then Boris danced offstage to see his instructor and some friends, and Katya was left alone, clutching the open piano for support as she tried to fit again into her inadequate body, the day once more turning stagnant around her.

Eventually coming to, she noticed a young man standing on the steps, watching her. He took long drags on his cigarette, narrowing his eyes each time, then angled his square head away to exhale through one side of his mouth, as though to avoid blowing smoke directly at her. She had no idea who he was, but this apparent consideration impressed her.

He didn't alter his gaze for the long seconds it took him to take a final puff, flick his cigarette down, grind it with his heel, and walk toward her with heavy, methodical steps. He was average height and sturdy beneath his collared shirt, which strained only a little at the buttons above his belt. Yet he moved as though gravity worked harder on him than on other people. It made him seem serious—mule-like, even. He stopped directly in front of her and put his hands in his pockets.

"I found this piece to be motivically cohesive," he said with a jut of his chin. "It was good. I liked it. There were aspects of the main theme within the structure, yes?" His voice was deeper than she'd have guessed, a low-pitched key that made her think of the old oktavist tradition from the tsar's court.

She blinked at him. He didn't look like a musicologist or a musician, but what did she know? "Yes," she said, and it came out small and hoarse. She cleared her throat. "Thank you."

"Welcome," he said. He lit another cigarette and offered it to her.

She shook her head no. She'd tried smoking once; it had bothered her to hold her fingers like that. But she didn't want the refusal of his cigarette to end their conversation. "Are you at the conservatory?"

"No," he said, again turning his head to exhale just as a gust of warm air caught the smoke and blew it in her face anyway. "I am going to be an engineer. Still, I understand musical structure. Sometimes I read Schenker."

She, too, had read the theories of Heinrich Schenker, though only because she'd been required to. Whoever this young man was, she thought, he must be very intelligent. Up close, his eyes were the color of the canal, dirty gray and swirling. She saw herself reflected in them the way a dark sun floats on the surface of the water.

"Maybe you would like to have some tea with me," he told her. "I have some Estrada records . . ."

She was twenty years old. A virgin, and not necessarily by choice. In high school she had been almost serious with a boy who lived in her apartment building in Zagorsk, but she had ended it when he complained about her abandoning him for the conservatory, to her father's relief and her mother's disappointment. *You need to think of your future, Katen'ka. You should have a husband, a family! And what about me? I have only you. It would be nice for you to make me a grandmother!*

Boris had kissed her once when he was drunk, and she might have gone to bed with him had he not passed out against her shoulder. A similar opportunity had not yet arisen naturally, and she was too shy to proposition him. Since she'd arrived in Leningrad, two years before, no other boys had shown any interest in her.

"I don't know you," she said gently.

"I am Mikhail Zeldin." He didn't move to shake her hand, only continued to look at her appraisingly. Then he shrugged and gave a slight grin. "Now you know me."

She giggled. She found his confidence appealing. She liked how he looked at her, as if he knew she was sometimes lonely, like he might be lonely sometimes, too, even though he didn't seem the type to admit such a thing. "Okay," she said.

He turned and started down the steps as though he'd forgotten he had just invited her to have tea. She hurried to catch up, aware again of the tightness of her shoes, and then he slowed his pace so she could walk beside him. As they went along, mostly in silence, Katya registered an unfamiliar tension that pulsated between them in spite of—or perhaps because of—the fact that they hardly spoke.

He led her to his third-floor apartment in a dingy yellow building near the square and explained that he shared the two rooms with three other students from the Leningrad Polytechnic Institute, where he was studying civil engineering. "Road building is my specialty," he said. "Very important work." He didn't apologize for the heap of clothes on the floor next to the sofa, or the dirty cups that lined the windowsill, or the full ashtrays, or the faintly sour odor. Instead, after they removed their shoes, he motioned for her to sit and then went to the small kitchenette to put a kettle on to boil.

She cleared a stack of papers from the sofa and perched on the edge. Some instinct to help him welled up inside her, whether maternal or romantic she didn't know, and she sat on her slender fingers to keep herself from tidying up the awful room.

"Do you know Luba Vasilevna?" he asked.

"The singer?"

"Who else." He pulled a record from its sleeve and put it carefully on the turntable. Soon a high, warbling voice rose above the crackling, singing praise to the Motherland. Mikhail closed his eyes and nodded along. Katya didn't especially care for this style of music, yet she enjoyed watching him listen to it with such obvious admiration and wondered if he'd listened to her so attentively earlier. Perhaps he understood what it was like for her to play, to travel outside herself on the music, to hear colors. She thought briefly of the old German, how he was blind to the world but was still able to see music. Standing there, Mikhail became more and more attractive even as he seemed once more to forget her. The song ended just as the kettle screamed, and there was a frantic feeling in the air.

"She's good, yes?"

"She's very patriotic," Katya said, the kindest thing she could think to say.

"I like the Morse code in the background." He handed her a cup of strong, sweet tea. "Luba Vasilevna," he said wistfully, then shook his head and plopped down next to her on the sofa, as though they'd been married for years. He spoke the singer's name again, softer, and although Katya knew that Luba Vasilevna was enormous and age-spotted, with thick, black brows that made her look even less feminine than Leonid Brezhnev, she felt an inexplicable pang of jealousy.

"My name is Ekaterina, by the way," she said. "In case you're wondering."

He looked at her carefully before setting his cup down next to the others. "I would like to kiss you now," he told her. "Katya."

She liked the sound of her name in his mouth, deep and deliberate. It was the color of eggplant, and though nothing so exotic was ever available to regular citizens, she wanted to taste eggplant, and so she put her cup next to his and let him lean close to her. Her heart beat *in rilievo* as his mouth pressed against hers, and she could feel his heart beating faster, too. Was he as nervous as she? He rested his hands on her shoulders like he didn't know what else to do with them, and this display of uncertainty bolstered her own courage. She was ready to shed the burden of innocence. She threaded her fingers into his hair, lightly tapping out a measure of Rachmaninoff's third piano concerto against his head, and pushed the tip of her tongue into his mouth. He made a small gasping sound, then slid his hands down to her waist and pulled her closer. They kissed tentatively at first, wordlessly asking and granting permission to advance. A damp heat rose around them as their lips and hands moved more freely, more passionately, until each was nearly panting into the other's open mouth.

Katya became aware of a throbbing sensation between her legs that she had never felt before. She had touched herself there many times, often after playing a lengthy or demanding piece of music, but it was always prescriptive and quick, like scratching an itch. What she felt now was nearly an ache, a *need* not just for a touch, but to be touched by Mikhail. She moved one of his hands from her breast to the inside of her thigh.

"Oh, Katya," he moaned.

"Misha," she whispered back, claiming him with the diminutive of his name.

Without breaking their kiss they pulled themselves onto the floor on top of those dirty clothes, unbuttoning each other's shirts. She moved her hands over his chest and arms as he kissed her earlobes, the hollow at her throat, her nipples. Her stomach muscles constricted as he kissed down the length of her belly. When he paused to unfasten her skirt, she helped him pull it loose and peeled off her pantyhose and underwear. He looked at her with what seemed like awe, so instead of being embarrassed by her nakedness she slowly shifted one knee aside, opening herself to him, offering him a better view. Then he did something she hadn't known was even possible: he knelt between her legs and kissed her there until she thought she would explode and then did.

"Misha," she said again once she finally caught her breath.

"Yes?" He was kissing her belly as it heaved up and down.

"You've done this before?"

"I can't remember now," he said, and smiled at her.

She laughed, sat up, and kissed him, then unbuckled his belt and slipped her hand into his pants. She felt the hard length of him jump at her touch. "Now this," she said, and pulled him down on top of her.

There were more than twenty-nine thousand notes in the Rachmaninoff piece that had started playing in her mind when they first kissed; it took nearly forty minutes to play it from start to finish. She heard all of it twice in her imagination as she and Mikhail discovered and rediscovered each other, on the pile of clothes, the sofa, the narrow cot he slept on. Once they were finally too tired to continue, it was deep into the evening.

They dressed, and Mikhail made a fresh pot of tea, Katya accepting her cup with a tiny smile. Now that their clothes were back on, she felt shy again. Still pleased, yes, but a note of shame welled up as though she could hardly believe her own behavior, how unlike her it was. Perhaps it meant that she had found the man she was supposed to love. Usually, falling in love preceded making it. Could it work out of order, too? It seemed that she had a moral duty to try.

She watched him set the needle down on another record, his brow furrowed in concentration. Based on what she could know about him in a single afternoon, she liked Mikhail. What would it be like to love him?

Clara walked slowly backward, steadying the piano as Peter, Teddy, and their other brother, Alex, pushed it through her new apartment complex. "Bump," she warned them. They slowed down and one-two-three tipped the dolly over a buckle in the paved walkway. Feeling its heft jostle beneath the padded blankets, Clara didn't know which she resented more: that she couldn't afford to hire professional movers or that she was moving the piano at all.

"Careful," she said when they turned a corner and maneuvered around a curve to the staircase leading up to her second-floor apartment. Clara studied the pale stucco building, the roof that was missing a few red tiles, the chipped paint on the balcony railing, but at least it had a view of the community pool; the units behind hers looked out onto a Walmart parking lot. She heaved a sigh from deep within her chest. "I feel like Sisyphus at the bottom of the hill."

"Let's just hope we're not doing this for all eternity," Peter said. When he looked at her, she knew he wasn't referring only to the move. He wiped his forehead with the back of his sleeve, then squinted at the steps, his mouth moving as he counted to fourteen. "That landing's pretty small."

"It's okay," Clara said, "I already measured it. The hard part will be the turn at the top."

They got the two-by-fours from the moving truck, laid them parallel on the stairs at the width of the piano legs, and rolled the Blüthner so the keyboard side was facing the building. Peter said, "Alex, you and I'll go first and pull. Teddy and Clara, you'll push from the bottom." He looped a heavy nylon strap around the piano and wrapped one free end around his hand and gave the other to Alex to wrap around his, so that even if the weight shifted and slipped, the cargo wouldn't slam right back down to the bottom.

"This would be a hell of a lot easier if we had a crane," Teddy said.

"Or if you put on a little muscle," Alex said, giving his biceps a squeeze.

"Cut it out," Peter said. "Clara, you stay here, next to the building, and Teddy'll go on your right. It's heavier on your side, Teddy, so be careful. Alex and I can manage most of the weight, but we need you guys to guide it up." They got into position, Peter and Alex on the third step, their broad backs tensed and ready, Teddy and Clara below. Clara checked the alignment of the casters and the two-by-fours then tested the integrity of the metal handrails on either side of the staircase by giving them a stiff shake.

"Ready?" Peter asked.

"Okay," Clara said, "go."

"Stay with me," he responded.

They made it about halfway up, all of them grunting under their mostly coordinated effort, before Alex said, "Stop for a sec. I need to readjust." He rewound the strap more tightly around his hand, his fingers now turning white. "All right, ready to roll."

On the next step, Teddy pushed his side of the piano harder than he needed to, perhaps to prove something to his brothers, or maybe to Clara; Peter took a false step up to compensate for it and Alex tried on instinct to match it, but slipped. The piano, all five hundred and sixty pounds of it, swayed, and Clara braced herself against the railing with her left hand, ready to use her own small body to protect the instrument. If the Blüthner started to crash down the stairs onto the ground below, it would have to go through her first.

"Hold it!" she shouted.

Peter and Alex planted themselves to block its movement, but it tipped to the right then overcorrected and tipped even harder to the left, smashing against Clara's hand and pinning it to the railing. She screamed, high and tight, and, as if in commiseration, the piano released a cacophony of notes from inside its thick wrap.

"Teddy, you asshole!" Peter said. "Lean it back, get it off her!" Clara squeezed her eyes closed as hard as she could until she saw lights bursting behind her eyelids—her trick for stopping tears. The guys, yelling at one another in Greek, managed to right the piano and haul it onto the landing, their adrenaline a proxy for Clara, who stayed where she was with her throbbing hand draped almost casually on the railing and chanting to herself, "It's okay, it's okay, it's okay."

The scaphoid, the small bone above the thumb on her left wrist, was fractured. The ER doctor said it wasn't severe, but he wanted to put her in a plaster cast up to her elbow to make sure it would heal correctly.

"I can't wear a cast. How could I work?"

"Well, what sort of work do you do?"

"I'm a mechanic." She held up her unbroken hand, with its rough skin and perpetually grease-stained fingernails, as proof, though he was looking at her like she'd told him she was a lion tamer or a mermaid. It wasn't an uncommon reaction. New customers were usually surprised to see her hoisting tires and swapping out parts, but she was strong for her size, and she knew what she was doing.

"Well," he said, letting his eyebrows slide back into place, "in that case you might want to take some vacation time."

"Aw, shit, Clara," Peter said when she walked back into the reception area. "I'm really sorry. Damn Teddy. I should've known he'd screw something up."

"It's not your fault," she said. "Not Teddy's, either. It's mine. You guys were doing me a favor." She cradled the cast with her other arm, moving her swollen fingers tentatively.

"How long do you have to wear that thing?"

"He said six weeks. Maybe a little less. He wants to do another X-ray in a few weeks to see."

"I can help," he said. "I can bring food, drive you anywhere you need to go."

"I'll be okay."

"I know you will. But you don't have to do it all on your own." He took her unbroken right hand into his and covered it with his other as if were holding a lightning bug that he didn't want to let go of. His hands were so large that they enclosed hers entirely. She closed her eyes and, for just a moment, flattened her palm against his until she could feel the calluses that matched her own. It was far too easy to imagine letting him gather the rest of her up in his embrace. As gently as she could, she withdrew from his clasp.

"Thanks for being such a good friend," she said.

After Peter dropped her off, Clara stood at the base of the stairs leading up to her apartment, feeling the heat of the day radiating off the cement, and awkwardly rested her cast on the railing before slowly climbing up the steps. Inside, where a new coat of paint looked too glossy on the old walls, it felt like somebody else's apartment. An unfamiliar slant of light came in from the east-facing window, illuminating the dust motes swirling around the cramped room and her haphazard stacks of boxes. But wasn't that how it always felt when she was starting over? Nothing ever seemed right, not at first. Sometimes never at all.

The quiet was unsettling, but she didn't feel up to digging through the boxes to find her portable stereo. Instead she went to the Blüthner, which the guys had pushed against the wall by the door. She lifted the bench lid and pulled out one of her old pieces of sheet music: a simple version of Beethoven's *Moonlight* Sonata. The first movement was played mostly by the right hand, and the sorrowful, ghostly melody matched her mood. She sat down and adjusted the bench, then lifted the fallboard and put her fingertips on the yellowing keys, remembering what her first teacher had told her about curving her hands as if each were holding a ball.

From her first lesson, Clara had planned to devote herself to learning her father's favorite piece of music—Prelude no. 14 in E-flat Minor by the Russian composer Alexander Scriabin, which he'd looped repeatedly on his CD player at home. It was wildly energetic from the start through its abrupt and dramatic ending and very difficult even for an accomplished pianist to play well, her teacher had told her. Abbie Fletcher, who always smelled pleasingly like a swimming pool, said she admired Clara's choice but suggested they not get ahead of themselves. "Scriabin is wonderful. And it happens that he loved Chopin as much as I do," Mrs. Fletcher said. "In fact, when Scriabin played his Prelude and Nocturne for the Left Hand Alone, they called him the left-handed Chopin—*le Chopin gaucher*. Perhaps someday you'll be able to play Scriabin, dear, but for now let's focus on the fundamentals."

Clara played a few notes of the sonata, forgiving the piano for being so far out of tune. It had just survived a near-fatal crash, after all. Tentatively she continued, but because her memory of the piece and her technical skill were both lacking, she couldn't fix her eyes on either the music or the keyboard and had to keep glancing back and forth between them. The result was a staccato and discordant stabbing that made her feel even worse than the silence had. Besides that, her left hand ached from trying to spread her thumb and pinkie across an octave to play the bass part, so in the middle of the seventh measure she snatched the papers off the music rack and ripped them in half again and again until the thickness made it painful for her broken hand, then hurled the pieces toward her boxes and watched them float like big confetti flakes before settling on the floor.

She leaned forward, put her arms on the keys—creating a brief discordance—and rested her forehead against the hard cast. The ivory keys went out of focus, and she closed her eyes. Maybe Ryan had been right. What good was having the piano if she couldn't play it? She'd taken lessons for years, practicing diligently to become the pianist her father had so desperately wanted her to be. But the songs never sounded right. She was fifteen years old at her first recital, where she played "A Little Russian Song," which Mrs. Fletcher had arranged so it sounded more difficult to play than it really was. Her aunt and uncle clapped enthusiastically when she finished, along with the parents of the elementary school kids who were also performing, in spite of the mistakes she'd made. Even when she could play all the notes, they came out more mechanical than musical. By then she was working with Jack at the garage, so she knew her hands were good for something, yet she was never able to make them translate the emotion behind a piece of music through her fingers. Whenever she sensed that her music teacher had given up hope, she found a new one. Then, finally defeated, she gave up, too. The Blüthner became little more than a piano-shaped paperweight, keeping what was left of her childhood memories from floating away.

If she'd saved up all the money that all those years of lessons had cost, not to mention the tuning and moving expenses, it certainly would have covered a six-week forced vacation while her hand healed. Now she'd have to go into debt just to survive until she could work again. She pushed herself away from the keyboard and stood up, then wiped off the smudges on the case with her sleeved forearm. Then, because she had loved and hated the piano equally for the fourteen years she had owned it, she made a fist with her good hand and brought it down once, hard, like a gavel on the lid.

What would've happened if they hadn't been able to stabilize the piano earlier? What if it had gathered enough momentum from its wobble that they couldn't keep it from breaking through the railing and falling—what, ten feet, maybe twelve?—to the concrete slab below? Would it have crumpled in on itself the way cars do during crash tests? Or would it have smashed into splinters? What would that have sounded like? All the potential music that was trapped inside it would be lost amid the clatter and bang of the ebony case shattering and the heavy innards spilling out, muted forever.

The image of the Blüthner falling to its death gripped her, much like the time or two she'd stood on the precipice of something and thought, against all logic, of jumping. How would she have felt to see her piano broken open, its countless interior parts—unnamable to her—strewn everywhere? She'd be stunned, of course. Shaken. But maybe she'd have discovered something else there in the splintery mess. Maybe akin to relief. If the Blüthner were gone, she'd never again have to move it or tune it or suffer its silence.

An idea she'd never before entertained came to her and calmly settled in. She unpacked her laptop and found an online auction site then created a new listing:

> For sale: Antique upright Blüthner piano built circa 1905. Ebonized case in good condition—see photos for specific markings. Needs tuning, possibly new strings and hammerheads. Asking $3,000.

She had been told by one of her teachers that her Blüthner would've been common in Russia or the U.K., but very few tsarist-era uprights would have been imported to America. He'd warned her that, if she ever decided to sell it, not to go through a dealer; they might pay her an undervalued price before turning around to sell it for a considerable profit that should've been hers. Serious pianists, he said, would want only a grand, though she could probably sell this one to a collector for $1,000 to $3,000 because it was rare and in such good condition. But compared to the newer designs available, her old Blüthner was too big and ugly to have any value or appeal to anyone in the general market.

Clara really had no idea if $3,000 was a fair price, because she couldn't find anything comparable for sale. She chose the higher price not so much because she needed the money, although she did, but to mitigate the guilt she'd begun to feel when uploading the pictures of it she'd taken with her phone. She closed the computer, lowered the fallboard over the keys, and went about the unhappy business of unpacking her boxes with only one hand.

Mikhail stood in a shopping line in the wet, gray snow at nine one morning so his wife, Katya, could stay home with the baby. Their son was only six weeks old, too young to be outside all day in the cold, especially with influenza going around like a plague. Already the line was long, wrapping around the building, people grumbling as the reports filtered back: *They've run out of sausages; They say they'll close in an hour—that's not time enough to get to all of us; Somebody bribed the butcher, so the cashier let him buy a whole suitcase of bacon*. Occasionally people tried to jump the line, claiming a friend was holding their place, and citizens farther down shouted, "Get back! Don't think you're special!" Mikhail often shouted the loudest.

Finally, when it was almost five o'clock, he rode the trolley back to the grimy, seven-story concrete *Khrushchyovka* where they lived in a three-room apartment. It was dark, and he was nearly frozen, with only a few items in his *avoska,* the string "maybe bag" he always carried in case there was anything to buy. At least the apartment was heated. He could be grateful to the Soviet regime for that.

He let himself in, quietly. Whenever he heard Katya playing through the door, he liked to steal a moment watching her before she noticed him. The baby was swaddled and sleeping on the floor near her slippered feet. Her dark hair was down, swaying like a curtain in a gentle breeze along with the music. She looked thin, despite the swell of her belly that still remained. This made him feel guilty, even though he preferred to blame the Party for all their troubles.

"Here I am," he said when she was finished. He pulled off his wool hat and she stood up to greet him with a kiss on the cheek.

"What did you bring?" She peered at the contents through the string. A bag of rice, cigarettes, soap, a tea towel stamped with blue and ocher-yellow wildflowers, two bananas, six cans of green beans, a portion of meat. "No milk?"

"They ran out. I can try again tomorrow."

"You have to work tomorrow."

"Afterward, then."

She nodded and carried the *avoska* into the kitchen. Mikhail opened the cupboard and pulled down two glasses and a bottle of vodka.

"Mama?" he asked.

Katya turned on the burner to heat water for tea. "Resting. She didn't feel well today."

"Katyusha," he said in a lower voice. She turned to him. "We have to go. I can't do it anymore." He poured a finger of vodka and handed it to her.

"I can't. The baby," she said, and pivoted away. "Please, let's don't talk about this now."

He poured more into his glass and drank it in one shot, then poured himself another and watched it settle until it was as still as the frozen Neva. Soon he would be able to feel his toes again. He sank into one of the metal kitchen chairs. "We have to talk about it, Katya. Listen to me. We can have a new life in America, a better life. Someplace warm. We can buy produce and meat and milk and butter whenever we want."

"No," she said softly, her back still to him. "No. I keep telling you. Leningrad is home, not America."

"Leningrad is a beautiful city, but it's a terrible time. It doesn't feel like home anymore. It's no good for us."

"What about our parents? Our friends?"

"Irina and Pyotr are going."

"How? We can't even change money. Did Pyotr say they were leaving? Are you making this up?" The kettle began to scream.

"There are ways. I've been asking around." Mikhail stood up, took the kettle off the burner, and put his hands on Katya's waist. "Remember when we met? Such big dreams we had! So many plans! You would be a famous concert pianist. I would be a top engineer. But look, now you can only play for *Goskontsert*, making no money, even though you are so good. You didn't go to the conservatory only to play music the Kremlin allows, did you? You taught me that. Why should Brezhnev be the highest musical authority? You are twenty-five already, Katya. We must think about the future."

She pulled away from him. "Our future is here, Misha. In Leningrad." She thought of the International Tchaikovsky Competition. Held only once every four years, it was like the Olympics of classical music. The next one was just over two years away, in 1982. She had been practicing for it already.

"I can't move up," he said. "I'm the best one there, but I can't move up. They call me *Zhid* now, did you know that? That fucking Vasily, telling everyone. Fucking KGB. I don't even have a nose like my father, but still they all know. How can you expect me to rise up, Katya? It's hard enough to feed ourselves. Now we have the baby. In America there's no communism, no limit. You understand?"

"No," she said, "it's not fair. You're not saying this because of Grisha. You only want to go because of you."

Mikhail put his hands together and shook them, pleading. "No, it's only for you, Katya. You deserve much better than what you get here. It will be an adventure, starting over. Make a new home in a happier place. We will be happier in America."

"I don't want to go," she told him.

"I can't do anything here, don't you understand that? I'm a Jew—we're Jews!—and now I won't get the positions I deserve!" He kicked the chair from beneath the table, crashing it against the wall. The apartment was so small that the sound woke the baby and Mikhail's mother, sleeping in the bedroom.

"Misha, please," she begged.

"You can't tell me no." Though he lowered his voice, it still carried the weight of his frustration. "Anyway, you won't be playing concerts anywhere for a while. You have to take care of Grisha. By the time we get to America he will be bigger—then you can play. But I"—he pounded on his chest with a fist—"I have to take care of everyone. You can't say anything about it."

"Why do you get to make the choices, Misha? Why don't you think about me?"

"I am thinking about you! Aren't you listening?"

Katya's mother-in-law carried her grandson into the kitchen, but when she saw the chair on its side and the look on her son's face, she handed him to Katya and hurried out. The baby began to cry, so Katya righted the chair and sat down to feed him.

"Besides," he said more quietly, "it is too late now. I filed the application yesterday." Then he sat down next to her and put his hand on her son's small head as he nursed. "They made me quit work."

"Quit work!" The baby started, his tiny hands flying up by his face as though to defend himself. "They will charge us with parasitism!"

"It is required. While we are processed."

"It could take years to get approved for exit, Misha. You think I don't know what's happening? All this time while we wait, we will be enemies of the state, enemies of the people. You know the Moral Code: he who does not work, neither will he eat. We will lose friends. We will lose water and electricity. How are we supposed to take care of a baby then, eh? What will we do for money?"

"I have a little saved, not much. But your father is doing good. The piano-tuning business always seems to be doing good. You can ask him for money if we need it."

"Papa's just as poor as us! I won't ask him for money!"

Mikhail shrugged. "Then we'll find another way."

"How? By sweeping streets? Begging?"

"Stop! That is being selfish. I won't accept this kind of talk. It's too late, I told you."

Over three years of marriage, after a tender beginning, she had learned not to cross the threshold of his anger. She calmed her voice, but her heart was still beating *ravvivando,* like it used to out of passion. Now it happened only out of fear. "How long do we have to wait? What will happen? Where will we go?"

"Austria first, I am told. From there to Italy, until America gives us entrance visas. Maybe it will take a year? Maybe longer."

"What are we supposed to do in these places, Misha? Where will we live? How will we eat? And what am I supposed to do with my piano, eh? Carry it around on my back?"

He shrugged. "I am talking to others who are also waiting to leave. There are agencies to help. Jewish agencies to help us find what we need. We can take a small amount, maybe three or four suitcases each. But no piano."

"No piano!" She leapt from the chair and, with the baby's mouth still attached to her, ran the few steps into the small front room, where her Blüthner took up most of the space. She sat down on the bench, as though to hold it in place. How many times had she sat there since the old German bequeathed it to her? How many notes had she played on its keys, first one by one, and later the beautiful, complicated pieces that transported her to a place inside her mind like nothing else could? From the time she was eight years old, the Blüthner had been her constant companion. She had played it nearly every day for the past seventeen years. When she'd moved from her parents' home in Zagorsk to study at the conservatory in Leningrad, she'd insisted on taking it on the eight-hundred-kilometer journey. Besides her family, it was her only treasure. Even if she was forced to go, the piano was something she could not—would not—leave behind.

Mikhail stepped up behind her, resting a hand on her shoulder. "Katya, I will find a way. We will take the piano. Yes? Are you hearing me? I love you."

After a moment, she nodded. She closed her eyes and cried through her fingers. Then they moved across the sleeping baby, a silent performance of Beethoven's sonata *À Thérèse*. There were so many sharps in that piece, the crosses could fill a cemetery.

C lara sat at her Blüthner on a large stage, wearing a formal black dress. Her white cast glowed under the spotlights, and she had the urge to hide it. A large audience sat in hushed rows. Her father, up front, sat on the edge of his seat, clapping and whistling into the amphitheater's curved space. Next to him, her mother told him over and over to settle down. Clara lifted her hands above the keyboard and began to play the Scriabin prelude, but her fingers kept slipping off the keys, which were slick, and the only note she could play was a C with one finger on her left hand in quick, rapping salvos: C C C C C followed by a pause, and then again. She looked up to see if it was snowing, and it was—falling flakes of sheet music melting on the keys when they landed. She looked down at the mystery of this snow and saw that both of her hands were sheathed in plaster casts from her elbows to her fingertips, except for the one index finger that was able to tap out the C in bursts of five. Profoundly embarrassed by her performance, she gazed into the audience, ready to mouth a desperate apology to her parents. But her father had turned and was whispering to a woman next to him, someone she didn't recognize, and her mother was tapping cigarette ashes onto his lap and saying, loudly, "See?"

"Clara!" She turned her head toward her name. "Clara!" But it wasn't someone in the theater; the voice was coming from someplace farther away, so she departed the stage of her dream and followed it, begrudgingly, through the strange portal into consciousness, becoming slowly aware that the C's were actually knocks on her door, and the person calling her name was Peter.

She opened the door a few inches then staggered back to the futon. Peter, carrying a large Tupperware container, elbowed the door wide open. "I brought you *avgolemono*. Greek chicken soup."

"I'm not sick," Clara said, her voice muffled by the pillow she'd dragged over her face.

Peter went into the kitchen and opened cabinets until he found a bowl. "*Avgolemono* is good for anything—colds, flu, broken hands." He pushed aside empty Chinese food containers to make room on the tiny counter. "Besides, you can't live on takeout forever."

"Why not? What time is it, anyway?"

"Close to eleven."

"Shit, I had no clue it was so late. I've got a lot to do."

Peter looked around and opened his hands in a wide, questioning gesture. "What do you have to do? You're almost done unpacking. It's Sunday. You got soup. I was going to hook up your television so we could catch the race. Should be a good one. Kansas Speedway redid their track—now nobody's got an advantage." He walked over and handed her a bowl and a paper towel. "Here," he said.

She pushed off the pillow and sat up, holding the bowl in her right hand and trying to maneuver the spoon with her left, but soup splashed onto her lap. "Don't watch. This is humiliating. Also, I can hook up the TV."

Peter laughed. "Yeah, I know." He walked over and picked it up anyway, set it on the little bar that separated the kitchen from the front room. Clara watched him moving his bulk around as if he were half that size. He was tall, well over six feet, and broad, with big bones and solid muscle and thick hair that was as black and glossy as motor oil. That, along with his steady, placid gaze, made him an imposing figure. In the garage, he could pick up tires and engines without grunting, yet he could also somehow slip in and out of a room without drawing attention to himself. "You need a better set," he said. "A flat-screen."

"Sure, when I win the lottery," she said, raising one eyebrow, then taking another spoonful. "This soup is good. Did your mother make it?"

"No," he said, "I did." His back was to her, but she could see his ears turn pink at the top.

"Well," she said. "Thank you."

He shrugged and continued threading the cable into the port behind the television.

A few months after Clara had broken up with Frank, a massive power outage had darkened most of the city, and Peter had driven over to bring her a battery-powered space heater. "It'll get down into the thirties tonight," he said, almost apologetically, when she opened the door. They'd been working together for over a year and were now close friends. They shared an October birthday two years apart, as well as a passion for fast cars and fixing engines, Bakersfield's hometown NASCAR champion Kevin Harvick, and long drives with no destination in mind. They also shared a love of music and the failure to make it; Peter's mother had insisted that he learn to play the traditional Greek bouzouki, but his friends at school had teased him about it until Anna let him quit. Over beers after work, they developed enough trust to tell each other their important stories and eventually agreed that they probably knew each other better than anyone else did.

But Clara never let their friendship become romantic until the night of the storm. Something about how Peter stood at the doorstep of the apartment he'd helped her move into just a few months before, with flashlight and heater in hand, filled her with an unexpected tenderness.

"Do you want to come in?" she asked, and he nodded, slowly, as a cold wind blew his hair into his face. She looked at him as though for the first time, noting his strong jaw and straight nose, his deeply kind, coffee-colored eyes. Without thinking, she reached up to brush his hair back and felt a shimmer of electricity flash from her fingertips through the rest of her body. He must've felt it too, because he looked at her with an expression of wonder. She took his hand and led him into her bedroom.

Before dawn the next morning, with Peter's sleeping body curled around hers, Clara woke to a feeling of despair. She crawled out from beneath his arm and shook him awake. "I feel like I'm at a funeral," she told him.

He rubbed his eyes and tried to make her out in the darkness. "What? Why?"

She could hardly speak, with the sensation of impending loss welling up inside her.

"Clara, what's wrong?" He reached for her, but she pulled away.

"We can't do this," she said. "Not ever again."

"I don't understand."

"I don't want to lose you." She felt twelve years old once more, the same way she'd felt back when she still had to remind herself upon waking each morning that her parents were dead.

"But you *won't* lose me, Clara." Again he reached out, but she turned away.

"Yes I will. If we do this, things will eventually go sideways and it'll end. It always does."

"You just haven't been with the right guy until now." He smiled and pulled her back into his arms.

She wrested herself from his embrace and clambered out of bed. "That's right." She began gathering up and dividing their discarded clothes. "And for good reason."

"What are you doing? Why are you doing this? This isn't just a one-night stand, Clara. I want to *be* with you." He threw the jeans she'd handed him back onto the floor.

"This was a mistake, Peter. Okay? A mistake."

He flung off the covers and nearly leapt out of bed to stand in front of her. "What the hell are you saying? We made love all night! Do you know how long I've wanted to do that with you? How the hell can that be a mistake?"

She turned away from his naked body. "Because you're my best friend, and if I lose that I won't have anything." The sadness in her voice stunned him into silence. She turned around and handed him his shirt. The soft flannel slipping from her hand felt like a good-bye, but she refused to take it back. "If we stay friends—just friends—then we won't ruin it."

After a long pause, he said, his voice cracking, "*This* is the mistake, Clara. Not last night." He put on only his jeans, grabbed the rest of his clothes, and stormed out into the dark, cold morning, slamming the door behind himself.

He didn't speak to her for more than a week. While she refused to give in, neither would she give up. She invited him to dinner, bought him tickets to a Lakers game and a monstertruck jam, borrowed a customer's Harley-Davidson for them to take on a joyride. Gradually, over the next few months, they tentatively resumed their friendship, until it almost seemed like things had returned to normal between them. Then, toward the end of summer, she met Ryan.

"So I decided something yesterday," Clara said, and Peter glanced at her over his shoulder. She caught his eye then looked down at her cast. "I put up an ad for my piano."

"What do you mean?"

"To sell it."

Peter stopped working on the TV and turned around. "You're kidding. Why?"

"It's time," she said. "Plus, I need the cash."

He sat down next to her on the unmade futon and ran his hand over his face. It wasn't even noon, and already he had a five o'clock shadow. She could hear the whiskers rasp against the calluses on his hand. "If you need money, I can help."

She shook her head. "I'll be okay, but thanks. I'm tired of that damn piano anyway. Dragging it everywhere I go. Up and down stairs. Every time I move it costs a fortune to get it tuned. And I can't even fucking play it." She lifted a shoulder. "So."

"But we just moved it up here."

"Don't worry—if someone buys it, I won't ask you to move it again. If somebody actually pays the three grand I listed it for, I'll be able to afford professionals this time."

"That's not what I meant, and you know it."

"What, you don't think I should sell it?" Clara leaned forward and put the bowl down on the floor, then gathered her hair into a ponytail and struggled to twist the band around it. Until yesterday, she hadn't considered the movements that went into such simple efforts as holding a spoon or tying her hair. With a deep sigh, she shot the elastic band across the room with her good hand.

He walked over, picked it up, dropped it in her lap, and went back to connecting the cable. "Actually, I think it's probably a good idea."

She tossed the rubber band on the futon and pushed her hair off her face. "You do?"

He swiveled the television around to face the futon and turned it to ESPN, where the camera panned the crowd and the commentator said, "Today's Hollywood Casino 400 at Kansas Speedway will be one of Danica Patrick's ten NASCAR Sprint Cup races this year . . ."

"Yeah. I mean, we've moved it"—he closed his eyes, counted—"three times now. I don't know how many times you moved it before you broke up with Frank, but I for sure know it's been a pain in your ass."

"It hasn't been quite that bad."

He wiggled the fingers of his left hand. "Okay, maybe not for your ass, exactly." Then he looked down at her unmade futon with an unreadable expression—though Clara could guess what had crossed his mind. He dragged the twisted covers up before sitting down next to her and settling chastely against the wall. Directly across from him, the Blüthner matched his shiny black hair, his bulk, his untroubled nature. They were like a pair of sentries, each of them looking after her.

Her father had given her the Blüthner the week before he died. She hadn't asked for a piano, never once had thought of playing one. But she remembered how excited he seemed when he brought it home. He pulled out the bench seat so they could sit side by side. "This is for you," he told her, beaming, resting a hand on the keys, his other arm around her. "Something very special, so you know how much I love you."

She squeezed her eyes shut. She'd been too hasty. "I'll be right back," she said to Peter, standing up.

"The race is gonna start."

"I know. I just need to take the ad down."

He put his hand out to stop her. "Clara, leave it."

"I can't."

"Yes, you can. I know why you're hanging on to it, but you don't need it."

"No, it was a stupid impulse. I can't imagine not having it after all this time, you know? I'd miss it."

He made a huffing sound through his nose and shook his head.

"What's that supposed to mean?"

He stabbed the remote, turning up the volume. "Nothing. Forget it."

She took the remote from him and switched it off. "What?"

"You're focused on the wrong stuff is what. You just got dumped and your hand's broken. But look. You're in a new place, new part of town, new paint on the walls. It's time to shake the dust off and start over. Think about the future for a change." When she didn't reply, he let his hands drop into his lap. "Hey, it's your piano, do what you want with it."

Clara tossed the remote onto the futon. "I will." Then she got her laptop and sat back down next to him. She opened her e-mail to find the link to delete her listing, and near the top of her in-box was a new message whose subject line read:

CONGRATULATIONS! Your item sold! Send an invoice now.

"What the hell . . ." she muttered, then looked at Peter. "Somebody bought it."

"For three thousand dollars?"

"Apparently. Wait, maybe it's a joke. Or one of those phishing scams. But why would anybody pretend to buy a piano?"

"Can you e-mail them back to see if it's legit?"

"Yeah." She clicked on the link to see the buyer's contact information. "Greg Zeldin, New York, New York. Does that name even sound real to you? It's probably fake."

"So Google him."

"No, I'll send him the invoice. If it's a scam or something, he won't pay it. Anyway, now I don't have to take the ad down, because it says 'Sold.'"

"I know how much you like signs. You should take that as one."

She shot him a look. He winked at her.

With Peter leaning in to watch, Clara went through the few steps to complete and send the invoice. In the field for special instructions, she typed: *I forgot to put that the cost of shipping from Bakersfield is the buyer's responsibility.* "I don't know how much it would cost to pack and ship it to New York, but

I'm sure it's a lot. No way he'd pay that much plus shipping on top of it. It can't be worth that much to anybody except me."

Peter glanced at her briefly and sighed, turned the television back on. "Let's watch the race," he said.

After the NASCAR wreckfest ended, with Matt Kenseth in first place and Danica Patrick a disappointing thirty-second, Peter went home, and Clara opened a beer, put on a CD of Chopin's nocturnes by Arthur Rubinstein, and opened her laptop to check her e-mail.

From: Greg Zeldin <grisha@zeldinphotography.com>
Date: October 21, 2012 at 11:59 P.M. PDT

To: "clarabell1986@gmail.com"
<clarabell1986@gmail.com>
Subject: Re: CLARABELL has sent you an invoice
Greetings:
I have submitted payment in the amount of $3,000 and will make arrangements for the shipping. My assistants will be able to pick it up about a week from now. What upcoming day will work best for you?
Regards,
Greg Zeldin

From: Clara Lundy
Date: October 21, 2012 at 3:14 P.M. PDT
To: Greg Zeldin <grisha@zeldinphotography.com>
Subject: Re: CLARABELL has sent you an invoice
Hi Mr. Zeldin,
I'm very sorry to have to tell you this, but I can't sell the piano. I'll refund your money plus the amount for the payment service fee.
I hope it's not a problem. Clara Lundy

*

From: Greg Zeldin <grisha@zeldinphotography.com>
Date: October 21, 2012 at 3:21 P.M. PDT
To: Clara Lundy
Subject: Re: CLARABELL has sent you an invoice
Ms. Lundy,
I'm afraid that *is* a problem. I've already remitted payment and, therefore, the piano is technically mine. If you'll please let me know where my assistants can pick it up, they will be there on Saturday, October 27, between 1 and 4 P.M. I hope *that* won't be a problem.
Greg

From: Clara Lundy
Date: October 21, 2012 at 3:23 P.M. PDT
To: Greg Zeldin <grisha@zeldinphotography.com>
Subject: Re: CLARABELL has sent you an invoice
Dear Greg,
Like I said, the piano's not for sale anymore. I'll refund your payment. Sorry for the inconvenience.

Clara logged into the payment account and saw that Greg had indeed sent her $3,000. More money than she'd ever had all at once. When her parents died, Clara inherited their savings and a small life-insurance distribution from the university, but her aunt and uncle used some of that to cover the funeral expenses and then, thinking of her future college expenses, invested the rest. Jack, acting on a stock tip from a longtime customer and fellow Texan, even added a large portion of his own savings to Clara's inheritance and bought shares in a Houston-based company called Enron. They never recovered financially after it collapsed three years later, in 2001, and once Clara was on her own, she had never been diligent about saving the modest income she earned as a mechanic.

Now, seeing that $3,000 figure gave her pause. Like the nocturne she was listening to, with its two melodic strands playing in counterpoint to each other, she felt equally pulled between the two voices in her head: keep the money, return the money, keep it, return it. Then the piece ended with a coda that sounded to Clara like longing, or perhaps homesickness, and she looked over at the Blüthner. Then moved her cursor to the Refund This Payment icon on the computer screen and clicked.

Katya took the kettle off the burner and poured boiling water over the coffee grounds. How much longer would they have electricity? It had already been eight months since Mikhail had filed their exit-visa application; she expected the power to be turned off any moment, and it was almost winter again. She was without help, too. With no money coming in to support all of them, her mother-in-law had returned home to Kolpino and her factory job at Izhorskiye Zavody. Mikhail offered no help with their son, even though he wasn't working. He had applied for a job as an elevator operator in a hospital, but he was waiting to hear about that, as well. Such menial jobs were quickly filled by Jews living in refusal, all of them with specialist degrees. So he spent the daylight hours brooding and the nighttime ones sitting in the restaurant at the Hotel Leningradskaya, where a Jewish bartender he'd befriended let him finish the drinks of paying customers after they'd left.

He was there this afternoon, she assumed. Meanwhile, her old friend Boris Abramovich had surprised her with a visit, bringing a bottle of good Armenian brandy and a cache of needles, thread, and buttons, all of which were *defitsitny* in the local shops. Katya was so happy to see him, to finally have friendly company to talk to. Grisha was good-natured but still could only babble. She and Boris hadn't seen much of each other since they'd graduated, almost three and a half years before, in 1977. He did send her letters, usually from cities abroad where his ballet company toured, but also from within the Union. The year before, he'd done the impossible: having a bouquet of hothouse flowers delivered to her after he received the People's Artist of the USSR award.

"You are beautiful as ever," he said.

She touched her hair, smoothed her sweater, hid a smile. "I was very happy for your award," she said. "Tell me, what will you do now? How has the world changed for this great choreographer?"

When he leaned back in the kitchen chair and clasped his hands behind his head, she worried that the cheap metal legs would collapse but said nothing. "This is my wish, Katya. I want to build a repertoire that shows the disorientation created by Communist thinking. A movement metaphor for the oppression of the human spirit," he said. "It's good, yes? A perfect cover for a social revolution. What will they think of that, eh?" He laughed in a high voice, almost a giggle.

Katya put the coffee and brandy and teacakes on a tray and sat it on the table. "They will think you are anti-government. A social revolution? It would be very dangerous for you."

"For us."

"Who is *us*?"

Boris shrugged. "A group of us, thinking the same way. We certainly appear innocent, yes? Nobody suspects a traveling ballet company." He let his chair fall forward again with a thud. "Maybe I'll produce a Tchaikovsky ballet, but not one of those silly dramas with fluffy swans and sleeping beauties. I mean one about the life of the revolutionary Nikolai Tchaikovsky. Or perhaps a psychological ballet based on *Doctor Zhivago*. Or *The Gulag Archipelago*. Something important." He reached out and grabbed her forearm as she poured his coffee, looking at her with fanaticism in his eyes. "You can help me, Katya."

"How?"

"Like we sometimes did at the conservatory. I create the choreography. You can compose the score."

"And then what? Let the KGB drag us to Siberia?"

"Have you forgotten your ideals, Katya? It wasn't so long ago we used to talk together about making a better life in Russia. Remember the night we stayed up reading Nekrasov's poem *Who Is Happy in Russia?* Our duty is to remind one another of our human dignity. We must do something to defend the future of our children, because the present time is no good. Think of your son, eh? Don't you want him to have the right to read and think what he wants? To stand up for his own convictions? Not to be an obedient tool of the government?"

Though she admired his passion, she was no activist. "You don't have children, Borya. You don't know what you're talking about. It's different when you have someone to protect."

"I'm talking about protecting all of us, Katya. I'm talking about changing the world."

"Through ballet?"

Boris again leaned back in his chair. The slippers she had given him at the door were too small for him, and one dangled off his toes when he crossed his lean legs. "Yes, ballet. You think that can't change the world? You think it all has to be violent revolution?"

"So you want to fight Brezhnev with music and dance? Sneak *samizdat* texts inside the programs at the theater?" She shook her head. "There's no point. You can't win—you'll only get punished. Remember what happened to Rostropovich for denying official musical policies? Or Shostakovich? The wise thing is to keep your head down, I think."

"Or leave, yes?" His eyes were mean all of a sudden, and she went cold under his glare.

As students, they had been very close friends, performing together, sharing meals, and occasionally attending parties, when he could convince her to come along. They took long walks and often ended up at the Tikhvin Cemetery, wandering beneath the trees among the graves of famous ballet masters and composers: Balakirev, Petipa, Rimsky-Korsakov, Rubinstein, Tchaikovsky. Things changed between them the night after one of her final performances, when Boris threaded his fingers into hers—hers tired from playing, his chapped from clapping—and declared his love. He had been foolish before, he told her. How had he failed to recognize his true feelings for her? He wanted them to marry, to conjoin their passions, to form their own ballet company, to travel and discover the pleasures and excesses of the world, to have children if she desired. They would have her dark hair and his gray eyes, and they would be able to create music as well as dance. Even as he begged her, she was forced to tell him: she was already devoted to Mikhail by then, though she loved Boris still and wanted them always to be friends. Of course he couldn't take back the passionate plea, which ultimately embarrassed both of them, and ever since she had been careful to keep him at an appropriate distance.

It occurred to her then that this surprise visit might be a test. Anyone could be an informant. A *stukach*. It was one of the few means to get ahead—by helping the KGB with the day-to-day work of keeping watch over the Soviet people, reporting on dissidents, rounding up so-called prisoners of conscience. Just the year before, witnesses had seen two agents force a popular Ukrainian nationalist composer, Volodymyr Ivasyuk, into a KGB car. Three weeks later, his body was found hanging from a tree. His eyes had been gouged out.

"I don't want to leave, Borya," she said carefully. "I never wanted to leave."

"But your husband does. He has been petitioning. And you will go with him, yes?" It was posed as a question, but it sounded to Katya like a threat, like a dare. She had no idea where Boris's loyalties lay: for or against the Kremlin? For or against her?

Then, after a bit of silence, the clock ticking softly on the wall above them, the coffee gone cool, he said, in a soft and pleading voice, "Play me something, Katya. Please? It has been such a very long time."

She stood without a word and led him into the other room, and then she paused, contemplating whether she should take Boris to her bed. Would it protect her and Mikhail? Their child, who was right then sleeping on a pallet on the floor? But she couldn't imagine such a betrayal. No. She took a breath and gestured to the narrow sofa against the wall. He sat, and she could feel his eyes on her as she took her place in front of the piano.

She'd play, as he'd requested, but would be cautious. There would be no fluffy swans, yet nothing revolutionary, either. After a moment of consideration, she chose the second movement of Pyotr Ilyich Tchaikovsky's Piano Sonata in C-sharp Minor, written in 1865, during his last year at the conservatory, 112 before she and her guest graduated.

Boris made a small huff of acknowledgment. "Good one," he said. The sofa squeaked a complaint as he settled back against the worn cushions.

She imagined that he closed his eyes as she played the simple, marchlike theme, in a gesture of Soviet patriotism. She hoped the enthusiasm of her performance would conceal her deep unease.

The phone rang.

"Is this Clara?" The voice was low and melodic, like a radio personality's, and the use of her first name sufficiently intimate to raise goose bumps on her arms.

"Who's this?"

"It's Greg Zeldin."

She glanced at the dead bolt to make sure it was locked. The leasing office had boasted about how the neighborhood was turning around, but Clara knew there had to be a reason the rent was so cheap. "How did you get my phone number?"

"It was on the bottom of your invoice."

"Shit," she said. "Why are you calling? Didn't you get my e-mail?"

"I did, yes. I thought we should talk about this in person."

"What?" Clara spread the blinds with her fingertips and peered through the twilight to be sure he wasn't standing outside her apartment. Just because his address said New York didn't mean he was actually there. "Look, I'm sorry," she said, letting the blinds go with a small clatter. "The deal's off. I never should've listed it for sale in the first place."

"But I've already paid you. I've already started making the arrangements. You can't just call the deal off."

"Yes," she said, "I can. I refunded the payment. So you keep your money, I'll keep my piano, and we can forget this ever happened. Good night, Greg." She was about to hang up when she heard his voice keening through the tiny speaker.

"Wait! Please!"

She put the phone back to her ear and sighed into it before flopping down on the futon and looking at the ceiling.

"If it's a matter of money, I'll pay more." His radio voice turned breathy and went up a few notes, as if he were trying and failing to sound calmer than he was.

"It's not about the money."

"Clara, please. Listen to me." He cleared his throat. "I *need* that piano."

She tossed her good hand up in a gesture of frustration. "There are thousands of other pianos for sale. Better ones. Cheaper ones."

"I need *that* one."

She closed her eyes. "So do I."

He said nothing for a moment. Clara could hear him slowly exhaling. "Okay. How about this. Let me rent it."

"Rent it? For what?"

"For a week, two weeks tops. Keep the money, and let my guys come pick it up. When I'm finished, I'll have it delivered back to you."

"I didn't mean for how long, I meant why."

"Does it matter?"

She thought for a moment. "Well, it might if I were considering renting it, but I'm not. I'm sorry. I have to go now."

She let it go to voice mail the first time he called back, and the second. The third time she picked up right away and said, "Please, stop this."

"Let me explain," he said, rushing his words. "I'm a photographer. I do commercial work, fashion, portraits, the occasional wedding if I need the money. And music—instruments, concerts, CD covers, that sort of thing." He paused. "There's a photo series I've been thinking about for a long time that would feature an antique, ebonized upright Blüthner. I've been looking for one for a while, and there just aren't very many of them around. It would mean a lot to me if you would consider letting me use yours."

She stood up and paced the length of her small living room.

"Clara?" Greg said. "Are you there?"

"What kind of series?"

There was another pause on his end. "Well, I'm trying to depict the absence of music."

"With a piano? How does a piano show an absence of music? It makes music."

"Does it?"

She looked over at the Blüthner. Its silence was both an answer and a rebuke. "I guess not all the time."

"I'm fascinated by the instruments used to make the music. And the people who play them to make the music. But what happens to the music if the musician dies? Or the instrument's destroyed? What then?"

"I don't know." She made a small laughing sound, an audible blend of discomfort and curiosity.

"Have you ever been in a car or at a party where loud music was playing, then suddenly it got turned off? There's this after-echo of silence that you can feel. You can even see it, like there's been some physical shift in the space. Do you know what I mean?" He took a deep breath. "So I want to use the piano—your piano—as the symbol of what it feels like to inhabit the world when the music stops. I want to show it just being there, nobody playing it, just an ordinary object."

She was intrigued by his idea: that was exactly what the Blüthner was in her life. But she was still unconvinced. "I still don't understand why you need *this* piano."

When he answered, his voice was strained. "My mom used to play an upright Blüthner when I was a kid, and I've never forgotten it. I guess I'm sentimental."

Goose bumps flared up again on Clara's arms. She hadn't heard anyone speak as ardently about music since her father died. It was the one thing he'd ever seemed passionate about. She thought of her mother: arms crossed, no-nonsense shoes even on Saturday mornings, shoulder pads under all her blouses and jackets like a football player or a soldier suited up and ready to take the field. Then she thought of her father: a ghost even before he died, a shadow behind an unfolded newspaper, a disembodied voice on the phone saying, *I'll be home late, don't wait dinner for me.* Even if her parents were ignoring each other and her, too, she'd give anything to be back inside their yellow cottage, lying on the living room floor as some strain of classical music and cigarette smoke floated through the air above her.

"Where would you do it? In New York?"

"No, in California. Not too far from Bakersfield, actually. Like I said, I'd only need it for a week and a half or so, maybe not even that long if everything goes right, and I'm sure it will. The guys I'll use to move it are really good. They've worked for a set designer in Los Angeles for years and I've used them a couple times before on big jobs," he said. "That's not such a bad deal, is it? Three thousand bucks for less than two weeks' rental?"

No, she figured. It wasn't.

"So what do you say? If you let me rent it, then we both get what we want." He sounded so convinced, so sure of himself, that by contrast Clara immediately realized how uncertain she was about everything: the crappy apartment, her financial situation, her breakup with Ryan, her future. Even the damn piano she couldn't play and couldn't part with. *I hope you figure out whatever it is you want, I really do.*

"Fine," she said, "you can rent it. But it'll cost you five grand, not three, plus extra if you keep it longer than two weeks. It goes out of tune whenever you move it, and it's not cheap to fix. Okay?"

"Okay," he said with obvious relief. "That's great, Clara. It's terrific. Thank you." Her name from his mouth was like a caress in her ear. She pressed it harder against the phone. "I'll send you the money now. My guys'll be there this Saturday, the twenty-seventh. Does that work for you?"

"That'll work," Clara said. "By the way—well, maybe they'll expect it if they're professionals—but it took three friends and me to get it up a flight of stairs."

"They can handle it."

"And you promise you'll take good care of it?"

"Yes," he said, "of course. I'll sign a rental agreement if you'd like."

"How can I be sure that you'll be careful?"

"How can we be sure of anything?" he said. "I guess you'll just have to trust me."

After they hung up, Clara looked him up on the Internet. His website featured collections of work in the various categories he'd mentioned, and she clicked through all of them. His style was distinctive. He seemed to like stark contrasts: big swaths of sky and earth and human figures stirring between them. She was especially drawn to the landscapes, which conveyed movement that had been stopped in time: wind in trees, waves on a beach, water spilling over a cliff, storm clouds boiling in the sky. She found it interesting that in the portraits few of the subjects' faces were clear; instead, their identities were obscured in profile or beneath heavy shadows or simply blurred. The work appealed to her. Unfussy, straightforward, clean.

She clicked on the biography tab.

> *"I record what is there and what is not, so that you may see what it is that I hear."*
>
> —*Greg Zeldin*

Greg Zeldin was raised in Los Angeles. He moved to New York in his early twenties to study music and fine art photography. He spent several years assisting many of the world's top advertising and fashion photographers before opening his own studio five years ago.

Greg has drawn upon traditional and modern photographic techniques as well as his understanding of musical composition to develop a synesthetic style that New York Times *art critic Euben Goethe has called "an interpretation of the mysterious forces of music, nature, time and humanity that is as deeply lyrical as it is visual."*

Greg is available for documentary, editorial, and commercial projects. For additional information concerning bookings, exhibitions, or ordering prints, please contact us. Thank you for visiting.

"When we separate music from life we get art."
—John Cage, composer

Unlike the obscured faces in his portraits, his own head shot was startlingly clear: his torso was angled aside, but his face was turned directly toward the camera, one thick eyebrow arched in an expression at once arrogant and vulnerable. It seemed in conflict with itself, and he might've looked menacing except for the baby-bird quality of his translucent skin and the downy fuzz that his receding hairline had left behind. His lips were full and pouty against a square jawline, and while they suggested a smile, there was no hint of one at the corners of his intensely light blue eyes. The sly gaze was so unrelenting that Clara felt as though he were right there in the room, staring at her.

So that you may see what it is that I hear. She looked at the piano and thought about that. She had known people who always heard music in their minds, always humming or whistling or tapping along to a beat that drummed only in their imaginations. Her father had once taken her to a performance of Rachmaninoff and Prokofiev by a young American pianist. Clara couldn't remember anything about the concert except for his comments about it afterward. He said that the way the pianist's hands flew across the keyboard, how she shifted her entire body with the pull and sway of the music, made him feel the concertos right down to his bones. He also said he'd be able to hear them again anytime he wanted in his mind, that he wished he had a talent for making music but didn't, so he was grateful for the mental recordings. "Do you keep music in your head like that, Clara?" he asked. Searching her imagination for an answer and finding none, she simply nodded. "Then you understand," he said solemnly, and drove her home in silence.

She wondered now what having a jukebox in your mind would be like. Whenever anything did get stuck in her head— a jingle from a television commercial, some popular tune—she found it claustrophobic and couldn't wait for it to stop. When music was playing on a stereo or in the garage, she could tune it out or switch it off if it got tiresome, but now she wondered if this was a shortcoming on her part. If she'd been able to hold a song in her mind, perhaps she could've learned how to really play the piano. She might've been like that concert pianist they'd seen, whose hands were probably delicate and clean instead of callused and grease-stained and broken.

Katya threaded her hands into her hair, yanking it at the roots. Mikhail watched without betraying his growing anger as small clumps of it fell to the rectangle of carpet that looked newer than the rest. "What have you done?" she screamed. "What have you done? What have you done?"

Grisha was on the floor, crying along with his mother; next to him, where she'd dropped it, the *avoska* spilled the whole chicken she'd stood in line for two hours to buy.

"What have *I* done, Katya?" Mikhail's voice began its trembling ascension. "What have *I* done? I told you I would think of how to take your piano out of Russia. I could've pushed it out of the window or burned it for fuel, but I told you I would find a plan, and I did. You should be on your knees in front of me, thanking me in every way you can imagine for my brilliant solution to your problem—not shrieking at me like this." His pale cheeks bloomed red, and he tapped the thinning patch of hair at his temple. "For a year you've treated me like a secondclass citizen. So gloomy all the time. Never smiling. You just want to rot here in this place, eh? You tell me you won't leave without that fucking piano, so I thought and thought and then after you tell me about the visit from your pansy ballerino, my mind gave me the idea you should be thanking me for. Now here you are, making my son cry, disturbing the neighbors, disfiguring yourself. Stand up! You disgust me."

Katya had sunk down onto the carpet where her piano had

stood for the three years they'd lived in this shabby apartment. Finished with her hair, she clutched at the fibers that had cushioned the Blüthner, absorbing the vibrations of her music.

"That night I went to see Boris, you should've seen his face!" At this, Mikhail laughed. "Let us say he was not expecting a visit from me. Such a guilty look on him! He's no KGB, I tell you. When he told you about his fancy ideas, did you wonder how he could ever get the money he needed? Maybe he is some Menshevik turning pirouettes into social reform, I don't know. I don't care. But I know something about him that you do not."

"What are you saying?" she asked without looking at him. "Just tell me what you did with my piano." Her tears fell into the fibers; it felt as though her entire soul would leak out from her eyes.

"Simple," he said, his voice brightening with his own self-regard. "I never could believe that a man like him, so light like a whisper, elegant as a tsarina, would have such love for a woman, but he does, Katerina, he does." Mikhail bent down next to her, his knees popping as he crouched. He reached under her chin with his thick index finger and lifted her face toward him so he could look at her. "And it is not you. It is the *babki* he carries in his wallet.

"To find weakness is not so difficult, you know," he continued. "Doesn't matter if you're talking about a structure or a circuit or a person. A good engineer knows what to look for, but a great engineer can see it without effort. Boris's weakness is as obvious as his dainty loafers. Nobody in Russia can afford such things, Katerina. When you lent him my slippers at the door the day he came here, did you notice how fine and soft his shoes were? Italian-made, without question. Even if a ballerino travels to Italy, he cannot afford these luxuries on a Soviet salary. Do you see where I'm going with this? Has your soft mind caught up with me yet?"

Mikhail laughed. "I will give your small friend credit; he understood very quickly. When I mentioned his fine loafers and suggested that the KGB might like to know where he got the cabbage for such things, he realized the dangerous situation he was in. It's not so hard to see, is it, Katerina? I didn't know exactly what he is buying and selling, but when I guessed that it was something he could transport in his ass while he was twirling across the border then sell to someone who would put it up his nose, his face told me I was correct. Maybe after he buys those fancy shoes he uses his drug money to fund his little revolution, I don't know. Good for him. And what he puts up his ass is of no interest to me, Katya. I'm sure it has been stretched out many times by a variety of objects. But the KGB has great imagination for such things. There is no telling how creatively they would explore Boris's cavernous hole if they had reason to believe he was hiding something there."

"Where is my piano?"

"*Chi-chi-chi.* I'm trying to tell you. I made a proposition to him. In exchange for my silence, I offered to sell it to him."

"Why?" she screamed.

"It's only temporary, Katya. My solution for getting your fucking piano safely out of Russia. We will go to Europe first, I told you. Boris also goes to Europe with his ballet company, as a cover to move drugs, yes? And also to buy shoes." He laughed again. "So I suggested he pack his opiates behind the—what do you call it? The iron frame? I think he even agreed it was much more logical for a traveling ballerino to hide his inventory in a musical instrument instead of inside his abused rectum. I'm surprised he hadn't thought of it before. Perhaps he could transport the same amount—who knows how vast his own emptiness is—but certainly it would be easier to feign innocence if the drugs were discovered inside a piano. And then he could still enjoy a decent shit along the way. And, when he finishes his smuggling, he gives us back the piano. Everybody's happy." Mikhail smiled broadly, baring his small, yellow teeth, and opened his hands in a gesture of triumph. "See, I promised you I would solve this problem. Now, stop with the crying before your misery becomes contagious. Soon we will go. We will all have a big adventure, even your precious piano."

Katya dropped her head, and a heaving sob escaped her, a grief that could not fill the space where the Blüthner had been. There was no reason to hope that she would ever see it again, no matter what Mikhail had done with it. She had never known that he could be so cruel. His anger, which had simmered steadily the longer they'd waited, she could forgive. But not his cruelty. And Boris, could that story possibly be true? She had no idea who to ask—if not her own husband, who was there to trust anymore?

The child, temporarily abandoned to his own fate, had stopped crying for a moment, just long enough to catch his breath before starting again.

The Saturday morning Greg's movers were to arrive, Clara drove to Kappas Xpress Lube for the first time since her accident a week before. Peter's mother was at the computer, completing an order, and when Anna saw her she pushed her chair back and walked over to Clara with her arms open.

"*Yassou, koukla*," Anna said, taking Clara's cast in both her hands. "You poor thing, look at you. And so *thin* already. You're eating the food I send you, yes? I tell Peter to take it to you."

"Yes, thank you." Clara hugged her, breathing in her familiar scent of baby powder and motor oil. Peter, she thought, was lucky to have a mother like Anna.

"But he made that *avgolemono* by himself," she said, and winked.

Clara laughed, and then realized she hadn't done so in a while. "He told me. It was really good, but he learned from the best."

"When are you going to come to dinner, huh? When are you coming back to work?"

"I'm ready to come back now," Clara said, "but I can't do anything." She held up her swollen hand.

"You come back. You can stay up front, do the register. Or be service writer until you're better. It's not good for you to be home alone."

Clara shook her head. "It takes me forever to type. And Teddy's the service writer. You don't need two." She shrugged and gave a half-smile. "It's okay. I'll be back as soon as the cast's off."

Anna leaned forward and whispered, "You need money? You need anything, you just say."

"Thank you."

Peter came up from the pit, his work boots heavy on the steep metal steps, wiping his hands on a grease-covered shop towel stuffed partway into his front pocket. "Hey," he said, smiling when he saw her. Then he turned to his mother and said something in Greek.

She nodded and winked at Clara. "Always somebody need something," she said, and slid open the glass door to shout to her husband, "I'm coming!"

"You doing okay?" Peter asked, bending toward her.

"Yeah, fine. Ready for this thing to be off." She tipped her chin toward the pit. "Why are you changing oil?"

"Alex always leaves a mess down there. I know how much you hate it when he does that, so . . ." He tossed the towel into a bucket. "You want to get some lunch or something?"

Clara smiled at how his eyes, turned down slightly at the corners, always revealed his emotions. "Can't, sorry. I just came by to borrow some of those moving blankets we've got somewhere."

"Shit, you're not moving again already?" He winked at her.

"Well, I did get five grand from that photographer, so maybe I should. Find a place on the ground floor to keep from moving the piano up another flight of stairs."

"Or you could let him keep the piano and live anywhere you wanted to, happily ever after."

She set her mouth in a hard line and gave him a go-to-hell look. "Will you please just give me a hand with the blankets? Greg's movers are coming to pick it up today, and I want to make sure they wrap it up right."

Peter looked like he was about to say something then

thought better of it. He just shook his head and went to find the blankets.

The surge of protectiveness she felt for the Blüthner took her by surprise. She imagined Greg scrutinizing it upon delivery, examining its yellowing keys, its scratches and scuff marks. Like a mother sending her child to school on picture day, she wanted to make sure it looked its best. So she put tiny dabs of toothpaste on a soft cloth and wiped each of the eighty-eight keys from back to front. "Now smile," she said, then closed the fallboard.

Examining the case, she paused at the treble end, where she noticed what had to be one of Peter's thumbprints. There was a smaller one overlapping it, and she wondered if it was hers. She sprayed on the special high-gloss piano polish she'd bought at Kern Keyboards and wiped them away.

She ran the cloth over every inch of the ebony lacquer, pausing at each of the major blemishes. Gone were the occasional water spots and fingerprints and smudges, but she couldn't quite buff out the accumulated scratches or the two dents on the top of the case that had been there when she got it. They were faint enough that they hadn't shown up in the photos she'd posted on her ad. She touched these as though noticing them for the first time. Would Greg be upset that she hadn't mentioned them? Would they show up in his photographs and ruin the effect?

Suddenly the idea of a stranger taking even temporary possession of her piano flooded her with panic—should she really let him take it away?—and she was still in the throes of doubt when someone knocked at her door.

Two men, stocky and serious-looking, nodded at her. "*Estamos aquí para el piano*," one of them said. He was bald and had a scar that ran from behind his right ear down his neck and into the thistle of hair poking out of the neck of his T-shirt.

He carried an armload of quilted moving pads. The other one was taller, with mocha-colored skin and wavy hair that hung halfway down his back. He rested his arm on the top portion of a padded and upholstered board that was clearly a piece of moving equipment.

She stood there looking at them. The bald guy stared flatly back at her, waiting. The other one checked the brass number screwed into the door just above the peephole, glanced at the paper in his hand, and said, "For pickup?"

"Yeah, sorry." She opened the door to let them pass. "Come in."

They wiped their feet before entering, although there was no doormat, then went straight to the piano, pulled it away from the wall, and began wrapping it in the heavy pads they'd brought.

"I have more blankets," she said, and the bald one looked at her and shook his head as if admonishing her.

She watched as they secured the pads with packing tape and gave each other directions in Spanish. This was just another job for them, just another day. It seemed they knew what they were doing, but they didn't seem particularly concerned about the piano; it was simply an object that needed to be moved from one place to another. Clara stepped forward and adjusted the pad where it had drooped off the corner of the case.

"You have to be careful with it," she said. "It's very . . . old."

"Yes, miss."

With the blankets in place, they maneuvered the piano onto the padded board, adjusting it until the bass end was snuggled up against the brace that came out at a right angle. The taller guy held the piano in place atop this platform while his partner ran thick nylon straps into slots in the board and fed them through to the other side. Each strap went over the piano and was buckled tightly to itself. When that was done, they squatted down slightly and buckled the second set of straps around their hips.

"Listo," the tall one said. On the count of *tres* they stood up, lifting the piano off the ground. The bald one looked at Clara with an unreadable expression, as if he had all the time in the world, despite the fact that he was holding up half of a five-hundred-and-sixty-pound load.

"Oh," Clara said, realizing that they were waiting for her. She moved quickly to hold the door open. The guys took careful, synchronized steps until the piano was over the threshold and then on the deck. They paused at the top step, then again counted and lifted and the bald man went first, descending the top two steps. The tall one held the piano steady and then slowly let it tip forward until it rested almost entirely on his partner's backside. The bald man looked strong but wasn't very large, certainly not big enough to bear the weight of the piano himself.

"Wait," Clara said, panic rising again. "Are you sure you can do this?"

They seemed not to hear her, because they continued their slow plod down the fourteen steps, a span that looked—that had been—treacherous to Clara. Surely the straps would come undone or their legs would give out and the piano would go crashing down. She held her breath, anticipating disaster, but they made it. Without speaking, they eased the piano down off the stairs. The bald guy used his foot to kick a four-wheeled dolly into position, and they moved forward and set the piano on top of it, then began rolling it along the sidewalk, toward the parking lot.

Clara let out her breath and jogged down the stairs. In spite of their apparent competence, she wondered how careful they would be when she wasn't looking. "Excuse me," she said to the bald one, shielding her eyes from the late afternoon sun. "What's your name?"

"Juan."

"Juan," she said, "can you tell me where you're taking the

piano?" He narrowed his eyes as if he didn't understand. "I mean, are you allowed? To tell me, I mean." He released the ramp from the truck and climbed up into the bed. "Of course you should be allowed to," she continued. "I'm only renting it to the guy, not selling it. It's not unreasonable for me to know where you're going."

They pushed the Blüthner up the shallow incline. "*Cuídate, Beto,*" Juan said to his partner. She knew enough Spanish to understand that this meant *be careful.*

She sucked in her breath, and Juan looked at her. "It's okay, miss. No problem." Inside the bed there were two duffel bags, a toolbox, and another stack of moving pads. The movers secured the piano to the rails along the length of the truck, then flipped the dolly over on its flat side so it wouldn't roll around. After getting out, they pulled the door shut and locked it. Juan walked to the cab of the truck, rifled around, and withdrew a map.

"Here," he said, pointing to a tiny town just west of Las Vegas that had been circled in blue ink. "Then here." He pointed to a large green area labeled Death Valley National Park, then swirled his finger over it. "And around here."

Clara leaned in and searched the map. "What? Why there? What's he going to do with it there?"

Juan lifted an eyebrow and shrugged. "Taking pictures. Then . . ." He made a flicking motion with his hands before dusting them together. Clara didn't know what he meant by that, but it did nothing to ease her concerns.

"I don't understand," she said.

Without changing his expression, Juan lifted his hands to his face and pretended he was holding a camera, clicking the shutter.

"No, sorry." Clara shook her head. "I know he's a photographer. I mean I don't understand what he's going to do with my piano in Death Valley."

Juan shrugged again. "Wherever he say." Then he tipped his chin at Beto, and they climbed into the cab, Beto on the driver's side, Juan on the other.

Clara stood there, hands hanging limply at her sides, trying to reconcile this odd itinerary with Greg's explanation of his photo essay.

Resting his arm on the open window frame, Juan turned to look at her and nodded with a vague smile that suggested she'd been tricked into this arrangement, that something ominous was going to happen. Had Juan's flicking motion been a symbol of finishing something? Or finishing something off?

As the truck started to pull away, Clara turned and sprinted up the sidewalk to her apartment, taking the stairs two at a time. She grabbed her backpack and cell phone and keys, locked the door—fumbling because of the sudden release of adrenaline—ran back down, slipping once and catching herself with her broken hand, which hurt but not enough to slow her until she was in her car and turning on the ignition and thinking, thinking, thinking: Which route would they take? East and then down Oswell, probably, instead of west to Mount Vernon—there was a construction project on the southbound side—and then they'd pick up Highway 58.

She caught up with them at the Virginia Avenue stoplight. Juan's elbow was still poking out from the passenger window, and the left blinker was on even though they were already in the turn-only lane. They probably couldn't hear the rhythmic blinking over the *cumbia* that blared from the truck's radio. The light went green and the truck pulled ahead.

"Come on, come on," Clara said to the car in between them. "Move over." She honked, and the driver glanced at her in his rearview mirror. She swished her hand at him and then pointed toward the truck. "I'm following them," she yelled, exaggerating the words as though he might actually hear her through the glass and metal. He flipped her off then moved into the other lane.

"Okay," she said. "Okay." She was right behind the truck. Now what? Make them pull over? Insist they return the piano to the apartment? Driving behind them, with the hairs on Juan's arm fluttering in the wind, the heavy beat percussing out of the truck, she realized this was a stupid idea. She eased off the gas and drifted back a little. *I should just go home.* But her broken hand refused to turn the wheel.

Katya stepped out of the car and squinted at the fierce sunlight. Even in Italy the sun hadn't been as bright as it was in California. Here, it glinted off of everything: the shop windows, the parking meters, even the sidewalks. She put on the sunglasses the woman from the Southern California Council for Soviet Jews had given her when she'd picked them up at LAX, just four weeks before. The same woman, Ella, was with them now, ushering her and Mikhail from place to place, helping them get settled.

"There," Ella said with a smile. "You look like a real American with those on." Katya didn't like them; they had heavy frames that covered her eyebrows and rested uncomfortably on her cheekbones. She wanted to throw them into the street, but didn't because she needed them. She resented this, and the resentment made her feel guilty, and the guilt made her feel even more depressed than she already was.

Mikhail beamed, happy as a child on his birthday, and led them into the United Desert Bank of California, where Ella would guide them through the necessary steps to open their first checking account. The money they would deposit—$400—seemed a huge sum compared to the amounts they'd subsisted on in Russia and Italy; it had been given to them by a local synagogue. "We didn't earn this money," she'd whispered to Mikhail when the rabbi's secretary had offered him the envelope filled with cash. "We can't accept it." But her husband wasn't embarrassed by charity. When, after they'd moved into a rental house paid for with an interest-free loan and she'd refused to go to the FEMA warehouse to pick up damaged canned food that supermarkets had donated, he'd gone instead. He said he planned to repay everyone as soon as he earned his first paycheck as an engineer for a top American firm. But first he had to learn enough English to get an interview; after a month in Los Angeles, he still knew only a few words.

The bank manager invited them to sit down at a large desk. "*Здравствуйте,*" he said. "*Добро пожаловать в Америку.*" He knew enough of the language to welcome them to America, because so many Russian immigrants had ended up there in West Hollywood. His bank was friendly to new residents in spite of their small initial deposits; he knew that Russians were viable. The doctors, translators, and engineers, even the blue-collar workers, often labored harder than their American counterparts because they were so grateful for their newfound freedom and their second chances. At weddings and other gatherings, their first toast was always to the United States. The manager knew they would be loyal customers, eventually taking out loans to buy houses and cars or open businesses. Hospitality toward them was a good investment.

Katya and Mikhail produced their passports and the INS-issued white cards that proved their refugee status. Ella helped them fill out the application: their new address on North Genesee Avenue, their proposed employment, their sponsor's information. They wrote their names awkwardly in English and signed the form.

Along the wall behind the desk were framed bank-sponsored posters of California landmarks: the Golden Gate Bridge, Lake Tahoe, Disneyland, Venice Beach, and more. As Mikhail completed some other paperwork, Katya stared at one image over the bank manger's shoulder.

After a moment he glanced back to see what had captured her attention. "You like that one?" he asked.

It was a strange image compared to the rest, all of which seemed determined to establish the state as one of perpetual Technicolor sunshine and happiness. It was the only one in black and white, a stunning photograph of what looked like a frozen lake with ice cracking into polygons in the foreground, pale mountain peaks beyond, and a wintry sky above. More representative of her homeland, she thought, it seemed out of place next to the others. Just like she felt herself to be. She gave a half-smile and nodded.

"That's Badwater Basin, the lowest point in North America. Eerie, isn't it?"

Katya nodded again. She would have to look up the word *eerie* in her dictionary at home.

"Like it says there, it's in Death Valley National Park. It's about a four-and-a-half-, five-hour drive northeast of here, right on the Nevada border. Kind of desolate, but worth a visit if you get a chance. We've got a lot to see here in California. You should take your son to Disneyland. It's a real American institution."

Katya nodded once more.

"All set," the man said, and handed Mikhail their temporary checkbook with a shiny plastic holder. "Let me know if there's anything else I can do to help you while you're getting settled in."

Ella translated, and Mikhail smiled broadly. "*Отлично. Спасибо. Спасиб,*" he said, nodding and pumping the manager's hand. Then he elbowed Katya, who again was staring at the black-and-white picture on the wall, and she came out of the reverie she'd slipped into and said, "Thank you also."

That night, after her husband and son were asleep, Katya tiptoed into the kitchen and turned on the light. She looked around at the gleaming fixtures, the white tile counter, the large refrigerator that could hold more food than they would eat in a week. In Leningrad, their apartment was only twenty-seven square meters, exactly nine per person. This kitchen alone was almost that big, and they also had two bedrooms, a large bathroom, a living room, a backyard with a patio, all filled with far more donated furniture than they needed. The walls had recently been painted a white as bright as their future was supposed to be. The large windows on the perimeter walls made Katya feel exposed, even though they looked out on the vine-covered fence or lemon trees or rosebushes. She thought of her mother, always hunched over a pot in a dank corner, trying to turn next to nothing into a decent meal. She would be overwhelmed by the magnificence of this kitchen and probably insist on sleeping on a cot next to the breakfast table so that others could live under the same roof. *I don't need to sleep in my own room, what a waste! This is more than enough for me. I could die here it's so beautiful.* Katya thought of this, and of the other refuseniks waiting for approval to leave Russia. They didn't care that they'd have to learn another language, a new currency, a new transportation system, a new set of rules. It was worth it. So what if they had to sell everything before they left? Maybe they didn't care that they'd never again see their relatives or friends who stayed behind. But Katya did.

At the airport, she'd sobbed until her head ached as she clutched her mother and father for the very last time. It was a fact. If you left, you never would return. And her parents, who'd never leave Russia, would be buried near where they'd lived their modest lives. She'd never even see their graves. After a year in Los Angeles, she would be given her green card and made a legal citizen instead of a refugee. In another five, she could take a test in English to become an American citizen. But the thought of getting buried in an American cemetery made her heart ache.

Why are you thinking of your death, Ekaterina? Are you ready to join me? She had heard this harsh voice in her head ever since she'd left Leningrad. She didn't know whose voice it was. Maybe it was a *domovoi* that followed her from house to house. Did Americans have house spirits? Probably not. They probably didn't want hairy goblins keeping the peace for them. She opened the oven door and peered in. No *domovoi* there. More likely it was the lost music who was talking to her. But it wasn't the music that could part the clouds and lift her into color; it was the music's absence that was whispering. Her country was on the other side of the world. Her parents were muted by the distance. Her piano, gone. Without those things, there was too much emptiness in her head.

"I would welcome it," she said aloud in the tiled kitchen, her voice bouncing back to her off the bright whiteness.

And your son? He is very young.

She lowered her voice. "Grisha will be fine. Many opportunities exist here. He won't need me."

Perhaps that's true. American sons seem to find success. But what about your husband?

"He isn't the man I married. Angry all the time, except in front of other people. For them, he is happy and kind, but he saves the worst of himself for me. He always says he understands music, yet never remembers it. The same with the language. English words are too difficult for him. He drinks more now, and his excuse is that it helps to loosen his tongue."

It will be—

"Stop."

She opened the refrigerator, the cold air hitting her nightgown, and peered inside at groceries she could hardly remember buying. She was hungry, but nothing looked appetizing. While Mikhail struggled to learn English, it came easily to her. Milk. Eggs. Orange juice. Lettuce. Mayonnaise. Carrots. Velveeta. She closed the door, sat down at the kitchen table, and laid her head down on her crossed arms.

The three of them had flown from Leningrad to Vienna with eight suitcases, wearing as many of their clothes as they could beneath their coats even though it was mid-May and already quite warm. Because they had almost no money, their parents had given them as much as they could afford, and they'd used it to purchase goods that were in demand in Europe: Russian vodka, caviar, quality babushkas, hand-painted ornaments, matryoshka dolls, linens. Others had told them that selling these black-market imports was their only hope to make enough money to survive the emigration.

After two miserable weeks in Austria, living in a tiny, dark apartment with two other families, all of whom were suffering from an intestinal flu that ruined the collective mood as well as the bathroom they shared, they were transferred by train to an Italian village on the Tyrrhenian Sea called Ladispoli. They had two rooms with damp, peeling plaster walls in a building filled with other Russian refugees waiting for permission to resettle permanently in the United States, Canada, or Australia. Katya remembered that first night in Italy. Standing on the balcony outside their walk-up railroad flat, she saw a full moon, yellow and heavy in the sky, that looked closer to the earth than it should've been. This scared her. The air was warm and smelled like the ocean, and it, too, scared her. She should have loved it, but she couldn't.

They lived in Italy for a year and nine months. They sold almost everything they'd brought along at the Sunday morning flea markets in Rome, but by the fall they needed more money to pay their rent and buy food.

"Give me your records to sell," Mikhail told her. Katya's small collection was by her favorite Russian composers: Tchaikovsky, Rachmaninoff, Prokofiev, Mussorgsky. Scriabin, Borodin, Taneyev, Shostakovich. All she had left of her home and her music, though of course they had no turntable on which to play them.

"No," she told him. "I'll starve first."

"Then you will find work. I'm tired of you moping around every day, letting me bear all the burdens."

Mikhail had been taking minor off-the-books jobs in restaurants and construction. "Road building," he'd said ruefully after a day of filling potholes on the Strada Statale. While Katya cleaned houses, an older woman in their apartment building looked after their son and told her she was lucky that she could find work, because not everybody was able to. She felt like a traitor, since she only wanted to go home.

"Misha, I want to go to the Death Valley," Katya told him a few days after they'd opened their bank account. She was tired of traipsing around the city with Ella, gathering castoffs and hand-me-downs with which to fill their too-big and already crowded house.

To her surprise, he agreed. Perhaps he, too, was tired of the city, even though he would never dream of admitting to anything of the sort. On a Friday morning in mid-April, they packed their thirdhand car, a tan 1972 Cadillac DeVille of which Mikhail was unusually proud, with snacks and drinks and extra blankets for their son, and drove four hours to Panamint Springs without stopping. They had a late lunch, filled the gas tank, bought a map of the park, and asked the man at the counter to show them the route to Badwater Basin.

"Now, you know it's a mighty big place," he said. "Lots more to see than just Badwater. You got the Mesquite Flat Sand Dunes, Salt Creek, Devil's Golf Course, Mosaic Canyon, Ubehebe Crater, Racetrack Playa . . ." He held up a different finger for each location; then he looked down at them and paused. "How long you plannin' on stayin'? I guess I should've asked."

"For today," Katya answered. "Then we go home to Los Angeles."

"Well, you might consider spendin' at least a night if you can swing it. There's a cheap place in Beatty on the other side of the park, got a casino and a swimmin' pool. If you can manage that, then here's how you could see a fair number of the more accessible areas." Katya and Mikhail looked at each another and watched as he circled and numbered a few landmarks and drew a line east into and around the park to the town of Beatty, then southwest back into the park to a couple other places and finally out to the southeast side. "You can go on home from there, get a little different view of things." They thanked him and, as they'd long been accustomed to doing, did as they were told.

They drove mostly in silence as civilization became just a speck in the rearview mirror and a wholly different terrain unfurled around them. Katya looked out over the hood of their tan car to the tan road that cut through low tan hills dotted occasionally with clumps of tan vegetation. She began to worry that she'd made a mistake; it seemed lonesome and deserted, not starkly beautiful. Was this why someone had named it Death Valley?

Grisha was too young to notice the landscape, but once they parked and got out of the car he squealed with delight and ran around in every direction. It made Katya laugh, too, watching him toddle over sand and rocks on his fat little legs. Even Mikhail seemed to relax. He did a series of stretches then squatted down and extended his feet one at a time, as if performing a slow-motion Cossack dance; over the lusty wind, Katya could hear his knees pop. He offered her a Coca-Cola, which had gone warm, but she drank it anyway, letting the carbonation sting her nose.

"I will take your picture," Mikhail said. He held up the Polaroid camera they'd borrowed from Ella—"Enjoy it!" she'd commanded them—and pointed it at Katya. She'd been dusting sand off her son's open hands and turned back toward her husband when he called to her; he snapped the shutter just as a gust blew her hair across her face.

"Take another," she said. "I wasn't ready."

But he shook his head and closed the camera. "We can't. It's too expensive. Only one picture at each place."

They had only one eight-pack of instant film and took five pictures that day before checking into the least expensive room in the hotel. They ate their leftovers from lunch in their room, and then Katya gave Grisha a bath. "I will go to the casino," Mikhail told her, tapping his temple and smiling shrewdly, "to win back the cost of the hotel and even more so we can buy a fancy breakfast tomorrow and another pack of the film."

But when he stumbled back to their room hours later, stinking of alcohol, he slammed the door and let loose a barrage of curses. They'd tricked him, he insisted in a slurring voice, gotten him drunk and taken advantage of him because they were afraid of his superior gambling skills. Katya hushed him, worried that he would wake the neighbors, and helped him to bed. There was no breakfast at all the next morning.

Back in Los Angeles, Katya kept up the habit of sitting alone in the kitchen after her family was asleep. She drank according to her mood: tea if she was melancholy; coffee if she was already anxious, though it might keep her awake for hours; vodka if the whispers of the *domovoi* or the lost music were too insistent in her ears. Tonight, a night in early May, with field crickets trilling outside her window, Katya poured herself a half glass of vodka from Mikhail's stash.

She spread out the eight photographs from their trip on the table and studied each one for minutes at a time. The film carton had said it could produce "Supercolor," but all the images looked as dull and tan as the faded finish on their car, Katya always standing either alone or with their son in front of jagged peaks, dry lakebeds, or undisturbed sand. No trees, no flowers, no other people—just empty landscapes that suggested a cold and unpopulated otherworld. Even she didn't look like herself. Mikhail had managed to capture her only when she was half turned, or with her eyes closed, or bent down over her son. There was only one in which her face was clear. She was standing on the dry salt-covered Badwater Basin, the place that had looked like a frozen lake when she'd seen it on the banker's wall. She was staring up at the cliffs above—Coffin Peak, she remembered one of them was called—with something akin to longing. Behind her, the scenery did appear frozen. That was how she felt inside—dead. As, in fact, she did in all the Polaroids. Even the bank manager had called this place desolate, a word she didn't know but somehow understood.

There's no music there, came the whisper in her ears.

The voice was right. These hot-weather vistas seemed frozen because they were trapped in time and silence. Just like she was.

Maybe it wasn't the case that she didn't look like herself in these photographs. Instead, maybe it was that she did.

On the highway, the eastbound traffic was dense enough that Clara could keep the truck in sight without being conspicuous. She'd decided to trail them for a while, since she didn't have anything better to do and the mountains were lighting up in a lovely fiery glow as the sun set behind her. She rolled her window down, then the passenger side to eliminate the annoying low-frequency buffeting that filled the car when she reached a certain speed. She would turn around soon, just not yet.

When Clara was young, her mother never rode in a car with the windows down; she didn't like the wind blowing her hair out of place, loose strands getting stuck in her mauve lipstick. But Uncle Jack always did. As a hobby, he fixed up old Chevrolet trucks from the 1950s, none of which had air-conditioning, and once Clara was living with them, he'd often take her for long drives during that lonesome stretch between dinner and bedtime. They would head out of Bakersfield toward the Sierras, driving past the oil fields, the bluffs overlooking the Kern River, the college. Occasionally they went as far as the big county park, where they might get out and take a walk, mostly in silence, looking for the peacocks that liked to wander there. Or else they went north into the Sierra Nevada foothills or south to look at the native grapevines, or west through citrus orchards and fields of almonds and pistachios. He didn't try to make up for the lost, empty parts of her life; he just drove her around at a leisurely pace with the windows down, letting the wind do the talking for both of them.

That was the comfortable rhythm she fell into now, secretly following the truck. The produce fields and vineyards scrolled by like moving pictures then opened into grazing areas and low, grassy hills. Half an hour out of Bakersfield, they approached the Tehachapi Pass wind farm; off to her right, the giant white turbines made their slow, synchronized rotations. She imagined the inner workings, the energy created by the blades turning the drive shaft, the gearbox increasing its speed to power the generator, which then converted kinetic energy into an electrical current, which flowed down a cable inside the turbine tower. Watching the machines relaxed her; she loved the complicated simplicity of the moving parts, the static elements that could wring megawatts out of thin air.

Her phone rang, startling her out of her reverie.

"Hey," Peter said when she answered. "You hungry?"

Clara considered this. It was almost seven, and she hadn't eaten since lunch. "Yeah, actually I am," she said. "But I'm not around. I'm . . . on the road. I had to go somewhere."

"Oh," he said. "So did those guys pick up the piano?"

"They did."

"You okay about it?"

"Not really." She sped up just a little, again feeling the need to stay close to the Blüthner. She attached her gaze to the truck and let it pull her. She wanted to be eight years old again, or six, or two. She wanted to be in the car with her mother and father back when they were a still family that was going to live happily ever after, all of them. She wanted to stretch out on the backseat and drift off to sleep, curled up in the murmur of their voices. She stifled a cry with a single sniff.

"Clara, talk to me."

"I'm fine. I just want to make sure they get there safely."

"Where is *there*?"

"Vegas, I think. And then they're going into Death Valley, though I don't know exactly where." Abruptly she understood why she hadn't yet turned around to go home. "I know it's weird, but I want to meet Greg."

"Fucking hell, Clara. You went with them? What's going on? Why do you want to meet this guy?" He paused. "Have you been talking to him?"

"I'm not *with* them. I'm behind them, in my own car. And no, I haven't been talking to Greg. This isn't about him, it's about the piano."

Peter's long exhalation sounded like a soft wind in her ear. "Sorry, I know it's none of my business, but it doesn't seem right, you taking off like that, going who knows where to meet some dude you don't even know. Where are you meeting him?"

"I don't actually know. Nobody knows I'm behind them. It was sort of spontaneous—"

"For fuck's sake, Clara. I'm leaving right now."

"Oh, stop it. I can take care of myself."

"It'll be midnight by the time you get there. Nothing good happens at midnight in Vegas."

"Well, whatever happens will stay there, right?" She tried to laugh, but it sounded forced. "Look, I won't do anything stupid. I just need to do this."

He was quiet for a beat. "Will you do one thing for me? Could you call me when you get there to let me know you're okay?"

She could picture him holding the phone against his scruffy cheek, hunched forward like he did when he was working, as if he could isolate and solve the problem by enclosing it inside his physical bearing. She smiled. "Yes, I will. I promise."

"And if you get tired, you know, just blow it off. We had a guy in here this week fell asleep behind the wheel and drove into a telephone pole. Lucky he wasn't going very fast. So, keep the windows open."

"I will."

"I know," he said.

By the time they hung up, the sun's remnant glow was nearly gone. She put in a CD that had been her uncle's favorite, one he'd called his driving collection, though they rarely played anything during their jaunts: James Taylor and Cat Stevens, Neil Young and Bob Dylan. She fast-forwarded until she found the song she liked the most, Simon and Garfunkel's "Homeward Bound," and she listened to it as the night engulfed her. The temperature dropped quickly in the foothills, but she kept the windows down anyway, her hair blowing against her face, catching at her lips. The red lights of the U-Haul moved steadily forward.

She began to feel sleepy, and her mind wandered back to her childhood home, as it sometimes did. It was only in these moments that she might catch a glimpse of her parents' faces. Their images had started to fade from Clara's memory almost immediately. The harder she tried to conjure them, the fuzzier they became. Within days, she couldn't summon the shape of her father's birthmark. She couldn't remember which side of her mother's face had the dimple, or if her eyes were brownish-green or greenish-brown, or what was the last time she'd given her a hug. She had hugged her good-bye before she went to her friend Tabitha's house that night, hadn't she? She could smell the cigarettes, could hear the music, but was it Chopin? Or maybe one of the Russians? Their faces, though, were slowly disappearing, melting like they must have in the fire.

A few years after they died, she did some research. As the flames lick a body, the outer layers of skin begin to fry and peel away. After a few minutes, the deeper, thicker layers of skin shrink and split, leaking the yellow body fat contained underneath, which further fuels the fire. Then the muscles dry out and shrink, and finally the bones, which take longer to burn, until all that's left is a charred skeleton, unrecognizable except to dentists and doctors with X-rays and other medical records. She had only one photo to rely on—the family albums had burned along with them—because her mother had sent it to Ila many years before. Someone had taken it on the beach near their house on a late-summer afternoon; the shadows in the image were long, the light low and glowing on their bodies. Her mother wore a blue one-piece and hat, the blunt ends of her reddish-blond hair sticking out from underneath. She faced the camera head-on, her weight shifted onto one leg. She was hiding a cigarette behind her back, but not well; smoke curled up over her shoulder like it was whispering in her ear. Her smile showed no teeth. Her father was in a pair of swim trunks, his midsection not yet paunched. His bucket hat shaded his forehead, and because both of them were wearing sunglasses they looked like they were in disguise. They could have been an anonymous pair of thirty-something parents, strangers plucked off the boardwalk and asked to pose, except that Clara was clearly herself in the picture, a toddler sitting in the sand between them, her eyes closed against the sun. She resented the picture for what seemed like a cruel withholding of the features she wanted most to see.

She blamed herself, of course. If she had loved them better, she would've been able to recall every detail of their living features. If she had loved them harder, then maybe they wouldn't have died.

They drove for another two hours before the truck pulled into a gas station off the highway. Now that they'd probably notice her and want to know why she'd followed them for three hours deep into the middle of nowhere in eastern

California, Clara was embarrassed. Wanting to meet Greg seemed like an inadequate explanation under the circumstances, so she tried to hide by pulling up to a pump a few rows down and standing where they couldn't see her while she filled her tank.

Both men stood outside the truck while Beto pumped the gas, stretching and making jokes she couldn't overhear. It didn't matter, as long as they didn't spot her or her white Corolla. They stopped laughing and settled into what looked like a companionable silence, and Juan's gaze passed over the pumps and the outbuilding and lighted, briefly, on her. She turned away. A minute or two later, she heard doors slamming and the truck starting up again, and she sheathed the pump nozzle and climbed back in her car, dark mountains and the impending strip lights of Vegas ahead of her.

But then, after forty-five minutes, just east of the California-Nevada border, the truck pulled off the highway and drove into a tiny town filled with shopping outlets and seedy casinos. Clara followed them down the mostly abandoned main street toward a cartoonish neon sign for Lucky's Golden Strike Inn and Gambling Hall, the kind of place she imagined would attract more insects than patrons. For a Saturday night, it didn't seem very busy. But maybe that was to be expected at a run-down hotel in the middle of nowhere. A few semis were parked in the big parking lot, and a middle-aged valet was slumped in a chair next to a pegboard where he'd hung a few sets of keys. Clara pulled in behind a semi and watched Beto drive up an empty row and make a wide, careful turn into a spot near the entrance. Juan hopped out and did a couple of knee bends, stretched his shoulders back, tipped his head side to side. Then he went around and opened the back of the truck. He pushed against the piano, shaking it gently as though to check the integrity of the tie-down. Apparently satisfied, he grabbed the two duffel bags and tossed one to Beto. Their voices carried on the crisp, clear air, but she could understand only a few disconnected words: *cansado* and *tomar algo* and *en la mañana*. Juan locked the truck, and they went inside the hotel, past the valet, with whom they exchanged juts of their chins without stopping, a greeting that suggested some sort of mutual recognition, not as individuals but as members of a social order that frequented run-down border-town casinos in the middle of the night.

She killed the engine and the headlights, and rolled the windows mostly up. She was hungry and tired and would've loved to stretch out on a bed—even one in a room that rented for only $29—but if the drivers weren't going to keep an eye on her piano overnight, then she would. She thought of Peter and how worried he would be if he knew what she was doing. How stupid he'd think she was behaving. Why babysit a locked-up piano in a casino parking lot? That was a downside of loyalty: logic didn't always disrupt its manifestation.

Reluctantly she dialed his number and was relieved when it went to voice mail. "I'm at a hotel," she said. "I'm going to crash, so you don't need to call back. Just wanted to let you know I'm all right. Okay?" She hated leaving voice mails. It made her feel lonesome, speaking into the void like that.

Katya took the Polaroids out of the drawer, laid them on her bed, and ran her finger around the white borders that had begun to fray at the edges. Throughout the five years they'd been in Los Angeles, she looked at the photos whenever her heart felt like it was breaking, whenever the blinding joyous sunshine was too much for her to bear. She thought that making herself feel worse might somehow make her feel better.

She tried to be happy. Ella had introduced them to the extensive Russian immigrant community, acquainting them with industrious, conscientious people who were eager to share meals and information. Ella invited them to the synagogue, though they weren't religious. She helped Katya enroll Grisha in preschool, where he learned English and made friends. She also went with her to the Salvation Army to buy a used upright Yamaha piano with a nice walnut finish. After being delivered and tuned it sounded all right but was nothing special. To Katya it had a hollow tone that lacked the essential warmth she was accustomed to, and the music she played on it barely stirred her. With Ella's recommendations, she acquired a few students. But none of them, even the Russian ones, had a passion for the piano. America was too sunny. Nobody wanted to stay indoors and practice. In Russia, the winters were long, and people turned to music for warmth and light. Music, if it was played properly, could melt the tundra. But who needed a piano when there were beaches all around?

To make things worse, her husband was now even unhappier than she. He'd failed to learn the language and therefore had no prospects in his field of expertise. Instead of becoming a top engineer, overseeing the construction of beautiful American roads, he was forced to drive on them behind the wheel of a yellow taxi. As his former comrades flourished, building wealth and establishing new roots, Mikhail withdrew from society. He was too embarrassed by his lack of success to enjoy the company of other Russians and became paranoid that his American neighbors would reject him if they knew what a failure he was. When he was at home, he kept the windows closed so they couldn't spy on him, and he forbade Katya from playing any Russian music, lest anyone hear her and think they were Communists. Although he was miserable in Los Angeles, he knew he would die of shame if for any reason they were sent back to the Soviet Union. Ironically, going back was what she wanted most. No matter how much time passed, she didn't miss her homeland or her parents any less. She still felt like part of her heart had been cut out, and she still couldn't forgive her husband for doing the cutting.

Grisha wandered into Katya's bedroom and sat down beside her. "Will you tell me the story?" he asked.

He was eight years old now, the same age she had been when the old German gave her the Blüthner, so many years ago.

"*Chi-chi-chi,*" Katya told him, still looking at the Polaroids. "You already know this fable so well already. You don't need me to tell it."

"But I want to hear it again," he said, turning onto his back and putting his head near her lap.

She sighed and shuffled the photographs until she found the one taken in the part of Death Valley known as Racetrack Playa. It had been a long and difficult drive to get there; the roads were bad, and their teeth had chattered against their will.

Toward the end their son began crying, pleading for them to stop the car, first in English and then in Russian. But Mikhail only gripped the steering wheel harder. "We have come this far already," he said.

In the foreground of the photo was a large, almost square rock. Behind it was a long trail in an otherwise undisturbed floor of dry mud that had cracked into polygon shapes that stretched out to the horizon. Because Mikhail had clicked the shutter too early, Katya could be seen walking toward the rock but was slightly out of the frame. They'd been told that these rocks were called "sailing stones" because they moved around Racetrack Playa without human or animal intervention, inscribing trails in the fine clay surface of the lakebed.

The rock reminded Katya of her Blüthner, shiny and black and alone. Like it was sailing away from her even as she chased after it. She wondered where her piano was right at that moment, if it was in a truck stuffed with drugs or shoved against some tavern wall or burned as firewood, gone forever. "This big rock looks like a piano, yes?" she said to her son. She said the same thing every time. "And the desert, it looks so lonely, because there is no one to play it. Lonely and frozen, no matter how hot it gets there." Then she sighed, and began:

"There once was a girl named Sasha who lived with her family in the far north of Russia where the reindeer herders were. It was always very very cold in her small village. There was ice and snow everywhere, and always blizzards during the harsh winter months. The villagers were not happy. They had no music or dancing, and could only tell each other stories to keep Death's cold hands away from their throats for another night.

"But then one day a foreigner was passing through, carrying his belongings in a wagon. A crazy man, a gypsy. He was trying to cross the world, but he had gotten lost and ended up in Sasha's village. The villagers weren't trusting of strangers, so when the foreigner went around begging for food and shelter, nobody would help him. When everyone had shunned him, he dropped his chin low to his chest and resumed his crooked journey, pulling his heavy sled behind him. Sasha saw this, and her heart ached. She ran to the basket where there was but one crust of bread left for her family, and she put it into a cloth along with some dried reindeer meat. She took a pouch that had just a sip of wine left inside, and she ran through the snow, following the tracks the foreigner's sled had made. When she gave him this gift, he dropped to his knees, took her hands in his, and begged her to accept a token of his gratitude for her kindness. They walked back to her tiny home, and there he unloaded something that none of the villagers had ever seen before: a piano. He told her he had been carrying it with him for thousands of kilometers. A prince had given it to him and, heavy as it was, it was too special to abandon in the woods or in the snow for the elements to destroy. But you, he said, are deserving of this music box, and he showed her how to press the ivory keys to make sounds.

"Sasha was enchanted and spent day after day trying to understand the piano. She pressed one key at a time, learning the notes, then added more, finding patterns. She listened carefully to the sounds in nature, to the wind hissing across the ice and the clacking and braying of reindeer and the whipping of fire flames. And she learned how to emulate them with notes coming from the piano. Soon she was blending those notes into melodies, adding layers of harmony, and changing the tempo to make the lonely sounds of hissing and braying and whipping into something different, something like how we think of springtime when the ice melts and colors burst where before it was only gray. Sasha was very happy making these songs, and her family was made happy listening to them.

"Then they noticed that the ice and snow around their house was melting, and in little patches, green things emerged for which they had no names. Then the sun itself pried away some clouds and showed its face to them. Well, soon the other villagers also noticed, and before long they were gathered around the piano, listening as Sasha played her strange music, which seeped into their skin like a chill, only it was warm and tingly, and it made them want to stand on their toes and sway and twirl! Sasha played wonderful, joyful compositions, and the villagers danced, and the patches of green expanded, and small animals came to nibble there and rest. In just a few weeks, the village had changed entirely. It became a place of enchantment and music and happiness, a warm asylum from Death's icy touch, and this went on for many years.

"The music drifted on warm breezes across the lands around them and to the northern seas, spreading hope and cheer. More foreigners came to visit, having heard strange tales from traders and trappers, or even the music itself, and some-times they chose to stay. One such visitor was a man who hid his greedy heart behind a handsome face. He was extremely charming and flattered Sasha by listening very carefully to her as she played and giving her many compliments about the beauty of it. When after several weeks he proposed marriage, she said yes.

"They lived happily together for a time, and at first Sasha didn't notice that a certain darkness crossed her husband's face whenever villagers came to sit or dance around her piano. He then decided that people should pay to enjoy his wife's music. Why should she give it away for nothing? They were poor. Why should they not profit from her playing? But Sasha dis-agreed. The piano had been a gift to her, and a gift before that. It was meant to be shared, just like the warmth of the sun shin-ing on the village when she played. Besides, all the villagers were poor as well and had nothing with which to pay.

"Then one day came a new stranger who was also enchanted by Sasha's music. A wealthy trader passing through, he shared her husband's mercenary view of the piano's magic, except he wanted it all for himself, thinking he could make himself an even richer man. He offered more money for the instrument than Sasha or her husband could ever have dreamed of, but she refused him. Sasha could not imagine being separated from her piano, nor from the joy it brought her and all the villagers. Yet the next day, when she was visiting her parents, her husband accepted the stranger's offer, and together they moved it into the tent he had set up during his stay. When Sasha returned and found her piano missing, she was heartbroken. Though she fell to the ground and wept, the husband was unmoved. 'With this money, we can build a bigger house and buy anything we want,' he told her. But Sasha didn't want a bigger house, nor did she want to buy things.

"As she lay weeping, an unfamiliar wind blew through the village. The sun, whose face had shone for so long, receded behind a thick curtain of clouds, and the temperature began to drop. Suddenly the villagers, by now accustomed to their warm climate, were shivering without their coats or boots. The husband did not worry; he was busy counting his money.

"On the door came a furious knocking. The wealthy trader who had bought the piano stood with a face red from anger and his fists clenched by his sides. The piano was broken, he said. He could not make music with it like Sasha had, could not make the flowers bloom nor the ground green, and he demanded his money back. The husband stood up to his full height, and he was much bigger than the stranger. He made no pretense of hiding his greed behind a charming face. He advanced toward the trader, threatening to kill him if he did not leave.

"The man ran away to save his life, and he took his anger with him. If he could not make music and he could not have his money, then he would burn the piano. He chopped it into pieces and put bits of kindling beneath the pile. He sat beside it for warmth as it burned, because without Sasha's music the harshness of winter had quickly returned. The villagers huddled together but could not stop the cold from seeping into their bones. Snow fell, and ice formed, and the villagers froze to death in their beds. The greedy husband died holding his money, and the wicked trader died when the last ember from the burned piano cooled to ash. Soon there was nothing but a stark and barren land, empty of animals and villagers. It was so cold that even the reindeer and their herders stayed far to the south.

"As for Sasha, she was frozen inside an ice coffin created by her own tears, but she wasn't dead. It is said that she is still there, waiting for a kind soul to bring a piano into the wretched cold, to thaw her heart and fingers so she can melt the snow with music and bring the village back to life."

In spite of her parking-lot vigil, at some point Clara fell asleep. Then there was a noise, a banging loud enough to wake her. It took her a moment to remember where she was, and why. She unfolded herself and peered through the thin layer of dew that frosted the windshield. The sun was starting to pink the horizon, and she was cold. She yawned and slowly sat up, rubbing at the tingling that started at her left elbow and traveled along a pins-and-needles current into her cast.

Bang! Bang! Bang!

She jumped in her seat and looked through her window, where a man dressed in black stood with his fists raised. She screamed and scrambled away faster than she could have imagined was possible, pressing her back against the passenger door and cocking her legs, ready to kick. She fumbled with her good hand behind her for the lock, but her movements were sloppy with sleep and adrenaline.

"Wait!" the man shouted. "It's okay. Are you Clara?"

Groping behind herself, she finally released the lock and then nearly spilled out onto the cool asphalt. She remembered something she had learned in the self-defense classes her uncle had made her take when she was sixteen: *Put something between you and your would-be assailant: distance, a large obstacle, anything to make it harder for him to get to you.*

"Clara, it's Greg. I'm Greg Zeldin." He held his fists aloft and Clara, blinking through her confusion, now saw that he was holding two paper cups with steam coming out of the white tops. Coffee. He lifted them even higher, a small white-flag gesture. "I'm the one who bought your piano?"

She recognized his coppery voice from their phone conversation. She took a breath but was careful not to let her guard down completely. "You mean rented."

He exhaled through his nose with a small huffing sound, and the air at his nostrils turned to steam. "Right," he said. "Rented."

"What are you doing here?" she said.

He walked around the front of her car. Instinctively she took a step back, but he reached out, undeterred, and handed her a cup. "I should be asking you that." He dug into his pants pocket and pulled out two creamers, two sugars, a small red stirrer. "I didn't know how you'd take it."

"Cream," she said, and tried to take a packet from him with the swollen fingers of her broken hand. Both dropped to the ground, one exploding white goo onto her sneakers and the hem of her jeans. "Great," she mumbled.

"Here." He took the coffee from her and set it down on the trunk of her car, then picked up the creamer that was still intact and emptied it into the cup. "You want another?" He pulled one more from his pocket and held it up to her with the aplomb of a magician pulling a rabbit out of his hat. She nodded absently, wondering, as he stirred, what else he might be able to produce from the pockets of his all-black clothing: T-shirt, jacket, jeans, shoes. He looked as if he might be capable of certain dark arts. She could imagine him as a circus sideshow performer. *The Great Zeldin*. All he needed was a hat and cape.

He was handsome, if unconventionally so: pale skin that reached well into his close-cropped and deeply receded hairline, thick brows that didn't move when he spoke, almost girlish lips. His neatly trimmed goatee had a burst of gray hairs in a small spot by his jaw. His light-colored gaze was striking, like a wolf's. Yet instead of feeling threatened, she found herself drawn in. Perhaps he wasn't so much attractive as he was mesmerizing.

"You're wondering how I knew it was you," he said, his eyes boring into hers as he handed her the creamed coffee.

She was wondering exactly that, but she didn't care for his didactic tone. "I assume your guys saw me at the gas station." She squinted through the coffee's steam and took a sip, willing herself not to look away, as though it were a challenge she somehow couldn't afford to lose.

"They did, apparently, but they didn't put two and two together until they came out this morning to check the truck and saw your car here and you asleep in it."

Clara looked around and noticed that all the semis were gone. Her car was exposed and alone in the middle of the lot. "Well," she said, then could think of nothing else to add. Feeling exposed too, she reached inside for the balled-up sweatshirt she'd found in the backseat and had used as a pillow. The temperature had dropped overnight and she was cold.

"I got in late myself," Greg said. "Flew into Vegas and rented a car. God, what a shithole that place is. Every time I go there, I feel like my soul corrodes a little bit. Besides, there's no point in gambling in those big casinos. They treat you like a king—okay, maybe a low-level nobleman—and some uninspired waitress who probably had a lousy childhood brings you rounds and rounds of drinks while you spend your money, blackjack, slots, whatever, and if you start doing okay, well, they don't care too much for that. The house guys in their cheap suits start moving in, watching. The house is always supposed to win in the end. Haven't you heard that saying, 'The house always wins'? But places like this"—he jabbed a thumb over his shoulder toward the crumbling gambling hall behind them—"they don't mind so much, at least for a little while. A little action fires up the indigents." He broke off his soliloquy to take a sip of coffee, watching her as he did so, as though awaiting a reply.

"I don't really gamble?" she said, curling the end up into a question like she wasn't sure of this herself. Immediately she wanted to say it insistently—*I don't gamble*—but drawing attention to it would only make it sound worse.

"So says the girl who followed a moving truck into the middle of nowhere." When he smiled at her, she blushed.

Behind him, the sunrise crept slowly over the serrated ridges of Clark Mountain, though nothing else indicated that it was morning. The gamblers must all have still been asleep, Clara figured. She felt strange standing in an almost empty parking lot at dawn, drinking coffee delivered by a stranger. But it also lent the day a vague sense of potential.

"Why are you here, then? In the middle of nowhere," she said, adding, "with my piano."

"I told you. I'm going to photograph it."

"Where?"

"Various places."

"Like casinos?"

"No. Outdoors."

"Out in the open?"

"Yes."

"But what about the elements? The dirt?" Her voice rose and she swept her arm toward the ground. She thought about Juan's flicking gesture the day before, the suggestion of danger in it.

"I told you not to worry. I'll be careful with it. Trust me."

She took a sip of coffee—it was hot but tasted old—and dumped the rest out on the ground. "I just don't understand why you're doing this," she said.

Greg's eyes narrowed slightly as he looked at her. He took his time answering. "I should think that five grand would answer any questions you might have about my plans for the next week or so. Or does minding your own business cost extra?"

Never mind that she'd found his plan interesting, or that his voice on the phone had been a comfort in the dark. Suddenly he was an adversary.

Growing up as an apprentice in her uncle's garage, she'd learned virtually all aspects of car maintenance and repair. She could fix anything. But what made her a good mechanic, what kept the customers loyal, was what her uncle taught her about dealing with them. "You gotta think from their position," he told her. "Their car's busted up or broken down—it's totally out of the blue. Now they're late for work, their whole day's gone off the rails, they're thinking about all the money it's gonna cost. They're pissed off. Not at you, but they're gonna take it out on you. You can't take it personal. You just tighten up your gut and take it like you're taking a punch. Then you just breathe out, nice and calm, no attitude, and you break it down in layman's terms what's wrong, how long it'll take to fix, what it's gonna cost. Show them some empathy, show them where the coffeemaker is, but don't ever try to tell them why they're wrong being mad or being ugly. It's called 'de-escalation.'"

"You're right," she said to Greg now. "It's your business. But technically, it's also mine. I'm not asking what you're going to eat for dinner or what time you're going to get up in the morning. I'm just asking about my piano." Then she forced herself to smile, and continued to look at him with what she hoped was a pleasant, de-escalating expression until he sighed and leaned against her car.

"I'm sorry, I shouldn't have been so insensitive. Obviously you wouldn't be here if you weren't concerned, but I assure you"—he reached out and touched her on the forearm—"it will be safe. Juan and Beto are good. We'll all be very careful."

He gazed at her with such earnestness that even his cold-eyed stare seemed warm.

She nodded. "So Death Valley, huh?"

"My mother's favorite place." He glanced down at the top of his cup—the first time, she realized, he'd taken his eyes off hers since he'd shown up.

"You said she played piano. Do you play, too? Your website says you studied music."

He shook his head. "Studied, yes. But I don't play. Do you?"

"No."

"Well, that's interesting, isn't it? Here we are bickering over a piano that neither of us plays." He drained his coffee and then crumpled the cup, looking around for someplace to throw it. Finding none, he shoved it into his jacket pocket, against whatever props or secrets he might be carrying. "I haven't even seen it yet. You want to show it to me before you take off?" Not *I* take off, she noted. Not *we*.

She shrugged. "Sure," she said. He led her to the truck and she noticed, walking behind him, that his gait was irregular. His left leg swung out in a tight arc each time he moved it forward, just enough to give the impression of a sashay. It didn't seem to inhibit him, however, and might even have added something to his self-possession. Maybe it was a dare, his striding ahead of her with his low-slung sway: *There's nothing you can think about this that I haven't already thought, but go ahead and try anyway.* Or maybe how he straightened his back above his swung-out leg and faced the dawn with a lifted chin was his personal emblem of triumph over something. Or maybe it was nothing, she thought as he unlocked the truck and heaved open the door. Maybe he was just an asshole with a limp.

The truck was parked facing west, so when the door scrolled up early sunlight filled the bed. Greg climbed inside, a little awkwardly with his leg, and then, almost as an afterthought, turned to offer Clara his hand.

"Need help?" he asked.

"No thanks. I got it." She grabbed the rail with her good hand and leapt in.

"What happened to your arm, anyway?"

Clara looked down. A week after the accident, her fingers were still swollen, and the skin was peeling a little at the edge of the cast. It was uncomfortable and irritating, but she was getting used to it. "Not my arm. My hand. Well, technically my wrist but it might as well be my hand. I broke it. While moving the piano, actually. Too bad I didn't have your guys to move it for me. They made it look pretty easy. Of course, if I hadn't broken my hand, I wouldn't have listed it for sale in the first place."

"In that case, I'm not entirely sorry you broke it," he said with a wry smile. "But I'm sorry if it hurt."

He released the ties, pulled the piano away from the wall, and began to unbundle it. His thick eyebrows knit together in concentration as he peeled off the layers of padding and tossed them aside, moving quicker and more urgently the closer he got to its bare surface.

It was fascinating to witness someone else showing such interest in the Blüthner. To her, it had abruptly become a part of her life, meaningful only because her father had given it to her. Those first few days, she had accepted it as she would've a new freckle on her forearm or an extra inch in height. But after he was gone, the Blüthner seemed inexorable. The unwitting custodian of her childhood. She had never imagined it being important to anyone except her.

Greg placed his hand lightly on top of the case and stared at it for a moment before dragging his fingers down its length, stopping at the dents on the treble end. He closed his eyes there, moved his fingertips into and around them, feeling their gentle topography as if he were reading the piano's history.

"I didn't see these in the pictures," he said, so quietly that Clara almost didn't hear him.

"I know, I'm sorry. I don't know where they came from. They were actually worse when I got it, but we had the case repaired and refinished."

"Yes," Greg said. He opened his eyes sleepily, then studied the rest of the case with his eyes, his hands. Clara watched him caress the piano, running his slender fingers over the fallboard and key block, down the leg trusses to the toes. "Yes," he said again, his voice barely above a whisper.

He pulled the piano farther away from the truck rails, exposing its back to the sunlight, and went around behind it and crouched down. A strange sound escaped him, a small bark between a laugh and a sob. Then he was quiet again. He nodded slightly, or maybe he was trembling; Clara couldn't tell. She stepped up close to see what had affected him. He was looking at the tiny engraving at the bottom of the bass end of the case. Someone—the manufacturer, she'd always assumed—had carved a single word or name into the ebony and, apparently, stained it so it wouldn't stand out.

She'd noticed that mark soon after she'd moved to Bakersfield with her aunt and uncle. The piano had to be stored in the garage until a bedroom could be cleared out, the one that would've been the baby's—her cousin's—had he lived. It had become a sort of junk room because her soft-spoken aunt hadn't been able to get rid of anything easily after his death. So for a few weeks, while her aunt and a neighbor slowly dismantled the room and emptied it of the things about which nobody spoke openly, Clara slept on a pallet in the living room and the piano stayed in the garage, with its keyboard facing the wall for safety. She didn't speak much herself for those few weeks—hardly a word, in fact, for several months—and hadn't yet developed that helpful relationship with her uncle, so she only really felt comfortable in the garage with the piano. She would lie down on the cool concrete and stare at the case's smooth sideboard. She pretended the shiny black was outer space, and she would look for images of her parents amid the indistinct reflections of the items behind her: the tool chest and gardening equipment and Christmas decorations. During one of those lie-downs she discovered the little carving in the corner, the one Greg was staring at now with an inscrutable expression: Гриша.

She'd never known why it was there.

T he doorbell rang. Katya was transferring cheese pastries from the baking sheet to the wire rack for cooling. She'd made too many, as usual. Maybe she would take some to her son's eighth-grade class. No, that would embarrass him. American mothers didn't do things like that. At least not after elementary school. The bell rang again.

"Moment!" she called, hurrying with the last few. "Moment," she said again, wiping her hands as she went to the door. She smoothed her hair and glanced around the living room, hoping it was one of the neighbors with an invitation to dinner or a party. She hadn't been to a party in a very long time. But it probably wasn't a social call; since her old friend Ella had died, she hadn't had many spontaneous visitors, and she hadn't been very good about cultivating friends. She worried about having people over, because she never knew when Mikhail would come home ranting loudly about rude customers and terrible tips, the traffic and smog and ruts in the streets. "I could make much better roads than these even if I had no eyes!" he would yell and, drink in hand, heave himself into a chair, which gasped beneath him. Mikhail's driving schedule was unpredictable, especially when he drank. He drank a lot these days.

The person on her small front porch was a man. Maybe it was someone coming to ask for piano lessons, she thought. She had put an advertisement on the community bulletin board at the park.

"Hello," he said.

"Hello."

"Are you Ekaterina Zeldin?"

Carried awkwardly on this man's voice, the sound of her full name was strange and rich. There was a shape to it that reminded her of the first measure of Scriabin's E-flat Minor Prelude. His face did, too. The left half was colored a deep purple, a *rodimoye pyatno* like Gorbachev had on his forehead, but thicker and broader, spreading from his temple down over his eye and beyond the ridge of jaw onto his neck. His eyelashes, she noticed, were so pale that she was moved to wonder if they provided his light brown eyes any shade. He was tall, much taller than Mikhail, and stood in a tentative, apologetic manner, holding an envelope in both hands. Maybe he was with the mail service? Or the police? But he wore no uniform, and his shoes were too clean. Did American policemen shine their shoes?

She had always believed that Mikhail had led her into this country incorrectly. Even when they had spent those weeks in Vienna, waiting, then the long months in Italy, where they had finally been given permission to enter the United States, it had seemed to her that they were riding on the tide of something illegal. Yet this worry had brought her no shame. Let the police come, let them send her back to Leningrad, even though now it was called St. Petersburg again. As long as she could take Grisha, after all this time she might have a chance to be happy. Oh, but it was too late to go home now. They had applied for citizenship by naturalization, studied for the exam, and sat all day in a federal building waiting for their turn to take the 150-question test. At the end of the exam, they needed to write a complete sentence in English. Mikhail chose the easiest thing, something suggested to him by others who had already passed: "I love the U.S.A." Katya borrowed from Tolstoy: "All happy families are alike; each unhappy family is unhappy in its own way."

"*Da*," she answered. Then she remembered where she was and said, "Yes."

"I was asked to bring you this." He handed her the envelope. The return address was that of a hotel in Finland. In the center, her name was written in Cyrillic and, in a different ink color and handwriting, her Los Angeles address in English. She slid her finger beneath the flap, her heart quickening.

Дорогая Катя!

Если ты получила это письмо, значит, ты уже живешь в своей американской мечте. В Калифорнии действительно много солнца? Может быть, ты думаешь, что я плохой человек, и, возможно, ты права. Но я не настолько плох, чтобы забыть о тебе. Не настолько плох, чтобы не вернуть пианино, даже спустя столько времени.

Может быть, когда-нибудь, я расскажу тебе, где путешествовал твой отважный инструмент. Он был надежным партнером, умел хранить свои секреты. И мои тоже. А какой сильный звук! Хотя никто не мог добиться от него такого звучания, какое удавалось извлечь тебе, Катя. Как зверь, покинувший любимого хозяина и вынужденный служить другому, он должен подчиняться, но дух его уже сломлен.

Твой муж разузнал кое-что обо мне, но он ошибся. Я не ак жаден, как он. Я всего лишь позаимствовал идеи у наших капиталистических врагов, чтобы заработать для более благородного дела. Пожалуйста, не суди строго; каждый несет свой крест. Сейчас гласность меняет нашу жизнь, не так ли? Возможно, ты была права. Балет не изменит мир. А гласность изменит. Как и те Mauerspechte, которые разобрали обломки старой стены и дали возможность пройти с востока на запад.

Что бы ни говорил тебе муж, я приобрел у тебя пианино только для того, чтобы когда-нибудь потом снова вернуть его тебе. Я не позволял никому играть на нем, если не был уверен, что руки исполнителя чисты.

Если бы оно могло говорить, то поведало бы тебе, что о нем хорошо заботились. Теперь оно снова твое. Пианино находится в распоряжении одного моего знакомого из музыкального отделения UCLA, который обещал его отреставрировать. Так что инструмент вернется к тебе в целости и сохранности.

Я все еще надеюсь, что однажды ты сочинишь музыку для моего балета. Может быть, его темой станет ослабление напряженности.

Твой Борис

Dear Katya!

If you are reading this, then by now you are living an American dream. There is a lot of sun in California, yes? You maybe think I'm a bad person, and maybe you're right. But I'm not so bad I forgot about you. Not so bad I wouldn't return your piano, even if it took a long time.

Someday maybe I'll tell you where your sturdy instrument traveled. It was a reliable partner and kept its secrets well. My secrets, too. And such robust tone! Nobody could coax music out of it like you could, though, Katya. It was like a beast that had gone from a beloved master to a new one; it might be obedient, but its spirit was broken.

Your husband discovered something about me, but he was wrong to assume that I was as greedy as he. I only borrowed ideas from our capitalist friends to make money for a nobler cause. Please don't criticize me too severely; we all have our own shame to bear. Now there is glasnost that changes the world, yes? Maybe you were right. It's not ballet that changes the world. It is glasnost that will change the world. And the *Mauerspechte*, who have taken away the rubble of the old wall and made it possible to pass from east to west.

Whatever else your husband told you, you should know that I only bought your piano so that I might somehow return it to you. In this time, I always made sure the hands that played it were clean. If it could talk, it would tell you that it was always handled with good care. Now it is yours again. It is in the possession of an acquaintance in the music department at UCLA, who promised to have it rehabilitated. He said he will get it back to you safely.

I still hope that you will someday compose a score for my ballet. Maybe with a new theme of détente.

Your Boris

Tears fell. Thirteen years and five months had passed since she'd last touched the Blüthner. Over the years, the very faint hope that Mikhail and Boris had not betrayed her, that the piano would be returned, had slowly dwindled until her mourning was not for her separation from the Blüthner but for its death, and she had finally stopped believing that she might ever see it again. The man on her front porch offered her a handkerchief.

"You have my piano?" she asked, with hope creaking her voice.

"Me? No. No, I don't have it. I just brought the letter. My colleague was going to deliver it but then had to leave town—his wife's mother is ill, I think—so he asked me to find out where you live. I guess the guy who had your piano knew you were in L.A., just didn't know where. Anyway, Andries—that's my colleague—happened to tell me this story about how this old choreographer friend of his shipped him a piano. Boris, was it? Yes, that's right. So somehow Boris got in touch with Andries—they hadn't talked in more than a decade, I guess. And apparently he's in some Siberian gulag for drug trafficking. I think he said it was Krasnoyarsk—"

"Prison! Boris is in prison?"

The man put his hands up. "Hey, I don't know anything. Andries told me all this just before he took off for Amsterdam. But yeah, he said Boris was in prison on drug charges or something. Anyway, this piano—your piano, I suppose—shows up in a big crate at the university with two letters, one to Andries and this one." He indicated the paper in Katya's hands. "He said he wasn't in a position to deal with it but said Boris told him it was urgent that he get the piano fixed up and returned to you as soon as possible. Between you and me, I think Boris paid him well to do it. It pretty much covered his family's tickets to Holland."

"Where is my piano?"

"Oh, right. He had some of his students take it down to Immortal Piano. Apparently they're the best when it comes to fixing up a banged-up instrument."

"What do you mean 'banged-up'?"

"Don't worry. After I found your address, I called them and they said it's good as new and all ready to deliver." He lifted his pale eyebrows like a shrug. "I can take you down there now if you want."

Katya rushed at him, landing with her cheek against the buttons of his dress shirt, squeezing him as though he were her savior, as though she loved him. Maybe he was, and maybe she did; he had found her and would take her to her beloved piano and bring her back to life, just like in her fairy tale. "Thank you, thank you!" she said.

He laughed. "*Пожалуйста*," he told her.

"You speak Russian?" She stood back to regard him.

"Oh no, just a few words here and there. I speak Czech and Polish, though. And English, of course."

"I will repay you for helping me. Help you with Russian, if you'd like me to. Or teach you piano. Do you play the piano?"

"No, no. I don't have an ear for it. I wish I did, though."

"I can teach you if you want. I don't have much, but I can do this as a thank-you for bringing my piano back to me." She leaned into him again, pressing her cheek to his heart, and he laughed again and hugged her lightly back.

Do you know what that marking is?" Clara asked Greg. He nodded, still staring at it. "It's a name," he said quietly. "*Grisha.*" After a pause he said, "I can't believe it. I can't fucking believe it."

"What?"

He turned on her. "Where did you get this?"

She was startled by the accusation in his voice. Or maybe it was panic. "It was a gift. From my father."

"When?"

"For my twelfth birthday," she said. Then, growing defensive: "Why?"

"And now you're . . . ?"

"I just turned twenty-six."

Greg's pale face blanched. "So that would've been in"—his brow furrowed as he calculated—"1998?"

"Yeah," she said, and he nodded, absently, for what struck her as an unusually long time. "Are you okay? Why do you want to know all this?"

"Do you happen to know where your father got it?"

"As a matter of fact, no. I never had the chance to find out. My parents died right after he gave it to me."

"In a fire," he said after a beat, staring at her.

Clara felt a chill that raised the fine hairs on the back of her neck. A rapid series of images flipped through her mind: Tabitha's mother, crouched next to her sleeping bag, *There's been a fire;* herself, wearing a stiff new dress and standing between her long-faced aunt and uncle at her parents' funeral; the glossy black Blüthner reflecting her curled-up image as she lay on the concrete floor of her uncle's garage. "How do you know there was a fire? Did you *research* me?"

Clara had once looked herself up on the Internet, wondering if there was anything out there. She'd found a social media profile belonging to a different Clara Lundy. A website that listed people's locations and net worths showed her still living in an apartment complex that was three addresses ago. There was an obituary for a Clara Louise Lundy who'd died in 1976, a thoughtful account of that other woman's life that had actually made her jealous. The only meaningful hit was in a comment somebody posted on a site that reviewed local businesses. Having overhauled the customer's engine, she was complimented as being "nice, knowledgeable—and hot." But there was nothing about losing her parents in a house fire. She'd been a minor when it happened, and they'd left her first name out of the news reports.

"No, that didn't occur to me. I didn't have any reason to. When I saw your listing for an upright Blüthner, it was exactly what I wanted—the right era, the right color—and I just thought maybe they weren't so rare after all. I would've researched you if I'd known your Blüthner was *this* Blüthner. But all this time I thought *this* Blüthner was gone, ashes to ashes, dust to dust. That's what my mother told me, anyway."

Clara shook her head. "I don't understand. How did your mother know about the fire?"

"Because before you got this piano, it belonged to her."

"What? How do you know that?"

"The marking. The one on the back. The name."

"Grisha," she said.

"*I'm* Grisha." He pointed to his own chest like someone pantomiming the fact to a non–English speaker. "I am Grigoriy in Russian. Greg in English. And Grisha's what my mother called me."

"So my father bought it from her?"

For what seemed like minutes, his face was still except for a vein that seemed to have come into relief down the center of his forehead. "Not exactly."

"What, then? Are you saying he *stole* it?"

"No, no, not at all. It was a legitimate transfer of ownership." He passed a hand over his face, squeezing his temples, and when he released them any hint of friendliness between them was gone and he again looked as he had in his portrait: cold, focused, aloof. "Never mind. The terms of their agreement aren't important."

"They are to me," Clara said. Her father hadn't told her the first thing about where he'd gotten the Blüthner, not why or how, or who had owned it before her. Of course it had never occurred to her to ask when she was twelve, and in the intervening years, its provenance had seemed irrelevant. She was privy to neither its music nor its mysteries. "Please," she said.

Greg closed his eyes, took a deep breath. "It's not a happy story, okay? My mother loved that piano, but something happened and her only hope of protecting it was to get rid of it. She didn't sell it; she gave it away."

Clara was so taken aback that for a moment she just looked at him, though her mind was swirling with questions.

"But wasn't it in the fire?" he asked.

"It was at the technician's, getting the case repaired."

He nodded. "Yeah, that makes sense." Then he looked at his watch. "The guys will be out any minute, and we need to get moving if I'm going to get all the photos done before our contract expires." He extended his hand and Clara automatically slipped her palm against his, which was dry and warm. He held it for just a beat longer than seemed necessary, looking at her carefully. She thought she felt something significant pass between them, riding on a current of shared history. But then he abruptly released her and said, "Nice meeting you" in a businesslike manner, and held out his newly free hand toward the open cargo door in an after-you motion of dismissal.

"Wait a minute," Clara said. "You can't just walk away after telling me your mother used to own my piano. You grew up in Los Angeles, right? So did I, in Santa Monica. How did your mother know my parents?"

"I didn't say she did."

"Then what *are* you saying? Why did she think the piano was in the fire?"

"Someone told her. It's no big deal."

"Who?"

Greg trapped her with that level stare, his countenance entirely calm. After a moment he brushed off the front of his pants, though there wasn't a speck of dust on them. He did it as though to mark the end of something, a gesture of resolve, and when he spoke again his voice had a decisive clarity. "That was a difficult time in my life. I have no interest in discussing it, not with you or with anyone else. It makes me angry, and I don't want to get angry."

Juan and Beto ambled toward them, both looking pink-eyed and a little blurry around the edges, following whatever late-night solace the casino had offered. She turned away. She felt silly standing there, obviously having slept in her car, and for thinking that she'd followed them without being noticed. She touched her hair, and thought of her breath and her need of a bathroom.

"*Vámonos*," Greg said to them in a fairly convincing accent. "*Quiero empezar temprano.*" Then he addressed her: "I'll take care of your piano." His mouth smiled, but his eyes didn't. "Enjoy your drive home."

She had no reason to balk; she'd gotten what she'd told Peter she wanted: to meet Greg, to make sure the Blüthner was in good hands. She didn't know how good his were, of course, but she could still feel the ghostly impression of his palm against hers and was a little embarrassed for thinking it might've meant something. She responded now with a jut of her chin, a gesture she'd picked up from being around men all her life, a way to acknowledge a person or a fact without exposing anything too intimate. Then she dusted her hands over the front of her jeans, wiping off the moment as he apparently had, and jumped down off the truck.

She walked backward to her car, watching the movers toss their duffels back into the bed, pull down and secure the door. They exchanged information with Greg, who pointed vaguely at the horizon in the direction of the border, where she herself would go. Then Greg limped to his own car, a black SUV that seemed bigger than necessary and—in spite or because of the chic make—was a model known to routinely break down. "Asshole," she said aloud. But they had all slammed their doors closed, so nobody except maybe the valet, back on duty, heard her.

She stopped at the gas station on the corner, filled her tank, emptied her bladder, bought a Slim Jim, a pack of peanut-butter crackers, and a half-pint of milk for breakfast, which she ate ravenously, sitting in the parked car, remembering that she hadn't had a thing in almost twenty hours. It was only seven-thirty in the morning, and already the day felt old. Her hand was throbbing, her neck stiff. She wanted a shower, a bed, some music to fall asleep to.

She thought about Greg's mother giving the piano away to protect it. From what? How and why had her father acquired it? Perhaps someone had known that he was looking for one to give Clara for her birthday. A mutual acquaintance? And then someone told Greg's mother that it had been destroyed in the same fire that killed her parents. The same person who'd connected them in the first place, or the co-worker who'd helped her father bring the piano home the night he gave it to her, or someone else from the university. It could have been anyone, really. If Greg's mother hadn't actually known her parents, it probably wasn't important. Or possibly she was just too exhausted and irritated to care.

If she drove straight through, she could stretch out in her own bed before noon. Then she thought about Peter and how worried he probably was. She checked her phone to see if he'd called, but it was dead. Too early to call anyway, she reasoned, and connected it to the charger. Deciding she'd text him later to let him know that everything was okay, just as she'd promised it would be, she started the car and headed home.

But she was on the highway for barely a minute when an image up ahead caught her eye, such an unlikely tableau that she drove a hundred yards past it before realizing what it was: Juan and Beto were unloading her piano on the side of the road.

She made a wide U-turn across the gravel median on the mostly empty road and drove by them on the opposite side, slowly this time—no, she hadn't imagined it—and then U-turned again so she could pull up behind them. She rolled to a partially hidden stop on the shoulder behind an earthmover and some other heavy construction equipment parked there. Her hands were shaking when she opened the car door, and her stomach roiled, whether from the junk food or her anticipation of having to defend the Blüthner against some act of aggression. She could feel the shout forming itself in her mouth when Greg beat her to it.

"*Cuidado!*" he yelled, lunging forward to kick away a rock that Beto couldn't see and might've stepped on, since he was on the bottom end of the piano as they rolled it down the ramp. Then Greg went to the side of the piano and steadied it as they tipped it back and settled it onto the off-road moving dolly.

Clara, somewhat appeased by Greg's stewardship, leaned

against the hood of her car and watched them maneuver the piano close to the blue-and-yellow sign with the golden poppies that welcomed travelers to California. She was too far away to hear what they were saying, but it was clear they weren't about to abandon it there on the San Bernardino county line.

They walked slowly, Greg because of his gait and the guys because keeping the piano secure on the sandy, bumpy ground was difficult. Greg pointed at a small rise. "Push it up to the top. That bump looks flat enough. Then take it off the dolly and set it down—otherwise it'll seem like just a prop. I want it to look like it's been here awhile. Like it has a *purpose*."

He directed Juan and Beto to shift the piano slightly in a variety of angles until, apparently satisfied, he backed away from it and held his thumbs and index fingers up, two L's put together in the shape of a rectangle, and peered through them. Next he pointed at the orange-and-white-striped traffic barrels, and Beto jogged over to pull them out of the imaginary frame. Juan picked up a stick and some rocks and litter lying on the ground, but Greg called out "*Déjalo!*" and waved his hand, so he shrugged and dropped everything more or less back where he'd found it.

They still hadn't noticed her, and she stayed behind the moving equipment in hopes that they wouldn't. It was interesting seeing her piano out of context like this, being handled and arranged by strangers. The Blüthner was as familiar to her as her own body, yet it seemed so different there on the roadside, like a version of herself that she'd never looked at before.

"Push it in a little deeper," Greg shouted, "but make sure it doesn't fall over. Good, okay." He patted the air. "Now come back toward me a little so you're out of the frame. That's enough. Stay there in case I need you to move it. *Entiendes?*"

She watched him crouch down and aim his fancy camera at the piano, the morning sun lighting up the Mojave National

Preserve behind it. He was very still, mostly cocking his head first to one side and then the other. Clara tried following his gaze, but she couldn't tell what he was picturing. She imagined that fashion-magazine photo shoots in New York City operated like this, though with angular models and unwearable clothes, people rushing around doing hair and makeup and setting up lights. All at once, the worry left her. Greg was obviously a professional, and it seemed like he really did just want to photograph the piano. How he'd run his hands over it earlier and shouted at Juan and Beto to be careful whenever they touched it, not to mention the fact that it had once belonged to his mother—she saw these as indications that he would probably take immaculate care of it. She resolved now to watch until he was finished and then go home. And when he returned the piano in a couple weeks, she'd ask him to show her the photos. She wanted to see through Greg's eyes how it looked, as he said, when the music stopped. It had certainly stopped for the Blüthner when she took possession of it. Maybe his images would reveal something about what it had been like before then.

Clara kept watching as Beto and Juan rewrapped the piano and got it back in the truck and Greg put his equipment away. But when he pulled out and pointed his SUV toward Las Vegas, spewing a rooster tail of powdery dirt off his rear tires as he sped across the median, she said, "Screw that."

There wasn't a hope in hell she was going to leave now, not after the revelation that her Blüthner had belonged to his mother. So what if Greg was sensitive about it? He was connected to her past and knew something about her piano—if not her parents—that nobody else did. And what if he decided it was his to keep after all? What if he carted it into Death Valley and refused to bring it back? Maybe that's what Juan's gesture had meant, that this was Greg's plan all along. Besides, without work or a boyfriend, why should she rush back to

Bakersfield? So when the truck pulled out onto the highway behind Greg, Clara once again fell in behind them.

Her phone buzzed. *Peter.* She yanked it out of the charger and blurted, "I'm sorry, I should've called."

"Not necessarily," said the voice on the other end. "I'm just flattered that you find me so attractive."

"What?"

"Well, it's not still about the piano, is it?"

"Greg."

"Ah, yes. Like that. Say it again."

"Don't be ridiculous."

"Oh, I don't think it's me who's being ridiculous, do you? I thought we'd settled things back at the casino, yet here you are again, filling up my rearview mirror."

She couldn't tell if he was teasing or angry. *I don't want to get angry.* She decided she'd rather not find out what would happen if he did. "I thought maybe I'd come along for a while," she said casually. "Turns out I'm not really needed at home right now."

"You're not really needed here, either."

She forced herself to think of a reasonable reply. "I'm a mechanic."

"So?"

"You're driving a piece-of-shit SUV and a moving truck into Death Valley. You might need my services." After a pause, she allowed herself a moment of optimism. She didn't need his permission to go wherever he happened to be going, but it would make for a more pleasant adventure if he agreed. "Besides, I just got paid a tidy sum in rental fees, so whatever you need, you got it, no charge." She even smiled when she said it and gave a thumbs-up sign in case he was looking.

He laughed. "You've got to be kidding. A woman mechanic with a broken hand? That's a liability, not an asset. I'm afraid I'm going to have to decline your very kind offer, but thank you.

Hey listen, have a safe trip back home and the guys'll see you in a couple weeks. Sound good?"

"Wait," she said, but he had already hung up.

They all drove on, Clara's eyes narrowed on the shiny black of Greg's SUV, its fancy exterior concealing a slippery, blue-collar transmission that seemed at the moment an apt metaphor for him. She wasn't offended by being called a *woman* mechanic; it was the broken-handed part that bothered her—the assumption that she wouldn't be able to handle any unforeseen problem. She'd always made it a point to be exactly the opposite: self-sufficient and self-contained, reliable instead of reliant. She banged her broken hand against the steering wheel, hard enough that she cried out, but when tears sprang to her eyes she blinked them away.

Who the fuck did he think he was, calling *her* a liability?

It was a Saturday and Katya was playing, practicing scales. In the six weeks since her piano had been returned to her, she'd played whenever she could. Everything else could wait: grocery shopping, cooking dinner, writing letters to her parents, even spending time with Grisha. When she wasn't playing, she was thinking about the sateen feeling of keys that had gone yellow again from disuse, the distinctive pressure of the dampers, the peerless tone. And the music! Now pieces she knew as well as her own hands suddenly sounded fresh. It had been many years since she'd composed anything, yet she could feel a new piece lacing itself into her imagination measure by measure. She wondered if this was what being addicted to drugs felt like. She hadn't played much at all on the substitute piano, which she'd been thrilled to get rid of. When the men from Immortal Piano had delivered her Blüthner, she'd tipped them well and asked them to drop the Yamaha off at the Salvation Army to be put back into circulation.

Once again she was floating above the dull world. Her fingers felt free, her mind as well. Her Blüthner was a connection to Russia—to home—that even the music itself couldn't match. Tangled up in the golden notes, she could forget about Mikhail's terrible temper, the exuberance and excesses of her fellow Americans, her own profound loneliness. She hadn't looked at the Death Valley Polaroids in weeks. And the wretched voice of the lost music that invaded her thoughts both day and night hadn't been bothering her lately. Maybe it had gone away forever.

"What are you smiling at?" her son asked her.

She didn't stop playing when she answered: "The tundra is melting, I think."

"When will you be done?" he said, sounding irritated. He'd been wandering around the room, waiting for her, growing impatient.

"In a little while."

He sighed theatrically. "Will you tell me the story?" he said, leaning against the piano.

She gestured for him to step back. "We don't need to tell that story anymore," she said.

"Then make up a new one. One for after Sasha was woken up."

"*Chi-chi-chi*. You're too old for silly fables now."

"Then let's go somewhere," he begged, sitting down hard next to her on the bench. "To the movies or the park or something."

"What about your friends from school, Grisha?" She loved him, but it was maddening how much he demanded of her. Especially now, when she simply wanted to float, pleasantly distracted from the life she'd been forced to accept as her own.

"I hate school," he said.

"You're fourteen already. Going to high school this fall! Time to find friends your own age to spend time with." Nonetheless, she stopped for a moment, and put her hand on his cheek.

He closed his eyes. "Nobody likes me."

She sighed. What a difficult child he could be. "Fine, we will go. But in a little while," she said. "After I'm finished practicing."

He missed her. Even though she was still here with him, as she always had been, she was different. Always smiling at nothing, always preoccupied. All his life she'd been his best friend, which he'd assumed was mutual, but now she had another. He wanted to crawl into her lap like he used to when he was younger, when she first taught him how to play. But she would tell him no, he was too old now, and too big. Instead, he lay down on the floor nearby in a shaft of afternoon sunlight and watched dust motes drift through the air, rising and falling along with the scales as she played them. He imagined them moving because of the music, each one tethered to a certain note, his mother directing them without even realizing it. He swatted at them like a cat, hoping that if he disrupted their choreography, she might finish sooner and take him down to the beach or to the mall, like the mothers of all his classmates did. Or at least talk to him before his father came home, angry or drunk or both, and ruined everything. His father hadn't liked it when the piano reappeared, but that was hardly a surprise. He didn't seem to like anything very much, least of all driving a taxi all day long then coming home to a wife who only wanted to play the piano.

The motes moved when he sliced his hand through them but without disruption, just drifting amicably away in different directions, like tiny clouds in a windy sky. His mother continued her major and harmonic minor scales, the right hand ascending while the left descended until they were four octaves apart, then reversing directions and moving her hands back together. Next, both hands ascending two octaves in parallel, then descending, then back to the contrary motions apart and finally together again. He knew the formula pattern because she made him do it too, during his practice times, which he'd already done today, right after breakfast. He wanted to love it like she did, but he didn't. He couldn't go as fast as she could, though it pleased her when he tried to.

The sun grew too warm on his legs, so he slithered across the floor on his side, onto a cool spot behind the piano. His mother kept it well away from the walls, though she'd pushed the Yamaha up against one of the living room windows, blocking the view. "Music needs room to breathe," she would tell him. "Like in the story?" he'd ask. "Yes, like in the story," she would answer. So the Blüthner sat in the middle of the room as if it were a grand.

Glossy and black, hulking in the center of the sunlit room, taking up too much space for its size, it both intimidated and fascinated him. He put his hand against the back of the case and felt the notes his mother played. Another set of scales, F-sharp minor this time: F-sharp, G-sharp, A, B, C-sharp, D, E, F-sharp, over and over again. He could hear the music, could even feel it with his hands, but he wished he could see it so he could know what it meant to her.

"Mama, what does music look like?" he asked above the scale.

"*Chi-chi-chi!*" she snapped. "I'm not finished yet."

"Ugh," he said, but low enough not to bother her.

He had a nail in his pocket that he'd picked up while walking home from school, along with an empty Bic lighter and two dull pennies. The point on the nail was like a sharp pencil but much stronger. As he lay on the floor, a cruel idea crossed his mind: what sort of mark would his nail make on the wood? Although he knew better than to do anything like that to the piano his mother loved—maybe more than she loved him—he found that once he'd thought this up he wasn't able to unthink it, and so he sprawled there with the dust motes and scale notes drifting around him and felt the nail being pulled almost as if by magnetic force to the bass end of the piano. He negotiated with himself. Something small, he thought, so small that nobody would ever notice.

He wrote his name very neatly. Tiny Cyrillic letters down at the very edge of the corner. He was extremely careful, tracing each one several times to achieve a uniform depth. The contrast between the black gloss and the dark natural wood where the finish had been etched away wasn't too striking. He liked the idea of claiming the beast that had claimed his mother. He continued, so focused on his task that he didn't realize that she'd stopped playing, that the notes he heard were simply echoes from his memory.

He was just finishing the final letter when his mother came around from her bench and screamed, "*Grisha! Что, черт возьми, ты делаешь?!*"

The road to Death Valley was long and flat, a three-hour drive up the western part of Nevada past sagebrush, power lines, and water towers. In the middle of a huge swath of desert, drained otherwise of color and distinction, an oversized red sign announced BROTHEL along with HOT SAUCE, PICTURES, SOUVENIRS, but there was no establishment anywhere nearby that Clara could see. In fact, the landscape looked mostly abandoned. It was peaceful, doing seventy-five through this expansive basin with low mountains in the distance and an eternal, raw blue sky stretching overhead. Eventually they drove through a small town, where a twenty-four-hour tire shop reminded her of her own garage, then crossed into California again.

They finally passed a marker welcoming them to Death Valley National Park. It was just after noon, the sun high and hot. This was the kind of place where people could get lost and die of thirst or exposure, Clara understood. She'd never been here before, but her uncle had once told her about a friend of his who had. He was camping, and a snake followed him into his sleeping bag, twining itself around one of his legs. When the man jerked out of sleep, the snake bit him, so he followed the old advice of cutting an X into the skin, then sucking and spitting out the poisoned blood. But he cut too deep. The bite hadn't been venomous, but the guy had nicked a vein, and after lying down to rest, he bled to death on the desert floor.

A few miles in, a sign told them PAY FEE, with an arrow pointing to a ranger station on the roadside. At the kiosk, Greg parked and paid for access. Once he was finished she did too. Twenty dollars wasn't exorbitant, but it made her consider her credit-card balance, her lack of income, her medical and moving expenses. Even with a five-grand windfall, she worried about how much this unforeseen adventure was going to cost. Greg pulled in at a rustic, Old West–style hotel and went inside with the guys, presumably to secure their rooms, and she sat in her car, trying to decide if she should do the same. After all, she could turn around and make it home by dinnertime if she wanted.

Her financial considerations were interrupted, though, when she heard Greg say, "Fucking check-in times." The three men were back in the parking lot. "Doesn't matter. I want to get two shots in before it gets dark anyway." Then he noticed Clara and walked toward her car, his obvious aggravation making his limp more pronounced. She unrolled the window and rested her cast on the frame.

He leaned in. "This has gone on long enough, don't you think?"

If he was trying to intimidate her, it wasn't working. She had made up her mind: she was going to stay, at least for a little while longer. "Why do you care? I'm not hurting anything."

"I told you before, you're a liability."

"I've been thinking about that. Exactly *how* am I a liability? You're not responsible for me."

He looked at her, hard. "No, I certainly am not," he said.

Then he took a step back and seemed to gaze around at the stretch of rocky wilderness beyond the hotel. "Look," he said after a moment, "you want to follow me around like a lost dog, I can't stop you. But stay out of my way, understand?"

He stood scowling at the barren landscape, the wind kicking

up silt and pushing at the wisps of hair he had left. He might be cruel, she thought, a cruel, crooked little man. But something told her that he wasn't as threatening as he pretended to be. What was it that made him so angry?

"Fine," she said. Then, as he turned toward his car, she asked, "So where are we going first?"

Greg lifted his sunglasses and leveled a glare at her that managed to be dull and piercing at the same time. "*We?*"

"Pardon me. *You.*"

"Well, I suppose you'll just have to wait and see," he said, then strode off.

Back on the two-lane highway that transected Death Valley, they drove about fifteen minutes, passing sporadic tufts of dusty green brush and a sign stating that the elevation was at sea level, until they reached a gravel turnoff marked SALT CREEK INTERPRETIVE TRAIL. How did Greg know where he was going? As decisive as he seemed to be about his route, he must have been familiar with the park. She wondered about the extent of his planning for this expedition, and this, in turn, increased her curiosity about his purpose in undertaking it.

After a mile or so, the road ended in a paved parking area where a wooden boardwalk stretched into the mountainous distance with a narrow creek on one side and sturdy, pale rock formations on the other.

Clara hung back—far enough so he couldn't accuse her of intruding, but close enough to watch—and read several signs that described the Salt Creek ecosystem. Greg ordered the guys to get the piano unloaded and start rolling it up the boardwalk. "Sunset's at six-oh-five, give or take," he said, looking at his watch. "I want to go south to Badwater for that, so we need to hurry. It's about thirty minutes from here." Juan and Beto stepped up their pace, which was much easier to do on a level boardwalk than up a rocky incline. As Greg hustled to keep up with them, his limp turned into a sort of skip, reminding her of the old sheepdog her uncle had when he and her aunt took her in. Shep had "a hitch in his giddy-up," as he put it, and whenever the dog tried to run it had the same staccato gait as Greg did now. She'd loved that dog.

"Here," Greg called. "Unstrap it and leave the dolly there. We're going to put it in the creek."

"What's that?" she called, pulled out of her reminiscence. "What did you say?"

"I was talking to them," he said, unscrewing and extending the legs of his tripod.

"Did you say you were going to put the piano in the *creek*?"

"Right over there," he called to Beto, pointing to the middle of the shallow water. Sunlight skittered on the surface, which was mottled with rocks of various sizes.

"In the water?" Clara asked. She stood in front of him so he couldn't ignore her.

He sighed. "Remember our agreement? The part about you not pestering me?" He attached a lens to the camera body and gave it a quick blast of compressed air from a can.

"Fuck your agreement. There's no goddamn chance I'll let you put my piano in the water."

"And how are you going to stop me?"

To the surprise of both of them, she snatched the camera out of his hands and marched back toward the parking area.

"What the fuck? Get back here! That camera's probably worth more than everything you own put together."

She could hear him coming up behind her—step, *thump*, step, *thump*—and broke into a jog, jumped into her car, and locked the doors. She had just finished rolling up the driver's window when Greg got there. She set the camera down on the passenger seat and jammed the key into the ignition. "If you put my piano in the creek, I'm leaving and taking your camera with me," she shouted through the glass.

Panting, Greg leaned against the window, resting one arm on the glass and wearing an indifferent expression in spite of his chest heaving up and down. "You think I don't have other cameras with me? What sort of photographer would I be if I only brought one?"

"Then I guess you won't care if I keep it," Clara said. She started the engine and tossed her arm over the seat, looking over her shoulder to navigate.

"Wait!" Greg shouted, slapping the glass as the car jerked away in reverse. "Stop!"

Her heart thundering, she arced the car around and then slammed it into drive like a stunt driver, a trick Peter had taught her one Sunday afternoon, and tore off up the gravel road. She heard Greg cry out but couldn't see him through the dust her car had whipped up between them.

"Stop!" she heard. "Stop!" But she wasn't sure if it was Greg who was calling or her own conscience. She slowed, and stopped, and looked at the camera, which had slid against the back of the seat. She picked it up and held it in her lap, feeling ridiculous and childish for having taken it. Then she turned the car around.

Greg was in the middle of the road, bent over with his hands on his thighs. As she approached, she could see that he was struggling to catch his breath. This made her feel even worse, realizing he'd probably tried to run after her. When he finally pushed himself upright again, his countenance carried the weight of defeat. She pulled up next to him and rolled down the window.

"I told you before I wouldn't let anything happen to the piano," he said to her. "And I'm not going to."

"Then why the creek?" The camera remained in her lap.

"Did you happen to notice, since you're so observant, how shallow it is, and that there's a dry elevation in the middle of it? No? Well, there is, and it's plenty wide to set the piano down without it getting its feet wet. In fact, the guys probably already have it in situ. They're probably standing there in the middle of Salt Creek waiting for me to photograph it, which I will do as soon as you give my fucking camera back."

"I thought you had others."

He took a handkerchief out of his pocket and ran it over his cheeks and the back of his neck. "You really are a pain in the ass, aren't you?" he said, staring down at her. It was odd how his voice conveyed so much and his expression so little, as though he were shielding his own vulnerability.

"No, actually, I'm not," she said, and held the camera out to him with her good hand. It was a relief to be rid of it. Greg examined the body and lens to see if Clara might've inflicted some damage, even turned it on and clicked through a few of the images to be certain they were still there. "Look," she said, "I'm sorry. I just—"

"I care a hell of a lot more about that piano than you could ever guess," he said, his tone shifting to a softer register. "It's not in my interest to ruin it now."

Clara was thinking about his rather ominous use of *now,* whether he meant it might be in his interest to ruin it later, when he turned without another word and started back toward the creek. Clara watched him go, the limp more pronounced, the sun beating down on him, his bald spot gleaming with perspiration. Despite his harsh and haughty bearing, his intrepid stare, his apparent conscription to unhappiness, she didn't entirely dislike him. In truth, she found him strangely appealing. In Greg, she recognized something of herself: a dull void where something had been lost. His forbearance suggested a wound deeper than whatever might've caused his uneven gait.

Considering his wounds made Clara think about her own, both physical and emotional. She walked down to the creek, wanting to see for herself that the piano was safe. There it was, on the dry spot in the middle where Greg had said it would be, with Juan and Beto standing beside it looking bored but patient, waiting for instructions. The sight of the water made her thirsty, and her thirst made her angry. At that moment she didn't want to need anything at all—not a drink, not a bathroom, not Greg's money, not a sense of control, and certainly not a piano she could neither play nor let go of.

She sat down on the boardwalk and watched from a distance as Greg set up his camera according to whatever mysterious calculations he'd made, then manipulated the scene by shouting to his helpers for what seemed to her inconsequential adjustments that only increased the risk of getting the piano wet. At one point Beto stumbled, and Clara, flashing back to the disastrous move up the staircase, made a small, involuntary noise that—once she saw that he'd recovered his footing and the piano was again stable—made her even angrier at herself. Cradling her broken hand in her lap, she fought against an overwhelming urge to cry. She lost.

Thick, streaming tears cut into the thin coat of dust and sand on her face. Once she started she couldn't stop, giving in to all the emotions that were behind and inside them, yet at the same time she was able to look at herself as if from a distant vantage—*oh, there's a woman who's crying*—and she felt a great inward tenderness as she bent forward, hugging her hand more tightly. This division of awareness allowed her to notice that the boardwalk was trembling along with her sobs, that her nose was running unattractively, and that the pathetic sounds she was making might have been loud enough to draw unwanted attention. Still, she let herself continue, let the frustration and thirst, the grief and embarrassment, and all the rest run down her cheeks and drop onto her jeans in fat splotches. Finally, after a few minutes, the well began to run dry, and the tears slowed, then stopped. She felt empty in a satisfying—though not entirely pleasant—sense. She no longer had to tangle with her emotions: the battle had been fought and was now over. She was like a car that had run out of gas, and the only option was to wait on the side of the road until she got the fuel with which to start again.

She looked over and saw that Greg had finished and was repacking his vest and backpack, and the movers had already carried the piano out of the stream and were positioning it on the dolly on the boardwalk. The sun was low enough to gild the setting with its eventide light, and she thought with a detached wonder how pretty and noble the piano looked. No wonder Greg wanted to photograph it. Whatever else there was to his relationship with the Blüthner seemed unimportant now; her curiosity had been supplanted by fatigue.

For lack of a tissue, she wiped her nose with the back of her good hand and realized how dirty she felt. Even though she was used to being filthy with car grease, this kind of road-driven wear and tear lacked dignity. Perhaps insisting on following Greg around did, too. She decided it was time for her to go home, but she wanted to blow her nose and wash her face and take care of her other human needs before doing so.

Slipping away unseen, she drove back to the motel with the intention of using the bathroom and maybe leaving a note for Greg to let him know he'd won, that she was getting out from underfoot. But pulling into the parking lot, she was overcome with fatigue and wanted desperately to lie down, even for just an hour or two, before driving the couple-hundred-plus miles home.

"Sorry, miss," said the man at reception. "We don't have any rooms left for tonight. They're all booked up way in advance this time of the year. Late October, early November's usually our busiest few weeks."

"Nothing at all?"

"No, I'm sorry."

She sighed, and thanked him, and followed his directions to

the public restroom. Then, while waiting for her meal in the hotel's restaurant, she wrote Greg a brief note on a paper napkin, apologizing again for having taken his camera, telling him she was leaving, and wishing him well. She read it over, then folded it up, tore it into small pieces, and dropped them into the breadbasket. On another napkin she wrote, *I'm taking off.—Clara*. It lay there on the table as she ate. When she was finished, she wiped her mouth with it and tossed it on her empty plate. She didn't owe him a damn thing.

Katya leaned in close to the bathroom mirror to apply the mascara to one eye then leaned back to check the result. Satisfied, she repeated the process for the other eye. There weren't too many wrinkles; she looked young for forty, she decided, even pretty. Then a bit of lipstick, not too much. She didn't want it to seem as though she'd made a special effort. This was the first time she had ever applied makeup or curled her hair or worn a pair of high heels to give a piano lesson.

Also for the first time, she wondered if it was appropriate to invite a student into her home. She didn't have many, so typically she was pleased to have them come. Most of them were elementary-age children whose mothers drove them over then sat on the sofa reading or knitting for the thirty minutes. Older children sometimes rode over after school on their bikes, dropping them carelessly in the front yard. She had a few adult students, women whose children were grown and gone and who wanted to finally do something for themselves or else to stave off the loneliness that had invaded their empty nests. One pair of students, a couple who'd been married for nearly fifty years, came twice a month at lunchtime, taking turns during a single half-hour lesson, each standing at the piano and offering encouragement as the other played. Never before, though, had an adult male come in the middle of the day, when her son was in school and her husband at work. But this was the only time slot that worked, since he had a busy schedule and a family of his own.

So why *wouldn't* it be appropriate? She was a teacher and her home was the only classroom available to her. That she would be alone with a male student had never been an issue before. This would be nothing out of the ordinary, simply another introductory lesson.

Katya put cookies on a platter and set out the makings for tea then straightened up the living room for a second time. She glanced at the clock: everything had been ready for too long already, and he wasn't even due until noon. She sighed and sat down at the piano. Playing always helped calm her nerves, especially now that she had her old Blüthner back.

She chose Liszt's étude "La Campanella" for its brisk *allegretto* tempo. Also, it was challenging technically, requiring finger agility for the large jumps with the right hand. The first few notes were played slowly, like a throat-clearing, the piece then gradually becoming faster, more urgent and, within a few minutes, complicated enough that she was so absorbed she forgot about the time and was startled when the doorbell rang. She jumped up and hurried to the door, then forced herself to pause and take a long breath so that when she opened it she'd appear calm.

"Hello, come in," she said, spreading her arm toward the living room like one of those game-show hostesses she'd seen on TV.

He smiled at her, his *rodimoye pyatno* changing shape along the crease at his left eye. "I hope I'm not too early. I was worried about the traffic and for once there actually wasn't any."

She smiled in return and cautioned herself to settle down. He was just a student. That he'd also somehow managed to make her knees go soft and her head light when he'd called, out of the blue, several months after he'd helped reunite her with her piano, and inquired about the offer of lessons she'd mentioned was not something she should pay any attention to. But how could she fail to pay attention? It had been so long since she'd felt butterflies because of a man that she couldn't even remember the last time.

"It's nice to see you again."

She led him to the piano and pulled the bench out for him. "Sit, please."

He did, and she sat next to him.

"The piano looks great in here. I bet you're glad to have it back after all that time, huh?"

"Oh yes," she said, smiling at him. "So glad."

He smiled back, and she could see his eyes darting over hers like a caress, and quickly dropped her gaze.

He clapped his hands together and rubbed them. "So how does this work? I've never taken a piano lesson before."

She straightened her already straight posture and nodded once. "Yes. First thing we must learn is posture, the foundation to all the expressive and technical skills, which will come later."

He mimicked her posture, which made him several inches taller, and they both registered that and laughed.

"Good," she said. "Now, basic playing movements. Your entire arm is relaxed. No tension in the shoulder, elbow, or wrist. Do this." She pivoted to him and pulled his right arm out of his lap until it dangled between them. She drew in a quick breath at the intimacy of touching him, then forced herself to focus. "Now, raise the arm—relaxed, like this. Watch." She demonstrated by lifting her own arm as if it were floating upward. "Keep the hand in a relaxed shape like this. Palm should be round like holding an apple. See? Okay, you try." When he did, he looked like a robot or a puppet being manipulated by strings. "Okay, good. More relaxed. Yes, now round your hand more. Like a . . . how do you call it? Dome? Yes, like a dome. Good. Now watch, stay relaxed, but each fingertip should be crisp and precise—not wobbly like a cooked pasta." She let her fingers drift to the keyboard and pressed a key with her middle finger. "Only press with the third finger for now, like this. Play deeply to the bottom of the key, then release. This will make a beautiful, deep, soft piano tone. Okay, now you." He did, pressing down as she had instructed, but too hard and with such a quick a release that it sounded harsh and percussive. "Very good," she said. "It takes a lot of practice. Try once more. And try with your other hand also." He played the same note several times with each hand, and they all sounded as terrible as the first one.

"How long have you been playing?" he asked.

"Since I was very small."

"Did you take lessons? I should've tried to learn when I was a kid."

"My father taught me at first, but mostly I learned by myself. Then later with teachers. I studied piano at university."

"You must be good, then. I mean you *sounded* really good. I could hear you playing through the door."

"Not so bad." She smiled as she shrugged one shoulder. The strap of her sundress slipped down, and she saw him notice it and then watch as she pulled it back up.

"Will you play something for me?"

"Don't you want to continue your lesson?"

"Yes, but it's pretty obvious that I'm not going to become a maestro today. You're a good teacher, I'm sure. But you're not *that* good."

They laughed.

"Do you have a special request?" she asked.

"Anything. Something you like a lot."

She nodded once, then shifted closer to the center of the bench, and he moved down to give her more room. She lifted her hands gently and paused before setting upon the keys with a strikingly fast and tempestuous piece that sent her hands flying up and down until it seemed she could strike sparks on them. Her feet worked the pedals and her body jerked with the energy being transferred between them and the piano. It lasted only two minutes, but when it ended—almost abruptly—her chest was pumping and a light sheen of sweat glossed her forehead. She turned to him and smiled. "Well?"

He answered by leaning in to kiss her just as she'd told him to press the key: deep, soft, right down to the bottom of the note before slowly releasing it, much better than his poor piano attack would've suggested. He opened his eyes and she blinked at him, still out of breath, stunned to silence.

"Forgive me," he said, standing up. "I'm so sorry. I don't know what came over me. Please—"

She also stood, fluttering one hand to her chest, her heart pounding so loudly she thought he could hear it.

"You play beautifully," he said, shaking his head and glancing around the room, then starting awkwardly for the door. "I'm really sorry about . . . Anyway, thank you." He lurched back toward her and stuck out his hand.

She took it and could feel it trembling—or was it hers?

"Thank you," he said again. "Okay. Good-bye."

He let himself out and was already down the steps before she realized he was leaving and hurried to the door. "Come back next week," she called out. "Same time."

He stopped and gave a sigh of relief that relaxed his whole body; then he turned slowly to her with a smile on his face. "Yes?" he said. "You sure about that?"

She nodded once, and bit down on a smile. "I will see you then," she said, and raised her hand before retreating back inside.

The sun had sunk behind the mountains by the time she stepped into the parking lot, the air cool and rich with desert smells carried on a stronger wind. She closed her eyes and breathed in deeply. Had she ever been so tired? The road strained toward the horizon, and remembering the long, monotonous drive earlier that day—was it really only this morning they'd arrived in Death Valley?—she felt her energy abandoning her. She knew she wouldn't be able to make it back to Bakersfield unless she took a short nap first. So she rooted in her trunk and pulled a towel to use as a blanket, cracked the windows to let the evening in, and lay down on the backseat. In less than a minute she was deeply asleep.

The sound of laughter awakened her. Even with the light pollution from the motel, the stars were bright points in the patch of sky visible through the window when Clara opened her eyes and looked out. The temperature had dropped. Pushing herself up, she groped around the seat for her phone and checked the time: 11:12.

"Figures." One minute past wishing time. When she was a kid, she'd frequently checked the clock until it ticked to 11:11, then would close her eyes and make a wish, but in recent years it seemed like she always missed it. She rubbed her eyes and yawned. It didn't matter; she wouldn't know what to wish for anyway.

She got out and stretched, looking around to see who was laughing: a few people sitting on folding chairs some distance away from the motel, the red ends of their cigarettes glowing. She wanted to splash her face with cold water but was too embarrassed to face the desk clerk again. There was a gas station just across the road where she could stop on her way out. When she was about to get behind the wheel, she noticed an envelope bearing the motel's name on the front seat. It contained a note, and a key.

Even lost dogs deserve a decent bed. Room 213 in Roadrunner Bldg.—G.

It wasn't until she'd rummaged in the glove compartment for her travel kit and was looking for the Roadrunner on the map on the wall outside the entrance that she wondered what had compelled Greg to such generosity. Then she remembered the clerk saying there weren't any rooms left, and there was no reason she shouldn't believe it; the restaurant and saloon were busy, and even at that late hour guests were coming and going from the various buildings that made up the compound.

Two young couples, all four people carrying laptops and laughing, passed her in one of the covered walkways as she checked the numbers on the doors. Abruptly, one of the women turned around and said, "You look lost. Do you need directions? The layout here's a little confusing."

"No," Clara said, with what she hoped sounded like nonchalance. *Yes. I'm lost. I'm confused. Tell me what to do.* "I got it, but thanks."

"Okay," the woman said, and lifted her hand in what was part wave, part salute. "Night."

"Night," Clara said and, flustered, turned back toward reception, and her car beyond it.

"Hey," someone else called. She looked over her shoulder and saw Greg standing in a doorway. "I see you got my note." He leaned back and crossed his arms. His voice sounded smug, but his face, as usual, was unreadable. She wanted to punch him.

"You're dreaming if you think I'm going to sleep with you," she said, loud enough to make him glance right and left and then scamper toward her.

"What are you talking about?" he hissed.

"You can insult me all you want, call me a lost dog, make fun of me for being here, but don't think for one second I'm that desperate."

His arms flew up as his eyebrows pinched together. "You can't be serious. You really think I'm trying to lure you into my room?" He looked genuinely surprised. She felt her face grow hot, but she didn't dare to release his gaze. Finally he let his shoulders drop, and closed his eyes for a moment while he took a deep breath and then exhaled. "I'm not hitting on you, Clara. I have no desire to sleep with you."

This made her miserable with humiliation. She didn't want him to hit on her—at least she didn't think she did—but somehow it was even worse being told that he wasn't trying to. Her face flushed with heat again.

"I told Juan and Beto to share a room so you could have the spare, which is down the hall. I didn't like the idea of you sleeping out there alone in your car. If you're going to insist on hanging around, you might as well be safe. My mother would've insisted on it." He leaned toward her and made a show of sniffing. "Besides, you need a shower. Good night, Clara." He stepped back into his room and closed the door, the chain latch sliding into place with a metallic rattle.

Clara slept hard on the narrow bed, better than she had in a long time. She usually fell asleep easily enough but throughout the night was fitful, bothered by too-vivid dreams, scouring her head against her pillow so when she woke up her hair was as tangled as her bedclothes. Today she woke up just before daybreak, feeling profoundly rested. She lay still, watching the light grow stronger around the edge of the curtains, and tried to remember the last time she'd had such as good sleep. It was probably that night she'd spent with Peter, years ago. Now it was Monday, so he'd be getting up soon, ready to open the shop by seven o'clock. She could picture him, his face peaceful with unself-conscious slumber. She sat up. Enough of that.

She opened the curtains and looked out at the mountains. There were dozens of tents and campers parked on the far side of the lot and, beyond them, a field of shrubs extending to the horizon that was golden in the morning light. The day, as calm as it looked, seemed to be posing a question: *What do you plan to do?*

On one hand—the broken one, maybe—there she was, at a hotel in an exotic and unusual setting, with no place else to be. It almost felt like a vacation. And wasn't she technically on a vacation, given that she was unable to do any meaningful work?

On the other hand, she'd never been the sort of person who took vacations. It wasn't that she was overly ambitious; she simply hadn't ever been part of a family that rewarded labor with getaways. Her parents had always been industrious. Even outside of their regular fall and spring semester course loads, they taught summer classes, did research, wrote papers. They were both so serious about their endeavors—about everything, really—that she couldn't imagine them setting their work aside, happily packing suitcases, and traveling anywhere that wasn't absolutely essential. In fact, she now wondered, perhaps for the first time, if either of them ever did anything just for fun.

Nor could she remember her uncle taking any time off. They had quiet evenings with her aunt and their long drives, but because Jack had a garage to run, there was never an opportunity to shut it down except for signature holidays. Besides his customers' vehicles, there was always something else that needed repair or attention, or the accounting needed to be done, or one of his employees had called in sick. Since they had no savings account to fall back on, her uncle was more inclined to do things that earned money instead of wasting it.

When she got older, and classmates talked about summer vacations or skiing over the winter break, she wasn't jealous. It was like talking about riding a llama to school or speaking in tongues. Interesting, but not something she even considered an option. So when Ryan surprised her with a weekend in San Diego for her twenty-fourth birthday, she felt guilty the whole time they were down there, like she should've been doing something more productive.

Through the window, she heard a door down the hall open and close. Then, a little farther away, a knock, an answer, muffled words in English and Spanish. The choice was simple. What could she do at home that was more productive than ensuring her piano's safety and possibly learning something about its—or her parents'—past?

Quickly, she brushed her teeth and got dressed. Greg, to her chagrin, had been right about her needing a shower. If only she had some clean clothes. She had no idea where the camera crew would go, or how long she would follow, so she gathered up her few things with no thought of returning to this room. She could leave anytime she wanted. No belongings to divide up and pack, no hard feelings to maneuver around. Just get in her car and drive any direction she wanted to go, just as she and her uncle used to do until they were ready to go back home.

She went to the small lounge behind the registration desk and was having a cup of coffee when Greg and the movers showed up.

"Good morning," he said, nodding at the banana and bottle of water by her cup. "A little sustenance for the drive home?"

"Actually, I think I'll stick around for a while." She smiled. Greg shrugged. "Suit yourself."

So she did. She was careful to keep her distance, but she tagged along for the next several days as Greg photographed the Blüthner in various locations around Death Valley. When driving from one place to the next, Clara was struck by the enormousness of the park. Something she guessed was a mile away—a sand dune, a variegated outcropping—in reality was probably four. Under the stark midday sun, the mountains seemed to flatten into two dimensions. At night, the dark was lavish with stars that looked low enough for picking. This sense that things were both closer and farther away was a disorienting illusion. Even the sky above didn't seem like the usual cupped vault; staring at it was more like gazing directly into outer space. And all of it was a fascinating setting for Greg's pictures.

Clara had never been interested in photography. People going around with their eyes pressed against viewfinders instead of seeing what was right there in front of them, and for what? To preserve an artificial impression that was more fragile than a real one? Even photos in albums could get lost, or burned, and then what was left? Just tattered half-memories that made the past seem even further away than it was. Until now—watching as the movers positioned her piano on top of dunes, against giant salt formations, in front of a mountain face that seemed composed by mounds of different flavors of ice cream—she hadn't considered that a photograph's artistic value might be enough to justify the effort.

For the most part, she and Greg didn't speak. She watched him work, and only occasionally did he register her presence. She was reminded of how she used to follow her father around the house, wanting to be near him, to know more about him. She learned to be quiet and not at all disruptive so she could study him. It was most rewarding, however, on those rare times when he would notice her, put down his papers, and call her to him for a kiss or a conversation.

Again and again the movers repeated their effort of unloading the Blüthner, placing it on the all-terrain dolly, securing it with straps, wheeling it out to wherever the shot would be, unloading and unwrapping it, and positioning it however Greg indicated. Clara was growing more comfortable with their handling of the piano, after watching them do it several times. She wondered if they were growing bored with their job. They didn't appear to have any opinion about it and simply performed the tasks as required, always keeping their conversation to a minimum and enduring Greg's demands with stoic indifference. When he was finished, the movers reversed all their actions once again. Then she would join their little caravan to the next destination, glad, for some inexplicable reason, to be doing so.

That first night, after a full day of shooting, she'd bought a change of clothes at the general store across the road. She hadn't asked Greg if the room was still available, but since he didn't tell her that it wasn't she let herself in with the key. Then, clean from a long shower and wearing her new Death Valley souvenir T-shirt, she went to the hotel restaurant for the second night in a row.

The hostess led her to a booth directly opposite the one where Greg, Beto, and Juan were examining the menu. She slid along the curved vinyl seat until she was partially hidden from their line of sight by the booth's high back. Juan, sitting next to Greg, glanced at her without acknowledgment, then looked back at his menu. Maybe Greg had told them to ignore her. She suffered another moment of humiliation at the thought of being the butt of some snide remark, though looking at them—Juan and Beto making quiet, spare conversation while Greg became absorbed by something on his phone—she figured that he probably wouldn't bother making chummy talk with them, even at her expense.

The waitress took their orders: hamburgers and orange sodas for the movers, a tuna-fish sandwich on wheat—"with the crust cut off, thanks"—and an extra-dry vodka martini up with olives for Greg. He was a fussy eater, picking at the bits of crust the cook had missed. He drank his martini and relieved the little plastic sword of its two impaled olives with his teeth, then raised his finger to signal the waitress for another. He spoke to Juan and Beto only once, and they nodded and went back to eating. It seemed that Greg didn't intend to build any friendships during this trip. Temporary allies, perhaps. Clara understood and even admired that kind of independence.

When he finished, Greg put his credit card on the edge of the table, and Juan and Beto shoveled down the rest of their dinner. Clara was still eating when Greg slapped the waitress's pen down on top of his signed bill and stood up. The movers wiped their mouths and dropped their crumpled napkins on the table and followed him out, none of them saying anything when they walked by her.

The following day was much like the first, at least in the beginning. They went to two different locations, covered many miles, took a break for gas and snacks, drove somewhere else. As the shadows grew longer, they made a long downhill drive to a place called Badwater Basin.

That seemed like a misnomer, as there was almost no water at all, only a small, shallow pond surrounded by what looked to be miles of salt. They drove a little beyond the parking lot and pulled off the road. Greg got out to scout the area, told the movers to wait and, to her surprise, motioned for Clara to join him.

He led her into the pan, where long-ago seawater had evaporated and left behind a snowy blanket of salt that was marked with irregular octagonal patterns from cracks and pressure ridges. Up close, those looked like crashing waves desiccated in time. He stopped a few yards out and, slipping his hands into his pockets, let his gaze roam over the tops of the mountains and down to the flats below. "Have you ever felt really low?" he asked, his voice thoughtful. "Like you've hit rock bottom?" Clara was taken aback by what seemed an admission of vulnerability. He was kicking at an encrusted ridge of salt that was like a miniature of the mountain ridges beyond.

"Yeah," she said.

"Well, now you've really hit it."

"What?"

"Here," he said. "This is rock bottom, right here. The lowest point on the planet. We're two hundred and eighty-two feet below sea level." He looked at her without any trace of guile, but his eyes did seem to crinkle at the outer corners. If they were friends—if he'd been Peter—she would've laughed, maybe given him a playful punch in the arm. But even though she appreciated the joke, she didn't want to let her guard down too far.

"No place left to go but up, then," she said, mimicking his deadpan expression.

He evidently considered this, and after a moment he nodded. "Maybe so. Maybe so." Then he lifted his hand and gave Juan and Beto a let's-go signal.

Clara, feeling less like a lost dog, if not quite included, watched him set up his tripod fairly low to the ground, digging around in his bag and muttering to himself, "Where's my wide-angle lens? Light meter. Yes, here. Okay." He crouched down, careful with his stiff leg, so he could peer through the viewfinder. He changed settings—"ISO 100, f/14, 1.6s," he mumbled—and focused the lens. He seemed completely absorbed in his work, and these tiny manipulations fascinated her. It made Clara think about her equivalent: going into the pit, removing the oil plug and its gasket from an engine, letting the oil drain out, changing the filter, replacing the oil. Menial, yes, but deeply satisfying—though probably nobody would find it interesting enough to actually watch. She was surprised at how much she missed the feel of oil on her fingers, missed finding the solution for a challenging problem, following every step, keeping things in order. Cleaning up after Alex, who always made a mess. Working with Peter.

Once he began taking pictures, Greg stopped talking to himself. Maybe, Clara considered, he needed to listen to something besides his own voice in order to capture each image. She thought of the line in his website bio: *I record what is there and what is not, so that you may see what it is that I hear.* Clara closed her eyes and listened, too. There was the rush of wind, stronger than the day before, shearing off the mountains. The steam-whistle scream of a hawk. The snapping of the camera shutter. Beto, standing behind them, striking a match to light a cigarette. When she opened her eyes again the sun had slid behind the mountains, and the clouds that streaked across the sky had taken on an orange-and-purple blush. The small stones in the shallow pond, which was still in shadow, seemed to float in a sea of reflected golden light. Her Blüthner's black finish gleamed against the white salt pan, while its doppel-gänger wavered in the pond. In the trick of this late light, the salt pan almost looked like a snow-covered valley.

That night, back at the hotel once again, Greg invited her to join him for dinner.

I don't want to be anywhere but here," Katya said, moving even closer to him and draping a leg over his, as though to trap him under the sheets. The window was open, and an ocean breeze moved the curtains *adagio,* like a slow dance in the dark. It was a new moon, and no light was coming in except from the digital clock on the bedside table. The beach bungalow belonged to a friend of his, a divorcé with more money than free time, so they had it to themselves almost whenever they wanted it, which had been nearly every Thursday afternoon for the past year and a half, for as many hours each time as they could get away with. Lately, they'd been staying until after dark, desperate for more time in each other's arms. It was a seven-mile drive for him if he was going from his office, a thirteen-mile drive for her: close enough that they could spend a few uninterrupted hours in bed or walking along the beach or in a café, but far enough away that they didn't have to worry constantly about being seen.

"Me either, my love. Let's just stay here. Move in."

She laughed. "Where will you put all your books?"

"Well, when we put your piano out on the curb for the scavengers to take, we'll have plenty of room for books."

She pretended to slap him on the chest, and he pulled her into a tight embrace. "Fine, no books. We can put the piano in the kitchen. I don't need to eat; all I need is you."

"That is better," she said, and kissed him.

"Our anniversary is coming up. Two years since our first lesson."

"You are a terrible student."

"The worst. But a wonderful lover."

"Yes, of course. The best." She bit him carefully on the shoulder.

"I love you," he said.

"I love you, too."

He rolled onto his side and propped himself on his elbow. "Why?"

"*Зачем?*"

"Yes, why. Why do you love me?"

"You don't know?"

"I do. I just like hearing you say it."

"Such a silly man."

"Your silly man," he said, and kissed her on the neck, just below her ear, where she was the most sensitive. "Tell me."

She tipped her head back to give him a better angle. "I will tell if you keep doing that."

He hummed agreement into her skin, and goose bumps rose up to meet him. "I love you for always coming here with me, every week, for your piano lesson." She giggled.

He licked her earlobe. "What else?"

"I love you for how you look me in the eyes for many minutes without blinking."

"I could look at you forever, you're so beautiful. And your fingers, the way you touch me like you're playing Scriabin or Tchaikovsky. You don't even know you're doing it."

She played the first few measures of Scriabin's E-flat Minor Prelude on his chest, *presto*. Each time she touched one of his nipples, he flinched in pleasure.

"And what do you love about me so much to bring you back all the time?" she asked.

"You want me to tell you in Russian or English?"

"English. So I can practice. They say 'pillow talk' is the best way to know colloquial speech."

"Well, we've had plenty of that, haven't we?" He rolled on top of her, shifting her body beneath his until she was flat on her back. "Anyway, I don't know enough Russian to express myself adequately. Okay. Well, your talent for one. You manipulate me like a puppeteer every time you play. Whatever emotion you want me to feel, it works. I don't even know how you do it."

"That credit is to the composer, not to me."

"You're wrong. It's you." He kissed her on the nose. "Then there's the conversation, the communication. I've never felt as free to talk and tease and joke with someone." He paused. They both knew that by *someone,* he meant his wife. "But with you I can be open. We can talk about the . . . mechanics of physical love. You've completely opened me up in that regard. And I love how amazingly you respond to me when I'm passionate. I've been with people who were horny, but never passionate. Not craziness that comes straight from the heart, not like this. You understand?"

She didn't, not entirely, not these nuances of his. But how he'd positioned himself over her, like he would protect and care for her, was enough. "Yes," she said.

"It's crazy how easy it is to be with you. Just like this, in bed together for hours. I don't think I've ever spent more than an hour naked with anybody without one of us picking up a book, or turning on the TV, or leaving, or falling asleep. Have you?"

She thought of the first afternoon she and Mikhail had spent together in his small apartment, making love until it was dark outside, twenty-one years before. They'd had a few more days like that afterward, as they got to know each other—maybe weeks; it was hard to remember—but he had the disposition of an engineer, not a swain. He was drawn to routine and efficiency; lovemaking soon became just another thing to check off a list. Had they even fallen in love? She didn't think so. They had simply succumbed to reasonableness and practicality.

Katya put her hand over his heart. "No, my love. Not like this."

"I want to be with you all the time," he said.

"So do I want to be with you."

He sat up and turned on the lamp. His dark red hair was disheveled, his day's stubble starting to show, sparkling silver in the light. Her own dark hair had started to turn gray, just a few strands here and there. She had asked recently if he thought she should dye it, and he said he didn't want her to do anything like that for him. He said he loved watching her hair change, that he wanted to watch it go all the way to white and her veins to gnarl the backs of her hands. He said he didn't care how the years showed on her as long as he was there to witness it. "I mean it, Katya. It's been two years. We know why we love each other, so when are we going to actually do what we need to in order to be together?"

She sat up too, punching the pillows into submission behind her back for support. Then she smiled at him. "How do we do this, huh? We do love each other, but are you really going to leave your wife? You really want to accept my son? There are many things about this arrangement that are difficult."

He didn't hesitate. "Yes! Of course I'd accept him. I've always said that I would."

She shook her head. "And what about your wife?"

"Remember me telling you that my colleague thought he saw her off-campus with a grad student?"

She nodded.

"I think she's seeing him. *Seeing him.* You know what I mean?"

"A love affair?"

"I think so, yes. She's been acting strangely. Well, she always acts strangely. But lately it seems different. She's more distracted than usual. Doesn't seem quite as angry. I don't know—it would be great if she was involved with somebody else."

"It wouldn't make you upset?"

He paused. "Well, I don't have much room to criticize her, do I? I'd like to think she's happier with someone else. That would make me feel less guilty."

Katya thought of the many lies they'd told since they began seeing each other, the energy diverted from their families so they could steal these few hours together every week. Phone calls during the day were easier to manage, but facilitating and keeping hidden the physical aspect of their relationship required constant vigilance and scheming. She also sometimes felt guilty, but not as much as she'd feared she would. She had decided long ago that Mikhail deserved her betrayal. It was her son she hated lying to, pretending she was driving to Mid-City every Thursday afternoon for adult chancel choir practice at a Presbyterian church where she pretended to work part-time. He was almost sixteen, both smart and suspicious. When he asked her why she played during choir practice but never during regular church services, she began sneaking away for a couple of hours every other Sunday morning. Sometimes, if her lover couldn't meet her at the bungalow, she would actually go to the church, although she had no interest in either religion or God. It didn't do much to assuage her guilt, but she gathered enough details that she could describe it to her son if ever he asked her to.

"In two years," she said. "Grigoriy will be graduated high school, probably going to university. Then I can leave Mikhail."

"Two more years," he said, as if it were a death sentence.

"It's not so long. It gives us time to invent a story to tell the children, to decide where we will live. Yes?" She put her hands on either side of his face and searched his light brown eyes. She ran her thumb over the rough skin of his purple birthmark, which she loved for reasons she didn't need to understand. "I can't leave now with my son still at home. I need to be there.

But when he's eighteen, he will be okay. He will be grown up, and he can take care of himself. You understand?"

He sighed, then leaned in and kissed her. "I do. I don't like it, but I do."

From within the pile of clothes on the floor, his telephone rang. "Shit," he said. In spite of the exorbitant cost, he had bought a cellular phone so he could take his wife's calls from any location without her knowing where he was. He had offered to buy one for Katya, too, but she hadn't needed one. Mikhail never bothered to check on her, and if she needed to talk to her son, she could call from a pay phone. It was challenging enough to pretend that she was getting paid for all the choir practices and performances; explaining how she had come by the extra money for one of these new phones would be impossible.

"I'll make this quick," he said. He flipped the device open just as he closed the bathroom door behind himself. "I'm just finishing up a dinner meeting," she heard him blurt.

Katya stretched out on the bed, feeling like a satisfied cat. There was a time, early on, when they'd spent a whole day in a hotel, making love, having a picnic on the rumpled sheets, drinking sparkling wine from paper cups. It had gotten late without them realizing it, and he'd suddenly panicked. What if his wife was worried? Or suspicious? Her husband was working, and her son away on a school trip, so she had no one to explain her absence to. But he trembled as he dialed his home number, and when his wife answered he sounded overly solicitous and affectionate. Beads of sweat appeared on his forehead, his cheeks flushing red. He held his hand over his mouth as he spoke, but Katya was right next to him. She heard him lie about his day, make false assurances and, at the end of the conversation, tell his wife that he loved her. It sounded more reflexive than sincere, like how Americans ask, *How are you?* as a greeting without expecting a reply. Afterward, he couldn't look at her directly. "I'm so sorry you had to hear that," he said. "I've never done something like this before. I'm afraid I'm not a very convincing liar."

It was new for Katya as well. Lying, cheating on her husband, stealing time from her son. But being with him—being loved by him—was her only reprieve from the melancholia that had tainted all her years since leaving Leningrad. She had fallen in love, truly. Yet the joy she felt with him didn't entirely eradicate the sensation that her doctor had suggested might be depression. She still felt it acutely, especially when they had to leave each other and return to their own families. She wondered if she'd be happier if they could be together openly, if they no longer had to lie. Perhaps someday they would find out, though in the meantime she was willing to tolerate all of it, including bearing witness to her lover's duplicity. It was surprisingly easy to get used to.

By now, it hardly bothered her at all.

M aybe you'd like to join us tomorrow," Greg said at the end of their meal.

She wasn't sure what had caused this turnabout, and while she'd enjoyed his company at dinner, she remained skeptical. "Why?" she asked.

"It's a long drive. Why wouldn't I want to have a mechanic along? Didn't you tell me I should?"

She looked away, took a sip of her beer.

"Clara," he said, laughing.

She felt heat rise to her cheeks and kept her face turned away, although it wasn't dark enough in the restaurant to hide her embarrassment.

"I'm sorry," he said. "Clara, look at me. Please."

She took a breath, chastised herself for being so easily played, and faced him.

He looked straight into her. "I'm really sorry," he said. "I didn't meant to hurt your feelings."

"You didn't," she said. Then she wiped her mouth, tossed the crumpled napkin onto her plate, and stood up. "Thanks for dinner. I'll see you in the morning."

"Good morning," Greg said. "Truce?" He handed her a cup of coffee, and she peered beneath the lid. "I made it how you like it," he said with a smile, then turned to the movers. "We'd better get going. It's going to be a long day." She followed them into the parking lot.

Greg walked with Beto to the U-Haul, pointing out something on the map. As Clara walked toward her car, Greg called, "You can ride with me if you want."

She was surprised to realize that she did. She didn't enjoy his presence as much as she was drawn to the complexity of it: the intensity of his eyes, his mysterious, limping constitution, how he seemed to be inviting her in even as he pushed her away.

"It's a long drive," he said. "Around seventy-five miles, but apparently the roads are so rough, it could take four hours each way. No sense in taking three vehicles. But of course, do whatever makes you comfortable." Then he turned his attention back to the map.

Eight hours in a car with Greg? Now, that could be interesting. "Sure," she said. "Give me a minute. I need to get some stuff out of my car."

When she turned seventeen and bought her first car—an old junker she and her uncle fixed up—he stocked it with an extensive emergency kit and warned her never to drive without being prepared to live on the side of the road for a few days in extreme heat or cold if she had to. "Never know when you or somebody else might run up against some trouble." So she always kept water, a thermal blanket, a magnesium fire starter, a fire extinguisher, old towels, a first-aid kit, sunscreen, sunglasses, and lip balm, plus a cache of tools. At least Jack would've approved of her grabbing her toolkit and roadside emergency bag. She might take a risk on being in the middle of nowhere with three men, but she wouldn't chance the environment.

"You have a spare tire, right?"

"Yep."

"For the U-Haul, too?"

"Yes, dear."

"Just checking," she said, and popped the back of his SUV. She noted that there were five gallon-jugs of water and a cooler alongside his photography equipment, which she tried not to disturb as she loaded her things inside.

"There's a picnic dinner in there," Greg said. "And snacks. Oh, and I bought a six-pack for the guys and some wine for us." He cocked an eyebrow and smiled. "Think we need anything else?"

Despite herself, she smiled back. The idea of a picnic and wine in the desert with an interesting—if irritable—guy seemed almost quaint. She shrugged. "I guess not."

"Then let's go," he said, hoisting himself into the driver's seat.

Everything in Death Valley seemed extreme to Clara, but thus far the six-hundred-foot-deep, half-mile-wide volcanic Ubehebe Crater in the northern part of the park was the most impressive; its array of colors and textures was nothing less than otherworldly. At the bottom of it, pink and brown mud-flats looked like dried-up lakes. In between, colorful layers of sandstone and other sediments, carved by millions of years' worth of debris flowing into the exposed red-orange bedrock, fanned out in deep gullies against the black volcanic terrain.

Standing on the crater's rim at an elevation of twenty-six hundred feet, Clara had to plant her legs in a stagger, one forward and one behind, to keep from blowing over in the great gusting winds that smeared thin clouds across the sky.

"*Miren,*" he called to the movers, pointing to the lowest spot on the southeastern rim.

"*Sí,*" Beto answered.

"I need you to take the piano around the crater to the other side"—he panned his hand across the northern ridge—"and unload it just opposite from where we are now. *Me entiendes?* Okay, good, but listen. It's probably a mile walk on soft, loose terrain, and it's going to be really windy. Once you get it out there, you're going to need to hold on to it. Just get it out as close to the edge as you can, but then you're gonna have to lie down behind it, both of you, still holding on. You know what? Use the straps. Just keep them on. They won't show in the photo at this distance. And given how the wall's angled, I probably won't be able to see the feet anyway. Here, take the walkie-talkie. I'll tell you what to do."

"I can go with them," Clara said, unable to disguise her concern. The gusts were strong, and she knew all too well how unstable the piano could be when it was off-balance. Her hand ached just thinking about it.

"Clara, don't worry. I wouldn't risk it if I didn't trust them," Greg said. "I told you they work for a buddy of mine at a set-design company. Movie sets. You know that one about the guy who falls off the apartment building? Where you see the whole story of his life as he's passing each floor? My buddy built that set. Won an Oscar for it, too. Anyway, these guys aren't piano tuners or anything, but they know how to move heavy shit around."

Juan smiled at her. "*Es* true," he said.

Without further ado they began hiking slowly around the edge of the crater, struggling to stay upright. During one violent gale, Clara thought she might fall over right where she stood and flung her arm out to brace herself against Greg, her heart pounding at the fleeting vision of the movers and her Blüthner being hurled over the volcanic edge, bumping and rolling until crashing into rubble at the bottom, six hundred feet below.

"They're fine, Clara." Greg heaved the SUV's hatch door open and reached in for his camera bag. Clara stood a few feet away and watched the movers wheel the piano slowly around the edge of the crater, wobbling on the loose ground, getting roughhoused by the wind just like Beto's long hair. How could he even see anything with it whipping into his eyes like that?

Finally, they were in position. Greg adjusted his tripod and bent down to squint through the viewfinder. He held a small device toward the piano and, after checking it, modified some settings and pressed his eye to the camera again. He pushed a button on the end of a cable that was connected to the camera, adjusted the settings once more, pressed the button. "A little more to your left," Greg said into his walkie-talkie, and the movers popped up from behind the edge like gophers. "Okay, hold it." He moved around, changing lenses and settings and the height of the tripod, wiping the lens clean. He told them to shift the angle of the piano a few degrees, which they did, and to disappear again, which they also did. As he worked, Clara noted the fluidity of his movements. He had the kind of comfortable authority over his own tools that she admired.

She stared at the Blüthner, sparkling in miniature across the chasm, and turned to him. "What does it look like?"

"See for yourself," Greg said. He stepped haltingly around from behind the tripod and pointed at the viewfinder. "The goal is to create a grand atmosphere. Normally I'd put the background as far away as possible to enlarge the piano, but in this case I wanted to showcase the fragility and danger of something on a precipice. See how I framed it? Big sky spread out above? Mysterious depths below? It suggests a potential for disaster. Can you feel it?" He sounded wound up, like he was excited by the danger he was describing.

Clara eyed him, concerned, but he pointed again at the viewfinder. "Take a look," he urged her, and she pressed her right eye up against the camera. Still distant, the piano looked lonesome and, yes, fragile, even though she knew it was being gripped securely by Juan and Beto, who were unseen behind it. After she'd spent a minute studying her piano in a context at once dangerous and beautiful, her left eye felt tired from being squeezed shut, and she turned the camera back over to Greg. Even above the wind, she could hear the shutter clicking. The rest of him was utterly still.

"Why are you doing this?" she asked him.

"Why am I doing what," he said without lifting his eye from the camera.

"Dragging my piano through the desert. It seems like a big expense and a real pain in the ass. Not to mention . . . precarious. I mean, I like your idea about showing what it looks like when the music stops, but why out here? Why Death Valley, of all places?"

He took a deep breath and exhaled it slowly as he unfolded himself from his crouch. "Okay," he said. "That's fair." Then he held the walkie-talkie to his mouth and said, "Okay, bring it back."

He replaced his equipment in the SUV. Before he began breaking it down, he rummaged around until he found a leather portfolio and handed it to her. "Go ahead," he said.

She unzipped it and withdrew something flat wrapped in a sturdy linen cloth stamped with blue and ocher-yellow wildflowers. She glanced at him and he nodded his permission to continue. Inside was a small hardcover photo album. Its white cover featured a single black-and-white image of a strange, frozen landscape with a desolate sky and mountains in the distance.

"You recognize it?" Greg asked. "That's Badwater Basin, where we were yesterday afternoon."

"Oh. Yeah, now I do. But it looks like ice instead of salt on the ground."

"My mother thought so too. She used to say it looked like the Siberian tundra, that she couldn't believe it wasn't cold. All of them, actually."

Clara turned the pages carefully. There was only one image on each one, a replica of an old-fashioned Polaroid picture with the white border and that slightly underexposed, dim, sepia-like quality.

"Is this your mom in these?"

"Yep. And me. Those are scans of pictures from a trip to

Death Valley we took right after we got to California. They're the only family photos we have, actually. Most of the time, my mom kept them wrapped and hidden in a drawer, but sometimes she'd take them out and look at them. She'd sit there at the kitchen table for hours staring at those pictures. I have the originals in a safety-deposit box back in New York. I made this as a backup."

Clara scrutinized each of them. She recognized Salt Creek and Mesquite Flat Sand Dunes, Devil's Golf Course and Artist's Palette, and several other places they'd been in the past four days. She was surprised, though, by the desolation the images seemed to embody. In fact, all of them, while beautiful, were jarringly stark.

"Wow, these are amazing. But really depressing. It's a lot prettier here in person."

"I agree. But she also said they looked like how she felt inside. Dead, just like the name."

"But I thought you said this was her favorite place," she asked, peering more closely at the woman in the photos.

Greg glanced at her, his forehead wrinkled.

"On Sunday, in the casino parking lot. That's what you said." He pressed his lips together. "Right. Well, I suppose I was being sarcastic. As far as I know, she only came here . . . twice." He shook his head, as though to rid himself of a thought. "We left Russia when I was a baby. It changed her, I think. She was so unhappy. I'm sure there was more to it, a real depression or something, but she used to say she was sad because she had to leave her Blüthner behind in Russia." He passed a hand over his face. "It was eventually shipped over, but until then those pictures were like a fetish for her. She said the reason the vistas looked so barren was because there was no music in them. She even made up a story about it, about a little girl, Sasha, who lived in Siberia. Everyone was miserable and cold until someone gave Sasha a piano, because once she played it the snow and ice melted and the whole landscape began to change. But then some terrible things happened, a bad marriage, a jealous merchant, and in the end the piano was destroyed and the tundra returned and Sasha froze inside a casket of her own tears."

"That's awful!" Clara said.

Greg huffed. "I loved that story. I probably wouldn't have asked her to tell it to me so often if I'd realized back then that my mother was the little girl. There we were in L.A., the warmest place she'd ever been, but inside she was frozen."

"Even after she got her piano back?"

"We weren't a very happy family, I guess." He shrugged his shoulders. "There were times she seemed okay. But happiness for her seemed, I don't know . . . fragile. Maybe it's like that for everybody to some degree."

Carefully, Clara rewrapped the album in the linen cloth and handed it back to him, just when two riders on a Triumph Roadster pulled up to the trailhead. They climbed off, peeling their long legs from around the motorcycle's wide tank, and pulled their helmets off. The woman shook out her hair while the man put his gloves into the trunk box. Their dusty leathers creaked as they walked hand in hand toward the rim of the crater, far enough upwind that they didn't need to say hello to anyone else nearby. Clara looked at the Triumph with envy. It was mammoth, even bigger and shinier than the Blüthner. Even at rest it seemed like a street fighter ready for a brawl, as if it wanted to tear off down the road, hovering over the asphalt. She wanted so badly to slide onto it and feel it roar aggressively to life beneath her. Just by looking she could feel the torque of the engine in her elbows, the sensation of speed in her gut. Then she glanced again at the couple. Their happiness didn't look fragile. They stood pressed together, the woman leaning back onto the man's chest as he wrapped his arms around her. Clara turned away but stole intermittent peeks while they pointed across the crater at the wonder of the piano that was being pushed along the rim. The wind carried their voices close, making them intimate. "Being out here and seeing things like this makes me want to believe in God," the woman said in a clipped British accent. The man responded by cupping her breasts and kissing her on the neck. She laughed, and they set off down a steep route inside the crater's western edge.

"What about you?" Greg asked Clara as he collapsed the tripod. "Do you believe in God?"

"I don't know," she told him. "Not really. You?"

"Fuck no," he scoffed. "Every time anybody talks about God, all I hear is their own brand of fanaticism, dogmatism, elitism, or bigotry. Some excuse to feel morally superior to everyone else. No thanks."

"That's religion, not God." She thought of something her uncle had once told her one Sunday morning. They'd turned off Weedpatch Highway and onto a dirt road, passed several TV antennas and microwave relay towers, and finally came to a gate. They had to hike the last few hundred yards, but when they got to Breckenridge Lookout, Jack put his hands in his pockets and scanned the slopes of the Sequoia National Forest below them. He looked at her and smiled. "I'm glad we could come to church today," he said.

Greg lifted a shoulder as he unscrewed a telephoto lens from the camera's body. "Same thing," he said. "Zealots and murderers and politicians are always justifying their actions by invoking rules made up by an imaginary friend. Or fucking athletes! They love pointing up at the sky during post-game interviews and saying crap like 'The Big Man Upstairs was watching out for me.' Could they actually believe that shit? That they're somehow superior enough to attract God's attention away from the other team? What do the other guys think, huh? If they're also into that, then they have to say, 'Oh, it's all part of God's plan' or some BS. Why doesn't somebody, any-body, ever say that one side worked harder or just got lucky? Why does it always have to be part of some divine plan?"

Clara, taken aback by his hostile reaction, by how his pale cheeks were blooming scarlet red, felt the need to both defuse his irritation and defend a more neutral position. "Well, what about the crater? Or those weird bushes behind us that look like grazing sheep? Or that hawk up there? What about the mystery of it all? No big plan."

"Maybe that hawk is God. Watching out for us." He pointed at the sky, then waved. "Hey, Big Man Upstairs! Thanks for everything, okay?"

"What's the matter with you?" Clara said.

He let go of his camera and put his hands against his head, then pulled them down his face as if he were wiping something away. "Sorry," he said. "I didn't mean to overreact. It's just that there have been plenty of times in my life when it was obvious I wasn't going to be winning any of the games. You know what I mean?"

The morning after her parents died, waking up at her friend's house, she remembered having a dream: she was wear-ing a sparkling blue leotard, bounding across a floor covered with a thick layer of powdery white sediment like the surface of the moon. With each leap she gained more air, leaving widely spaced footprints behind her. A crackling roar came from the spectators, the judges, and the other gymnasts, a sound that coalesced into a chant of her name: Cla-*ra*! Cla-*ra*! She was smiling as she took the final bound, so high that she escaped the gravitational pull completely and was released from one world to another, twinkling in her leotard like a star. Tabitha's mother's face was pained as she shook Clara by the arm and whispered, "Clara. Clara, wake up. Something terri-ble has happened. There's been a fire."

She let her gaze rest on the lunar-looking silt at the bottom of the crater then moved it up the jagged wall to the Blüthner inching toward them. Was the hawk flying anywhere nearby? No, it was gone. The sky was a shock of blue, empty except for streaks of clouds.

"Yeah," she said. "I know what you mean."

"You asked why I'm taking these photos here," he said. "It's because the second time my mother came to Death Valley, she killed herself." He shrugged. "And I miss her."

G risha?" Katya knocked on his closet door. "Your father is home. Come have dinner with us."

"Sorry, Mama. I can't come out right now."

He heard her hesitate, noted the disappointment in her voice. "Then soon, yes?"

"After I'm finished." He sighed. He did want to have dinner with his mother. But with only her.

Now that he was almost an adult, a recent high school graduate, Greg—he'd announced that he didn't want to be called Grigoriy anymore—had the habit of going to his room before his father came home from work; he couldn't stand the sight of Mikhail heaving himself into the worn easy chair, making rude demands of his mother, crumbs dropping from his mouth onto his mountainous belly. Instead, after Mikhail came home and assumed his bitter position in the living room, Greg spent the evenings in the darkroom he'd set up in his closet. He wanted to go to a good college somewhere else and study photography, though he was afraid that this would mean abandoning his mother. Instead, he'd enrolled at the community college near their home to buy himself time before making a big move.

He'd bought his first good camera, a Nikon F70, when he was a sophomore, with money he'd filched from his father's wallet over a period of six months. At first it was little more than a shield against the social swirl taking place around him. At school, whenever he felt embarrassed by cruel upperclassmen or uninterested girls, he could hide his blush behind the camera. But before long, as he trained his eye, photography became far more than just a barrier between himself and others. He took a part-time job at a custom photo lab to learn as much as he could, and to earn money for more equipment. When he wasn't working or in school, he spent his free afternoons on solitary hikes in the canyons, practicing the art of making pictures. He played with depth of field, perspective, rise and fall movements, exposure, distortion.

Besides landscapes, his favorite subject was her hands, especially when she was playing the piano, her thin fingers stretching across an octave. He also liked shooting the Blüthner's stark interior while she played, the blur of hammers and strings that translated her music into imagery. His mother's happiness, it seemed, was tentative and conditional, but she seemed most herself when she was at the keyboard. The tether between the two of them had grown frighteningly thin over the years; Greg worried that now that he was an adult, she wouldn't think he needed her as much, and it wasn't true: he needed her more than ever but didn't know how to say so. Instead, he took pictures of her. He thought if he didn't capture her making music, if he didn't make those moments real, make them his, then they might disappear. And then what would he have of her?

In his closet, under a special red lamp, he performed the steps: develop, stop, fix. Then he strung the wet papers up on a clothesline above the pans to dry and watched the images emerge. He felt powerful when using a camera, doing things that victors do—exposing and capturing. With music there was too much letting go. With photography he could be greedy, acquiring the things he shot, like a collector or a pillager or a thief. The piano gave. The photographer took.

Greg could hear his father yelling at her in the other room. Even with his door closed, the anger in his father's voice was clear. What was it this time? Was his dinner cold?

Had his mother forgotten to buy vodka? Had she sat too long at the piano again, instead of sitting in the dark with him while he drank and stared at American sitcoms he couldn't understand?

No, this was something else; it sounded worse than usual. Mikhail's voice was hoarse and crackling. It was bad enough that Greg opened the closet door while his prints were in the chemical bath, ruining them instantly with the light, but still he hesitated by the door. He had learned that it was better for his mother if he didn't get involved when they argued, but when Mikhail screamed, "You whore!" in English, Greg ran to her.

"You fucking whore! Who are you to do this to me? After everything I do for you?" Mikhail advanced, red-faced and shaking a rumpled handful of stationery at her. Katya backed away from him and slipped behind the piano for protection.

"What is this, huh? How long has this been going on? He doesn't even sign his name! What, I'm not going to notice my wife is whore when I find this letter that says, 'I love you'?" He looked at the bottom of the letter and read in a mocking voice, "'I love you,' he say. I love you? Someone say to my wife, 'I love you'? Nobody supposed to love you but me!" And he brought his fist down on top of the ebony case so hard that the piano bounced on the hardwood floor.

"No, Misha! Stop! It's not what you think!" Katya screamed, flailing her thin arms out. Greg held on to her as Mikhail balled his fist again.

"How long, eh?"

"Mama!" Greg yelled, and tried to pull her away before his father's next blow landed. He had never seen him this angry.

"There is nothing, Misha! Please, stop!"

"If nothing, then why is his letter in your drawer under your clothes? I think you must be keeping it like some kind of buried treasure, you can't say to me it is nothing!"

"Let me get you a drink. Some dinner. I will explain. It's

nothing to be jealous of, just a young student with confused feelings—"

"I bring you to America, give you sunshine every day. No queues, no dinner without meat. I work so many hours every day, at night all I dream is yellow from that fucking taxi. And you, what do you do? All day you play your silly piano or teach other people to play your silly piano, and afterward you give them bonus lesson, huh? Are you fucking this Romeo on my bed?"

Katya's eyes were dry and huge with fear; even her tears were scared to fall.

"You want to know what this letter feels like, Ekaterina? After everything I do for you all these years? This is what it feels like!" Mikhail, his faced bulging at his too-tight collar, spun around to tear the fire poker off the hearth—it was decorative, they'd never once had to build a fire in Los Angeles—and smashed it down on the piano's case.

The Blüthner responded with a shattered, rattling sound but held itself steady.

"Stop, Misha! Please!" Katya begged him, even as she allowed her son to hold her arms and pull her away. "You don't understand."

"What I don't understand? You want me hitting you instead? What good is that? That won't show you." Mikhail lowered his voice to a growl. "I break your piano like you break my heart. That will show you." He hoisted the poker above his head with both hands like a lumberjack about to fell a tree.

Greg let go of his mother and lunged at him, grabbing his father's thick arms with his own. He had inherited his mother's passions, but physically he was a strong teenaged replica of Mikhail. He couldn't stop the blow, but he softened it. Instead of splintering the case, the poker left only a blunt indentation. A wound, not a fatality.

Mikhail turned and fixed his prematurely rheumy gaze, his eyes wet with fury, on his son. Greg couldn't recall the last time his father had looked directly at him for any reason, and the intensity of his boiling stare made him think of a wolf on the hunt.

"No!" Katya screamed.

"You protect your whore mother, huh?" Mikhail moved toward him slowly, prowling, and lowered his voice to a terrifying *basso profundo*. "Such a child. Stupid child, trying to be grown up and still wanting to suckle at his mama's breast."

Determined to face him down, Greg tried not to retreat backward as his father approached with the poker aloft and fury in his face. Even when his bladder failed him and urine soaked his jeans, he didn't move. Then, with a speed and strength that seemed impossible for an aging and overweight alcoholic, Mikhail cudgeled his son's left leg with one brutal whack. His mother screamed, and he lost consciousness.

In the years to come, Greg would repeatedly return to that moment, trying each time to will his younger self to dart aside, to take his mother's hand and run, but of course he never could. Instead, the memory of his father and the iron poker and the sound that ricocheted around the room when the blow shattered his femur was like a sharp pebble that he would forever carry in his shoe, limping to minimize the pain of it.

After they left Ubehebe crater, Greg retreated into a somber silence. She wanted to know more but wasn't about to intrude. In the few days she'd known him, she had decided that the landscape of his emotions was as unpredictable as the desert they were driving through. It was like waiting for a storm to pass, trusting that the sun would return once the clouds had been emptied out.

They turned south, going uphill, and the smooth, paved road gave way to dirt. After several miles in a strangely comfortable silence, they passed a sign that recommended using four-wheel drive. The road didn't look all that demanding, but Clara noted the warning.

"The moving truck doesn't have four-wheel drive," she said.

"Sure it does," Greg said.

"No, it doesn't. None of them do. And the clearance is pretty low. How bad does this road get?"

"I heard it's bumpy, but not too bad until the last eight miles or so after Teakettle Junction. But between here and there it'll be okay. Supposedly there was a rainstorm in this part of the park yesterday, but there weren't any washouts on the roads. We'll just take it slow."

Clara picked up Greg's National Park Service map of the backcountry roads of Death Valley to see where they were. He'd circled a dozen or so landmarks—presumably where he intended to photograph the piano, as they'd already been to several of them. She found Ubehebe Crater and drew her finger along the route to their next destination. According to the key, the twenty-seven miles down Racetrack Road were "high-clearance" owing to loose gravel, washboarding, and rocks. "Flat tires are common on this road," she read aloud, "so be sure your full-sized spare is inflated, all parts of your jack are on hand, and tire tread is good. May require 4WD due to changing road conditions and irregular maintenance, so check postings."

"We'll be fine," he said.

"Did you check to make sure the spare on the truck was inflated? And that it came with a jack? Renters don't usually think about those things until it's too late. I'd have checked it myself if I'd known we were going off-road."

"Now, why didn't I think of that?" He looked at her and lifted one side of his mouth in a half-smile.

"You can mock me if you want, but we're smack-dab in the middle of nowhere, and if we get a flat I don't know how we'll get anybody to help us."

"But that's why you're here—right, Miss Fix-it?"

She sighed. "So you've mentioned." She watched the unruly-looking arrowweed bushes that dotted the foothills and mountains scrolling by her window. According to the map, this was the Last Chance Range.

The road topped out on a grassy mesa dotted with Joshua tree groves in all directions, their bayonet-shaped leaves tufting in strange Dr. Seuss configurations. Then, as it started dropping in elevation, the road surface swiftly crumbled into a rippled pattern so jarring that Clara thought she could feel her brain jackhammering into her skull.

"Stop the car," she said.

"Fucking hell," Greg said, gripping the wheel as he braked. Clara whipped around to see the moving truck thudding to a stop behind them. "I guess that's what they meant by *bumpy*," he added.

"We need to deflate the truck's tires," Clara said, opening the door. "Ours, too." She went to the back to get her tools.

"What? Why?"

"If we take them down to about forty psi, they'll flatten out enough to conform to the surface," she said. "It'll make for a smoother ride and help keep the piano from bouncing around. But we're going to have to take it slow."

"And how will we get them inflated again?"

"With the pump I brought." Clara held it up and smiled, enjoying a little moment of vindication. "You check on the piano while I do the tires. It's a good thing you're not bringing it out here for a concert; if it wasn't already, then for sure it's gone totally out of tune after this."

Juan and Beto leaned against the truck, dragging on their cigarettes. Juan tipped his chin at her in a gesture of solidarity when she crouched down to unscrew the first valve. She tipped hers back; this evidence of blue-collar expertise seemed to both increase his esteem of her and make her a peer. "*Le ayudo?*" he asked.

"I got it," she said, and he nodded.

She had finished and was loading her tools back into the car when her phone rang in her pocket. Without even looking, she knew it was Peter. "I need to get this," she told Greg, and sought some privacy in this miles-wide stretch of open land by walking down the road.

"Hey," she said into the phone.

"Hey yourself," Peter said in that slow, deep voice of his. "I don't want to bug you, but I just wanted to see if you were okay."

"I'm fine." She smiled. "Thanks for checking. How are you?"

"Me? Oh, I'm good. It's busy for a Wednesday." She looked at the clock: almost noon. His mother would start unpacking food for them soon, insisting they stop to eat something. "In a minute, Ma," he'd usually say. Clara could hear the familiar sounds of the garage in the background: the pneumatic whoop of lug nuts being unscrewed with an impact gun, Teddy laughing, the *laïko* music. "The Fast Relief 500 was Sunday," Peter continued. "I was wondering if you got to see it."

"No, I didn't." She hadn't even thought about it. She and Peter had planned on watching it together. "Did Johnson win?"

"Yeah. Pretty much dominated the whole race. Busch took second, Kahne third. I figured Johnson would win, but you never know what'll happen, right?"

Clara nodded. She looked back at the SUV, where Greg was reading a map, one hand stuffed into his pants pocket. "I'm sorry I missed it."

"It's okay. When I didn't hear from you, I guessed you weren't going to make it. But I saved you a seat just in case."

She pictured Peter sitting on his parents' couch, watching the race and protecting the promised space next to him by draping his arm over the back. Teddy or Alex might drift in and take a seat, and he'd say, "Not there. That one's for Clara. She'll be here any minute." He rarely dated, though she knew that any sane single woman would fall easily for him, if he gave her a chance. She'd seen a few of them try. A knot inside her tightened as she imagined the look on his face if she'd actually walked in the door. His eyes would go wide, and his lips would part and broaden, revealing his delight. Then, not wanting to scare her off, he would try to hide it, try to pretend he was just glad to have a buddy to watch TV with.

"Clara?"

"Sorry, I'm here," she said, pulling her thoughts back together. She was still a little offended by how readily he had encouraged her to let Greg buy the piano.

"About that. Where's here, exactly? I got worried when I didn't hear from you on Sunday, and I went by your apartment last night. It looked like you weren't home."

She could lie and say she'd decided to take a little vacation, to try her luck at a casino in Vegas for a couple of days. Or she could explain that Greg had turned out to be an interesting guy, really nice, and he'd invited her to help out with the photo shoot, which wasn't a complete lie. No, Peter would probably still be worried and certainly a little jealous. She thought of how his face fell whenever she said she was going on a date, not to mention the way he'd winced when she'd told him she was moving in with Ryan.

She sighed. Peter knew her too well to believe she was at a casino. The only gamble she would take was trying unfamiliar Greek food. Even moving in with Ryan hadn't been a risk; she hadn't had enough skin in the game for it to last. "I'm still in Death Valley."

There was a long pause before he said, "Clara."

"I know," she said. She could picture him closing his eyes, shaking his head. "You don't have to say anything. It's crazy and impetuous, and I shouldn't be doing this, but I couldn't stop. Remember how I said my piano was rare? It turns out this guy, Greg, his mother used to own it. Can you believe that? And then apparently she killed herself out here. How fucked up is that? Well, maybe it isn't—he didn't say why she did it.

"I don't think he wants to talk about it, and I'm not sure how he feels about me being here, but I just feel like I have to, for a little while longer."

"You don't have to—"

"Peter, I know you want to protect me. I know you think I'm a fool for coming out here. That I'm a fool for letting him rent it instead of buying it so I'd be done with it once and for all. Fuck, *I* think I'm a fool, but for the opposite reason. I can't believe I thought I could let the damn thing go after all these years," she said, and took a breath. "I hate it but I need it. I wish you could understand that. It's the only important thing I have. And now here's this guy with a connection to it . . ."

"Clara, you cut me off," Peter said, but not admonishingly. "I was going to say you don't have to explain it to me. I get it."

"You do?"

"Well, not exactly. But I understand you pretty well, I think. If you need to be there, or whatever, then do it. I'm not saying I want you to, but I'm not gonna try to talk you out of it."

She thought of him standing at her doorstep in the dark, space heater in hand. How kind he was. How thoughtful. "Thank you," she said quietly. "I appreciate that." Someone in the shop interrupted him, probably Teddy, and Peter murmured something in reply. "I'm a little surprised you're not mad," she said when he was back.

"Mad? Clara, I'm your friend. Not your father." Then, almost immediately, he said, "Shit, I'm sorry. I didn't mean to say that."

"It's okay."

"No, it isn't. I'm sorry."

"I'm just glad you're not mad. I'd hate it if you were."

"I'm not, okay?" His voice was serious. "But listen, be careful. You're tough and all, but just watch out for that guy. I don't even know him, and I don't like him."

She let out a small huff that was almost a laugh, thinking about Greg's frosty demeanor, his limp. He was what her Texas-born uncle would call all hat and no cattle. No threat whatsoever. "I'll be careful," she said. "I promise. And hey, we'll catch the Fort Worth race this Sunday for sure."

After hanging up, she wandered back to the truck, where Greg was illustrating the rest of their journey to Racetrack Playa by dragging his finger over the map. Beto nodded and Greg folded up the map. Turning, he noticed Clara and limped alongside her to the car.

"Boyfriend?" he asked.

"What?"

"Was that your boyfriend? On the phone."

"No. He's just a friend. Why?"

He shrugged. "The way you were talking. I couldn't hear, but it looked like you were talking to a boyfriend." He stared at her. Perhaps that was what made him a good photographer—his ability to see beneath the surfaces of things. And people. She wondered how he'd feel if the camera lens were turned around.

"Jealous?" she asked.

He opened his mouth as if to say something, closed it, then tried again. "Of course not," he said.

"Do you have a girlfriend?" she asked. "A wife? Or maybe a husband?"

"That's rather personal, isn't it?"

"So . . . no significant other," she said, though not unkindly. After he'd dismissed and teased her so unabashedly, it was amusing to see him blush. In fact, that small display of vulnerability was almost endearing.

He jerked his car door open and climbed in without replying.

When Katya brought her son home from the hospital the next day, Mikhail was in their bedroom, passed out—still? again?—from his characteristic cocktail of vodka and rage. Katya didn't know if he'd even gone to work. He hadn't gone with them in the ambulance or shown up at the hospital, that was for certain. Katya assumed that he'd stayed in the bedroom, where he'd gone, slamming the door behind himself, after his son crumpled to the floor, because he was ashamed and possibly afraid that she would tell the police what he'd done. But how could she? What if they didn't keep him in jail and he came back to hurt them? Or what if they did keep him? Her lover was still married, and she didn't make enough money on lessons to support her son and herself on her own. She had no idea how Mikhail would behave when he woke up. She hoped he would be tamed by remorse, at least for a while, until she could make a plan. But this latest act of violence was the worst thus far; she really didn't want to imagine what else he might be capable of.

While Mikhail was unconscious and Greg was asleep on the living room couch in the safe grip of the painkillers they'd given him after the operation to repair his shattered leg, she picked up the telephone and pushed the numbers quickly, before she lost her nerve. He answered in his professional voice, but when he heard it was her he sweetened it to a low whisper.

"Please," she said, whispering, too. "Please come quickly. I think you must take my piano away from here. It will be better if it's gone when he wakes up."

"Katya, let me take you and Greg instead. This is crazy."

"You know I can't do that right now. But please, at least keep my piano safe. This is the best solution."

"The piano isn't important. It's you who's not safe. And your son. I should be protecting you both."

"There's no time to explain. I don't know when he is going to wake up."

"He's there? Jesus, Katya, this is insane. You want me to come to your house while he's home?" He went back to his professional voice. "Do you realize what might happen?"

"Grisha's here, sleeping. Mikhail is unconscious from vodka, I think. I can smell it from the living room. He couldn't do anything even if he wakes up."

He sounded distressed. "Where do you want me to take it? It's not like holding your purse while you shop. I'll need help. A truck, some movers. Have you called that shop? Immortal Piano or whatever its name is?"

"No, I didn't call them. I called you."

He sighed. "Of course. I'm sorry."

"You are a smart man, a strong man. I know you will have the right idea. You will, yes?"

"Yes," he said. "I'll think of something."

"Quickly, please."

"Okay."

She looked in on her husband, who was under the covers with all his clothes on. His wiry, graying hair stood out from the pillow in every direction, and his foul breath spilled out from his wide-open mouth. She closed the door as quietly as she could. Then she checked on her son, his face a grimace even in sleep. She kissed her fingertips and touched his cheek, his cast. He didn't move.

Finally, she sat down at the piano to wait. It was so quiet she could hear the clock ticking off the seconds like a metronome. Softly, she began playing. Scales first, out of habit; then, one by one, she played the best pieces in her repertoire. Mikhail was too far under to be wakened, but her son, she hoped, would see them in his dreams. She began with some of the very short pieces by Milhaud from *La Muse Ménagère:* "La Douceur des Soirées" and "Lectures Nocturnes" and "Reconnaissance à la Muse." Then the titanic Prelude and Fugue no. 24 in D Minor by Shostakovich and Chopin's "Sunshine" étude. She moved on to Schubert's Fourth Impromptu in A-flat Major, which she loved for its balance between the strong left-hand melody and the right-hand arpeggios. Finally, Rachmaninoff's famous Prelude in C-sharp Minor, delicate and dirgelike, during which she, as the composer allegedly had when he'd composed it, foresaw her own demise. Heavy tears blurred her vision, so she closed her eyes and let the tears fall down.

Music was her only means of holding off grief. Even as a small child, she'd found her way to it every day. She thought of the terrible years when she'd had to live without her Blüthner beneath her hands, and the increasingly less miserable years since it had been returned. The pressure of her fingers on the keys was how she could tolerate herself and the world, yet she had no choice except to send it away. She couldn't bear to imagine its absence but knew, at least, that it—and her son— might be safe.

She began again, this time with her absolute favorite, the Scriabin E-flat Minor Prelude, its fevered rhythm demanding all of her concentration, and slipped so quickly into its eddy of color and punch that she didn't hear the knock at the door; nor did she notice that her son was awake and watching her with deep love and admiration.

"Mama, the door," he said once she'd finished.

She jumped up, smoothed her dress, stopped by Grisha

and again put her hand against his cheek. He closed his eyes. "This will be difficult for you to understand," she said, then opened the door.

For an awkward moment Katya stood looking at the three men there on her doorstep. Her face burned, and she darted her eyes over them like the staccato notes of Mozart's "Turkish March," saying a great deal without speaking, until one of the men coughed into his fist.

"*Privet,* Mrs. Zeldin," he said. "May we come in?"

After brief introductions, spoken in low voices so as not to disturb Greg, or to waken Mikhail, she led them to the piano and laid her hand on the case, caressing its fire-poker wounds. "Here it is," she said. There was much more she wanted to say—*take care of it, please; let no harm come to it*—but she couldn't bring herself to ask for any more than she already had.

One of them turned to his colleagues and revealed the cover story. "Beautiful. It is just as described. Just what I was looking for." He smiled at Katya, who turned away.

"Mama!" Greg said, his voice throaty and hoarse. "What's happening?"

"*Chi-chi-chi.* You're confused now. The medicine. Close your eyes, go back to sleep."

As the men began to manipulate the piano, testing its heft, deciding how they would move it without hurting themselves, Greg watched them with wide and wary eyes.

He was sleepy and confused, true, but he would not go back to sleep. He watched the men as they circled the piano like predators, deciding how to capture and kill it, grunting instructions to one another. He watched his mother bring blankets with which to drape it, good blankets they used every night that were made by his grandmothers and brought over during the emigration from Russia years ago. He watched his mother's eyes fill with tears when the men finally hoisted the piano—their prey, now killed and covered—with soft grips unaccustomed to such an effort. He watched until, struggling with their load, they moved past the threshold and beyond his view, and he watched his mother stand in the doorway with a hand pressed to her chest.

"Be careful," she said. "Take care." Then with desperation in her voice she called out, "*Я люблю тебя.*"

He did not know if her love was meant for the men or the piano, or both. But he knew that she began crying as soon as they drove away, and there was nothing he could do to help.

The next six miles down Racetrack Valley Road were the worst thus far: tedious, uncomfortable, and miserably slow. They averaged only about eight miles per hour, and every few hundred feet, when the car felt as if it were shaking apart, Greg slammed on the brakes. Each time, Clara looked behind them to make sure the truck was okay; each time, Juan gave her a thumbs-up. She was worried about the piano, though. The movers couldn't see into the bed and really had no idea what was going on back there.

Frustrated, she said to Greg, "I know braking's intuitive, but if you actually go just a little faster over the bumps it won't be as jarring. I'll drive if you want."

"I've got it," he said. He didn't acknowledge her advice, but did as she suggested. Twenty or so minutes later, in the distance they could see the nearly three-mile-long dry lakebed known as Racetrack Playa, where a huge, dark rock outcrop rose up dramatically out of the wide, flat, bright sand-colored surface. They drove along the western perimeter toward the southern end, outpacing the falling sun, which set early behind the adjacent mountains. The road began to smooth out.

"Let's stop here," Clara said. "We need to pump up the tires."

"Why? Won't we have to lower the pressure again when we head back out?"

"Yeah, once we're on that rough stretch, but now that it's smooth we need a normal psi."

"It's only a little farther. We're losing the light as it is. We can do it afterward."

"I don't think that's a good idea. When there's less air in a tire, it generates more heat and can weaken the rubber. We're risking a puncture driving too long like this."

"And if we stop now, I'll miss the shot. It's only another ten minutes or so. We'll be fine."

The cliffs to the west were already in shadow, and the lakebed's surface seemed to glow in the lower slant of light. But as they drove along without seeming to get anywhere, Clara grew increasingly nervous.

Finally, they arrived at a sandy parking area. Clara jumped out of the SUV to check the tires. Satisfied that there were no bulges or obvious signs of wear, she decided to let them cool down for a few minutes before reinflating them and wandered over to where Greg stood at the edge of the lakebed. Two hours of pounding on the rough roads had made her tense, and with her good hand she kneaded her lower back to loosen the muscles. Likewise, Greg was rubbing his lame leg.

"This was my mother's favorite," he said with a wistful reverence as he stared out at the playa. "Her favorite photo from the trip, I mean." He shook his head. "I must've looked at that one a thousand times. It didn't do the place justice."

The setting sun illuminated a strangely regular hexagonal pattern of dried mud. "Look at this," Clara said. From a distance it appeared smooth, but up close it reminded Clara of what the backs of her hands looked like after she scrubbed off the workday grease with Boraxo. Peter's mother had once taken one of her dry, cracked hands and tsk-tsked. "Rough skin, no good for a woman," she said. "You still a woman, *koukla,* even though you working here with the boys. You need to take better care of your hands." She brought in some heavy-duty hand lotion the next day and set it on the edge of the sink, but Clara wouldn't use it. It made her grip on the tools slick.

Now she felt the itch of dry skin beneath her cast; she'd massage her hands with a whole bottle's worth of that lotion if she could.

After a moment Greg nodded to the movers, his instructions by then implied by just the tilt of his head. "Come on. We need to hurry if we're going to get the piano set up in time. Those shadows are coming fast."

They walked out onto the playa toward a few scattered black dolomite rocks, Greg loaded with equipment, Juan and Beto flanking the piano and pushing it steadily into the wind. "We'll go to that first one there," he said, pointing at a small lump. When they reached it, though, Clara was surprised by how much larger it was than she'd expected. Another example of the park's tricky proportions.

"These are the sailing stones," Greg said, then pointed to a steep promontory on the southeastern end. "Over there's where the rocks start out. They crumble off that slope and fall onto the playa. And somehow, some of them start moving around by themselves across the lakebed. It's almost perfectly level from one end to the other—no slope at all, it's a real phenomenon—and they leave these long trails in the dirt, like wakes." Sure enough, there were trails behind several of the rocks that reminded Clara of the slug tracks she used to see on her uncle's concrete porch on rainy mornings. She crouched down to touch one. Though it wasn't very deep, it stood out against the tile-like polygons because its smoothed-out surface reflected the sunlight differently.

"How can they move by themselves?" she asked. "There must be something. Wind or earthquakes or some other force. Or maybe people push them." She tested the possibility by leaning against one and using her legs for leverage. It didn't budge.

"There are all kinds of theories about that. But here's the thing: nobody has ever seen them moving. It's one of the great mysteries of Death Valley."

She looked around and saw no signs of vehicle tracks. Beyond this were many other dark rocks of varying sizes, all leading their own meandering trails. They were like stock cars that had all stalled and been abandoned in mid-race.

"It looks like they're trying to escape," Greg said, as though reading Clara's mind. "They're refugees, all sliding away from one place to another."

"It's sort of eerie, like we interrupted them. You think that if we turned our backs they'd move some more?"

Greg made a low harrumph. "Maybe. But we'll lose the light if we waste any more time. We're late as it is, damn it. It took so long getting here with those crap roads." He told Juan to put the piano directly in front of a smaller boulder, so that the Blüthner, not the rock, appeared to have created the track behind it on the basin. It became just another one of those heavy objects silently fleeing their histories.

What if the Blüthner, Clara wondered, wasn't simply an insentient object at the mercy of its owner? What if it was a conscious entity frozen in animation? And if by some magic it could suddenly speak for itself, what would it say? Where would it go, if it could? Would it yearn to exercise its hammers and strings, or wish daily for minute flexions of its sound-board? Would it ache for the human touch that could make it sing once more?

And what about her? What would *she* do if the piano were to simply glide away, leaving Clara and her past in its wake? She shuddered at the thought of losing either.

She watched Greg photograph the piano amid the trails and sailing rocks until the shadows nearly reached this section of the playa. He seemed agitated as he worked, his limp more pronounced, his movements less fluid. He never seemed to walk with a light step, but now it looked like he was on a forced march. Though Clara admired his self-reliance, she recognized a burden when she saw one. She hadn't wanted to ask anything more about Greg's mother, but just knowing that she was gone made Clara feel more compassionate toward him. It also seemed to justify not only these quirky photographs but also his determination to feature her—and his mother's!— piano in them. Also, if her suicide had been recent, perhaps it also justified his erratic moods.

While Greg returned his gear to the back of the SUV, Clara plugged the portable pump into the SUV's power outlet and reinflated the tires on both vehicles. She gave a thumbs-up to the movers when she was finished, and Beto fired up the truck.

"So what's next?" she asked Greg as she buckled her seatbelt, hoping to draw him out of his foul humor.

"There's an idea I want to try out at the other end of the playa before we leave. I want to silhouette the piano in front of the last bit of light, maybe climb up on that outcrop we passed to get a higher angle," he said, without much enthusiasm. He started the car and they drove back out the way they'd come in.

Clara had been paying close attention. "Won't it look smaller if you're higher up?"

"Not if I use a wide-angle lens. If I'm above the subject and center it in the frame, the lens will actually emphasize it. And the horizon will look curved"—he made a dome shape with his free hand to show her—"like the piano's sitting on top of the world. If I can catch the last bit of sunset behind it, it'll look like it's radiating light." He thought for a moment. "But maybe I'll try both. Make it look grand and important with the wide lens, and then shoot it so it looks small and insignificant under a massive sky. Maybe that's a better metaphor anyway."

"I guess it depends on what you're trying to say."

"I want to say there's a point to all this." He swept his hand across the dashboard toward the horizon, possibly indicating everything under the setting sun. His voice cracked, and he suddenly seemed decades younger, wounded and desperate. "I want to say that there's a reason this piano exists in the world.

This *specific* piano. That there's something important about it, to the people who made it, to the people who played it and lost it and found it and lost it again, thinking it was gone forever. This Blüthner made music out of nothing, it thawed frozen imaginations, and then it burned down and showed up again with its old scratches and a new owner. This piano has been playing in my mind all my life, and nobody knows *that*. Nobody knows how it plays and plays and plays in my head, all the fucking time, and I can't make it stop, I've never been able to get it out of my fucking—"

A horn blared behind them, and Greg looked in the rearview mirror. "God *damn* it," he said, braking hard enough for Clara's torso to strain against the seatbelt. "They blew a tire."

They got out of the car and ran, Greg with his skipping, uneven trot, the fifty or so yards to where the truck had stuttered to a stop against a bank of dirt alongside the pockmarked road, listing to one side. Juan and Beto spilled out of the cab and stared at the right front tire, which was already flat, and then the right rear one hissed, exhaling air until it, too, was worthless.

"You've got to be kidding me," Greg said. "What the hell happened?"

"*Coño*," Juan said under his breath, shaking his head.

"The road, it is very bad," Beto said. "Lot of rocks."

Clara bent down to touch the front tire. "Yeah, they caught a sharp one with both tires. We can put the spare on the front. I might be able to patch the other, but I don't think it'll make it back over all those washboards. We're going to need a new one."

"What about the SUV's spare?" Greg asked.

"It won't fit. That wheel has a different bolt pattern."

"Fuck!" Greg said. He waved his mobile phone around in the air, checking it every few seconds to see if he'd gotten a signal; the deeper into the park, the worse the cell reception.

"Here," he told her. "Look on the map and tell me the number for the ranger station." He was so agitated that she did as he asked, though she resented being ordered around. If he'd let her reinflate the tires when she'd wanted to, they might not have been as susceptible to a puncture.

"Are you kidding me?" Greg was soon shouting. "What do we pay the goddamn park fees for, then?" and "So what am I supposed to do?" and "Fine, will you at least give me their number?" He pushed the End button so hard his thumb turned briefly white.

"What'd they say?" Clara asked. That they might be stranded in the middle of the desert didn't seem like a crisis to her. It was a beautiful evening, and they had food. Maybe they'd even get to see the rocks come to life and sail silently around the playa. Besides, what else did she have to do?

"They won't send anybody out here. 'Not enough staff,' she said. She told me to call a wrecker service in Beatty because they're the closest, but then she said nobody would drive this far out at this time of day. We'll have to wait till morning for anybody to get here." He leaned back and gave a rock on the ground a vicious, stiff-legged kick. That the rock barely moved only added to his fury. "I'm not staying here all fucking night. We'll just leave the truck and drive into town ourselves."

"We can't leave the truck," she said. "Not with my piano in it."

"Clara," he said, turning his anger toward her and sweeping his arm across the playa, "there's nobody here."

"Not right now, maybe. But what if people show up? Other photographers? There was a whole group of them back at the hotel."

"Yeah, photographers who'll see a moving truck with two flat tires and decide to break in just in case there's a piano inside they could shoot?"

Her uncle's advice: *The customer's always right, Clara. Remember that.* Not always, she thought. "No, of course not.

Only a lunatic would want to take pictures of a piano out here."

"Oh, great," he said, flapping his hand up and letting it drop against his thigh. "Fine. You want to stay here and stand guard? Be my guest. But we're leaving." He turned to the movers. "Lock up the truck."

Clara followed him to the SUV.

"Changed your mind, then?" Greg asked, his tone bitter. "Better to stick with the lunatic you know than the ones you don't?"

"Nope. I'm just going to get my stuff. And some water. In case you guys aren't back until tomorrow, I'll make myself comfortable. It's been a while since I camped out. Might be fun." She unloaded two gallons of water, her roadside emergency bag, her backpack, then reached into the cooler for a bottle of wine. "I'm sure you won't mind," she said. "Since you'll be driving all night."

"Take it all," he said. "You might want to share it with all the other piano photographers that show up." He grabbed the cooler and dropped it on the ground next to her gear. "Enjoy yourself. We'll see you in the morning." Then he turned to the movers and hitched his thumb at the car. "*Vámonos.*"

They looked at each other and then at Clara, obviously reluctant to leave her. She shook her head and gestured for them to go ahead. Beto walked over and handed her the truck keys.

She was neither surprised nor offended when Greg actually started the car and drove away, kicking up a spray of dust and pebbles. Clara watched them go, noticing with peaceful detachment through the back window that he kept his face forward, his eyes presumably just on the road. Juan, however, had turned to see her from the backseat. She stood there, half-thinking they'd stop and turn around but not minding at all if they didn't, until the car stretched the road tight between them, until it was just another dark rock on the move.

*

Clara dragged the cooler and the rest of her things to the playa side of the truck, so she'd be hidden from anyone approaching on the road. The few cars that had been parked near the sailing stones had been gone by the time they'd finished the shoot, and none had passed since they'd left. But she didn't like the idea of being exposed—not just to people, but to animals and the elements.

She looked up: clouds gathered, tore themselves apart, then gathered again, reflecting red and orange light as if the sky were on fire. The shadows were stretching longer over the packed, cracked earth, making the ground look like it was getting pulled apart at the seams. Except for the wind, Clara felt surrounded by an infinite and alien stillness. She considered the dual meaning of *desert,* the noun and the verb, and how appropriate it was that she would feel abandoned here. Watching the last light drain behind the mountains, she felt like the sun was dragging part of her with it below the horizon—the vigilant part that usually protected her from the slippery, empty feelings lurking inside her that she didn't care to acknowledge. But standing in the middle of a desiccated lake in Death Valley as the sky turned dark, she could not ignore the suffocating return of loneliness, and the vague fear that she would always be alone.

She had lost her parents, her aunt and uncle, her boyfriend. She didn't miss Ryan as much as she'd thought she would: she had been silently leaving him for many months before he finally realized the time had come; she was nearly at the end of that grieving when he asked her to move out. Now she felt that hollow space tugging at her, greedy with hunger, begging to be filled. Yet she was afraid of wanting anything too badly, because once she had whatever it was, it could so easily be lost.

She thought of Peter. Her current vulnerability worked

against her long-standing resolve to maintain a safe emotional distance from him, to protect and preserve their friendship, until she felt choked with longing. She imagined him walking toward her from beyond the dimming horizon, carrying hot soup or a blanket to drive out the cold that was making her shiver. He would wait to be welcomed before allowing the half-smile to become a full one. She would hold out a hand in invitation and he would sit down next to her. Then he would open his arms and draw her into the large, tender space against his ribs. She would nestle herself against him for warmth, for comfort, and that small act would abate the creep of isolation that always threatened her—even and perhaps especially when she was with someone. She reached for her phone to call him.

Zero bars on the screen. She walked north on the road, thinking the signal would be stronger the closer she got to the main road. How had Greg gotten reception? Still nothing. She turned and walked in the other direction. One bar appeared, briefly, then was gone again. The wind picked up, and the temperature was dropping, and she wondered if a storm was coming. By now it was dark, and she was scared. Jogging back to the truck, she felt for the keys in her pocket. No cell service, no sign of any other people. No voices on the wind, no headlights in the distance.

She rummaged through the cooler: sandwiches wrapped in wax paper, a block of cheese, crackers and grapes and a bar of dark chocolate. Plenty of food, but she'd only grabbed two jugs of water. Why hadn't she taken all of them? In fact, why had she insisted on staying behind in the first place? She kicked the truck's door and thought of the story her uncle had told her about the guy bitten by a snake in Death Valley. There might be other dangerous animals out there besides reptiles. Bobcats or coyotes or mountain lions.

She picked up her pack and the thermal blanket and both

bottles of wine. She'd save the water for later. She settled into the cab, locking the door behind herself. If the guys weren't back by first light, she decided, she'd hike out. Surely someone would find her.

I'd remember this one. Sure I would. Probably it was my old partner who worked on it—four years ago, you say? It was me, I'd remember it for sure. I see 'em all. Steinways, Yamahas, Melville Clark, Weber, Baldwin, what have you. List goes on and on. But you don't see that many Blüthners here in the States, especially not uprights, and especially not one this old. In Europe, sure. Common as Kleenex. That's how they talk about them, like we say Kleenex for tissue. They say Blüthner for piano. Well, that's certainly true in the U.K. But you got it from a Russian, you say? Yeah, Russians love them, too. In fact, I hear they're making a custom one right now for Vladimir Putin." The technician lifted the fallboard and played a short tune with one hand, then ran through the scales, listening. "I can take care of the tuning right now, sure. Be a pleasure."

The new owner shifted his weight, cleared his throat. "Well, actually I was hoping you might be able to take it back to your shop." Given how his wife had glowered at him when he'd brought it home, he wondered if maybe that hadn't been such a good idea after all. Maybe he should've taken it to work, or even rented a temporary storage unit.

"Oh no, that's not necessary. It'll only take an hour, ninety minutes tops," the man said.

"I thought maybe it would be easier to do it in a more, I don't know, professional setting."

"Hardly ever makes any sense to move it for tuning. The

transport'd cost more than the tuning. A total waste of your money. No, a tech's always gonna come to you for tuning."

"Well, isn't there something else that you might need to do? I don't know, maybe fix it up a little?"

The technician smiled. "This your first piano?"

He nodded.

"So let's have a look here." He opened the piano cabinet and peered inside. "This is a beautiful instrument, a real fine example of German engineering. An old one like this . . . let me check the serial number—yeah, this was probably made sometime between 1903 and 1907, not long after their fiftieth anniversary. Blüthners're good for a hundred, hundred fifty years because of the soundboards. Julius had a real talent for hunting down just the right wood. Legend has it he'd travel to northern Romania back in the day to hammer the spruce trees, checking for tone. Only chose the ones that had real tight rings and didn't leave any splinters, but they say he could tell by the way the tree fell if it'd make a good soundboard. So you got that going for you. A good soundboard like that improves over the years. The more it's played, the more flexible it gets. Kind of like it remembers the music, you know?

"Looks like it was probably restrung last time it was in the shop. See how the strings are still pretty bright?" He bent toward the action to inspect it. "Yeah, not much oxidation. That's a classic birdcage action there. It does sound kind of tubby, though. But looking at it now, I wouldn't say you need to restring it again. Usually you only do that once in a piano's lifetime, unless you have to replace the pinblock or the bridges. Yeah, I'd say everything looks pretty good. If you had it restored four years ago, I really think you don't need anything more than tuning. Pity about these gouges on the lid, though. Nobody ebonizes wood anymore. That's real craftsmanship right there. They used to add dozens of layers by hand back then. Now it's all production lines, you know?

Workers pressing buttons." He passed his hand over the top of the case, pausing at the deepest cuts. "You want, I can tune it now, then take the lid back to the shop. Build these divots back up, sand them down flush, and respray it. Tricky to match black like this, especially using modern techniques, but I'd do my best. Ever watch performers onstage, dressed in all black? They leave the house thinking their black pants match their black shirt and black jacket, but under the stage lights they all look different? Kind of discordant? I could respray the whole case to keep it from looking patched, but then you're talking real money. Depends on what you're hoping for, and what you're willing to spend."

"I guess I hadn't really thought about that." He pulled his hand down his face, momentarily emphasizing the dark circles beneath his eyes. "Actually, I really just need to get it out of the house."

"You thinking of selling it? Probably not much of a market for it, truth be told. You mind me asking how much you paid?"

"I don't want to sell it. I just need to get it out of here for a little while. It's causing . . . some friction between my wife and me, if you want to know the truth."

"Huh," the technician said, daring a glance around the sunny living room. "Well, I can't say I've ever heard that one before. All right, in that case I guess I can take it back to the shop and hold it for you there. For a fee, you understand. I only have so much space. The workshop's pretty small but I only have three other pianos right now, all grands, one I'm voicing and regulating and two I'm selling on consignment."

"That sounds fine. And go ahead and do whatever you think is necessary while you've got it. But I don't know if she'd want me to repaint the whole thing. Maybe just touch up the really bad spots if you can make them less visible. Could you do that?"

"Sure thing. And I subcontract with a good piano-moving

company. I can call and see if they can come out here today if you want."

"Please do that, yes. It is a beautiful piano, but it's really screwing things up for me right now."

C lara woke up to the sound of the wind. It was still dark. She pushed herself up, smacking the cottony residue from her mouth. She checked her phone: still life in the battery, still no signal. Thirsty, she thought about the water jugs she'd left beside the truck, but instead she drained the last sips of wine from the bottle. The wind whooshed in her ears, sending a shiver down her neck. It sounded almost musical. Gathering the blanket around her shoulders, she cocked her head. It wasn't the wind.

Her mind must have been playing tricks; sure, she was a little drunk, but there was a different kind of throbbing inside her temples, thumping in a rhythm she recognized from long ago, something that one of her piano teachers had tried to teach her. Chopin? One of the nocturnes? Yet even tangled as she was inside the grogginess of an interrupted sleep, she knew the sound wasn't just her imagination. She wasn't nearly talented enough to hold such musical detail in her memory—unlike her father, or others whose minds could play entire pieces note for note, earworms digging tunnels into their temporal lobes. She turned in her seat, trying to orient herself to the melody. The varying speed of the wind lifted and dropped notes, making the music both difficult to follow and sound muffled and profoundly off-key. Perhaps she was still asleep, simply dreaming.

The melody seemed to be sloping downward, like stones crumbling down the ridge and onto the playa; then a higher-climbing crescendo and decrescendo brought to her the jagged ridges of the mountains surrounding them, and the notes that trilled on the treble end of the scale became sparks of color against the dust that lay on the floor of the world. Then the wavelike melody conducted the movement of the clouds undulating darkly overhead. She was seeing what she heard.

Then it stopped, just long enough for her to realize that not only was the music real, it was coming from her piano, muffled because it was inside the truck. She got out of the cab. "Hello?" she said, sotto voce. Her heart began beating faster as she tiptoed to the back of the truck, which was still closed. Had the movers forgotten to lock it?

The piece ended, whatever it was, and she froze in the abrupt silence. Perhaps she really had imagined it. She held her breath as long as she could, waiting. When she exhaled, it was visible in the cold air just as another piece began, fast and emphatic, with a continuous, almost frenetic rhythm. Her heart leapt again, because this one she did know. In fact, even after so many years of determined but ultimately failed lessons, it was the only piece she could recognize instantly, even if it was coming from an out-of-tune piano, because it was the one that her father had played again and again on the stereo for the last year or so of his life, that had proved impossible for her to play, that had haunted her in her dreams ever since. Scriabin's Prelude no. 14 in E-flat Minor.

She remembered her father sitting in his study, his eyes closed and his hands grasping the chair's arms as though trying to keep himself from floating away, listening to this piece he was playing loudly enough to annoy the neighbors. Early sunlight from the window lit up his dark red hair like a halo. Her mother had already left for work; it was his turn to drive her to school. Clara had come in to tell him they needed to leave or else she'd be tardy, but when she saw his white-knuckled clench of the armrests, and the tears rolling down his freshly shaved cheeks, she knew not to disturb him. She was hardly ever late for school, so her homeroom teacher would understand.

Daddy, she thought now, and her uncertainty vanished. She might have been standing in the desert in the middle of the night, or she might have been dreaming, or she might even have been on the threshold of madness, but she didn't care. She hoisted the scrolled-down rear door, half-expecting to find the interior transformed and her father sitting there in his chair, waiting for her. She wouldn't let him get away this time. She would crawl into his lap, like she'd desperately wanted to for the past fourteen years and even before then, and rest her lonesome head on his shoulder.

But instead it was Greg inside the truck, sitting on the cooler and a stack of blankets in front of her Blüthner, playing.

The piece was short, only a minute or so of bursting color and flying hands. Greg bent forward, hunched over the keyboard, his bad leg held rigidly out to the left, his right foot working the pedals. He didn't seem to be aware of the door opening or the cold, dust-coated wind rushing in or Clara standing there with her mouth open. She could see a sheen of sweat on his pale, flushed face as he built up through the dynamic waves to the pounding climax, then fell down the cadence and came to an abrupt ending with a loud, slow crash. When he finished, he left his hands on the keys and put his head down on top of them, his torso heaving with gulping breaths.

A high-pitched yelp caught in his throat; then he released it in a fit of unself-conscious sobbing that pulled Clara to the edge of the open door. It may have been a terrible intrusion to eavesdrop on a grown man crying, but it seemed worse to let him do it alone. She lifted the edge of the blanket draping her like a cloak, pulled herself up into the bed, and sat down next to him on the improvised bench, tucking her feet underneath.

After a moment, he raised his face to wipe it against his

sleeve. His left hand remained on the keys, flat and defeated. The firm voice of her former teacher returned to her: "Hold your hand like this, round like a ball." Clara lifted her own hand, her good one, and placed it on top of Greg's, a move that surprised both of them.

For several seconds, he was still. Then he sniffed once and, without looking at her, pressed his thumb onto her pinkie finger with just enough force to convey a message: *Don't move, stay here.*

She stayed. "You came back," she said. The relief she felt took her aback. "Why?"

"Juan. He doesn't usually say much, that one, but he wouldn't shut up about leaving you behind once we took off. A few miles up the road I started to agree with him, so I let myself out and told them to go on."

"Guilty conscience?" she said.

"Always."

"Are they here, too?"

"No, I told them to stay in town until morning but to get out here around dawn. No sense having everybody camping out, and I gave them cash to buy tires." He paused. "I'm sorry I left you out here."

"I'm sorry I called you a lunatic."

"It's okay. It's probably a fairly accurate description."

She'd withdrawn her hand, and he took it again and put it back on top of his; then he began to play once more, very slowly. This piece had a different tone, predominantly but not exclusively of longing. His left hand, carrying hers like a passenger on a float, progressed through steady, repeated arpeggios while the right worked on long, flowing phrases that superimposed insane rhythms onto the meter. It sounded almost improvised, how the right hand flourished in contrast to the left. The piece seemed to shift back and forth in sections between happy and sad, major and minor, so perfectly mimicking her own emotional ambivalence that she thought he might be reading her mind. She wasn't sure what might be transpiring between them, but certainly she had never come so close to understanding what it felt like, physically and emotionally, to play her Blüthner.

"I thought you said you couldn't play," she whispered when he finished.

His eyes were deeply sad when he looked at her. "No. I said that I *didn't*."

"Was that first piece you were playing by Scriabin?"

"You know Scriabin?"

"Just that one," she said. "What are the chances that you'd be playing it?"

He sighed. "Pretty good, I'd say. It was my mother's favorite."

Clara leaned away and looked at him, her mind processing the coincidence. "Wait a minute. It was my father's favorite, too."

"Yeah," he said quietly. "That doesn't surprise me."

"What?" Now she was staring. "Why?"

He trapped her with that unblinking gaze that could hold hers, even in the barest glow of moonlight, perhaps a touch beyond civility. Then he stood up and ran his fingers over the top of the piano. "You know these other marks? These dings that didn't show up in the pictures you posted?" Clara nodded. "You didn't know why they were there, you said. But why would you? You weren't there the day that my father made them." At this, Greg's eyes turned to glass. "You weren't there when he picked up the poker for the fire and brought it down again and again, screaming at my mother the whole time. I thought he was going to kill her. He did, actually. Not right then. Not directly. But he wanted to hurt her, and so he decided to attack her piano. He didn't destroy it because I showed up, and he decided to use the poker on me instead."

He swung his leg out stiffly out to demonstrate the proof of this claim. "It never really healed properly, but at least it was me and not her."

"Oh, God."

"So in the days after what we'd refer to as 'the accident,' my father returned to his usual drunken stupor. I was in my own stupor from the pain meds, and my mother was in her private personal hell, trying to deal with everything. But I remember very clearly that she wanted to get the piano out of the house before he sobered up enough to demolish it."

"That's what you meant about her having to get rid of it."

Greg nodded. "I think she really believed it was the piano that made my father so angry. Even more than the fact that she had a lover." He cleared his throat. "So she called him—her lover, I mean—and asked him to come take the piano and keep it for a while, until my father calmed down or she could finally leave him. And he did."

"He calmed down?"

"No." He cleared his throat again. "I mean *he*—the lover—came to our house. He picked up the piano and took it home." Greg paused. "To his daughter."

Clara got up and took several steps backward, nearly tripping on a blanket. The world where she was standing began to recede, and she was pulled back into the shadowy depths of memory, where the days before the fire were kept. She recalled the night her father brought the piano home, the low voices of his colleagues, her mother's guarded posture, her wound-up tone when she asked, "What are you doing with that piano, Bruce?"

Clara took another step backward, then turned and hopped out of the truck bed, as if to distance herself from Greg's story. "That's absurd. That's absolutely absurd." She was pleased that her voice sounded so steady and certain.

"Is it?" he said gently. "You told me yourself you didn't know where he got it. Well, he got it from my mother, who was

his lover, and took it to your home to help her keep it safe."
She felt a cold heat climbing her neck, a metallic taste under
her tongue. She yanked the blanket off her shoulders and
tossed it on the ground. "My father brought me this piano as a
birthday gift. A *gift*. I'm not exactly sure what it is that you're
insinuating, but it sounds like you're calling my father an adul-
terer and a liar."

Greg followed her out of the truck, opening his hands in a
gesture of acquiescence. "I'm not trying to insult your father.
At the time, I had no idea about their relationship, either. But
from what little my mother told me before she died, he was a
great guy. She loved him. She trusted him. They were in love,
and they were planning a life together."

"A life together! Are you fucking for real? He was *married*!
He wasn't in love with your mother, he was in love with *mine*!"

"How do you know?"

The calm logic of his question enraged her. "Can't you even
hear what you're saying? My parents died together in a house
fire fourteen years ago. *Together*." She raised her voice in order
to silence her doubt. The investigators had called it a fire "of
suspicious origin." They were never able to determine if it was
deliberate or accidental, so she'd never known anything
beyond the fact that they were gone.

"Clara," he said, more softly still. "Look. I'm sorry about
your parents. Believe me, I know how much that hurts. But I'm
telling you the truth: your father and my mother were in love.
They met because of the Blüthner. We didn't get to take it with
us when we left Russia. It was years before she got it back.
Somehow your father helped in returning it to her, and they
became friends. I was fourteen then. You'd have been, what,
seven or eight? She told me that after they met, your dad
started taking piano lessons from her."

Clara shook her head. "He never took a single piano lesson.
Never! He couldn't play at all. He told me so himself."

"You're right about his not being able to play. My mother said she tried for two years to teach him, but all he could play was 'Chopsticks' because he never practiced. But he wasn't really trying to learn. At first the lessons were just a cover, to legitimize spending time together and the feelings they were developing. She told me they usually just talked, or else she'd play for him. Her favorite piece was that one by Scriabin, and he loved hearing it, over and over again. Eventually, things evolved, as they obviously do when people are attracted to each other." He shrugged. "Our parents were lovers, Clara. At least for the last three years of his life. That's the answer to your question about why your father loved her favorite piece of music. I might be an asshole for telling you, but it's the truth."

He looked so smug. What did he know about her father's life? His audacity made her furious. Without thinking, she lunged at him, striking him with her right fist directly on the chest. She followed that with another and another until Greg stumbled on his own lame leg and tumbled backward onto the cracked earth and she fell right with him, now raining punches and slaps and swats with both hands, even the broken one, on his chest, neck, face, ears. She used those self-defense skills her uncle had taught, even though the self she was defending wasn't an adult stranded in the desert, but a desperate twelve-year-old orphan that was huddled deep inside her.

Katya sat on the edge of the couch with her back straight, her son's broken leg elevated on a stack of pillows beside her. He was sleeping again, unaware of her or anything else, but Katya wouldn't leave his side. What else could she do, both of them aching so deeply for their own reasons? If she couldn't protect him, then at least she would keep him company. Mikhail had finally woken up from his drunken sleep and gone to work, mumbling an apology. If he'd noticed that the piano wasn't there, he hadn't mentioned it. A profound loneliness now permeated the house.

The old Polaroids of Death Valley were spread out on her lap, and she was caressing the border of the one at Racetrack Playa. Miserable once again, she felt herself moving fifteen years backward in time, looked at the stone in the photograph, alone in the barren playa, sailing away from her. She wondered where in Bruce's home her piano was. She'd been there a few times, in secret. It was larger than her house, but there weren't many big spaces. Had he put it in the front room, like she would've done? Did his daughter like it? Did his wife?

The phone rang. "It's time, Katya. It's been almost exactly two years since you told me 'two more years,'" Bruce said.

"We're not living honestly, not like this. You said you wanted to wait until Greg was out of high school, and he is. And now that Mikhail knows, there's no reason to wait any longer. It's not safe for you. It's only a matter of time before he flies into another rage against you or Greg. Or even me, for that matter, assuming he finds out who I am."

"He doesn't know your name. I told him it was just a letter from a lovesick young student, that I'd dismissed him when I discovered his true feelings. Then he wanted to know why I kept the letter, and I said it was only for evidence in case this crazy boy tried any monkey business."

"That was good thinking, my love. And yes, I do intend some monkey business." This was meant to be funny, she knew, but they were both too anxious to laugh. After a moment, he said, "Tell me you'll leave him."

"As soon as I can do that safely, I will." She wanted to and would; she'd been dreaming of it for almost four years, ever since that first kiss, sitting at the Blüthner in her living room. She'd tried to keep her feelings platonic, and for a time was almost successful. But soon it became unbearable to sit near him and not feel his lips on hers, his hands in her hair. The piano lessons became a euphemism: *Can we have a lesson tomorrow afternoon?* Or *That was a* wonderful *lesson!* They began talking about a future together soon after they first made love. But now that it was here, that it was a real possibility, she was afraid. She couldn't imagine Mikhail's rage if she told him she was leaving, and at least she'd need to wait until Greg could bear his own weight again.

"I'm telling Alice this week. Friday night, in fact. I'll arrange for Clara to spend the night at her friend's house, and I'll ask Alice for a divorce. She knew something was up when I brought the piano home. It's time."

"Will it be difficult?" she said. The year before, they'd gone to a concert and, afterward, to a small, out-of-the-way bistro for dinner. It was dark and romantic, the food delicious. Bruce held her hand across the table as they sipped their dessert wine. They talked about introducing Greg and Clara, where they might get married, maybe opening a small music school.

It was a perfect night until Bruce noticed his wife in the opposite corner—though she, too, was holding hands with someone else. By then Alice had convinced Bruce to try to reconcile for Clara's sake, and he'd felt guilty enough to stay, but it hadn't lasted. He'd called Katya four months later, only five months ago, begging her to meet him at the bungalow. Katya wondered, guiltily now herself, how Alice would feel once she learned that they'd resumed their affair.

He hesitated, and she could hear him take a breath. "Yes," he said, "it will be difficult, especially for Clara."

"Do you think she will understand? Still so young—not even twelve yet."

"I don't know. Not right away, certainly. But eventually she will. I know she'll love you once she finally meets you, gets to know you."

"I want very much for her to. I have always wanted a daughter."

"I know. And I hope Greg will understand."

"There is no doubt that he will. He is very unhappy. Mikhail and he, they don't get along so well."

"Obviously. Mikhail's a savage."

"Bruce?"

"Yes?"

"Do you still love Alice?"

"Not the way I love you."

"You are very brave," she said.

"What choice do I have?"

"Yes."

"And it's not me who's brave, Katya. It's you."

She stared at the sailing stone that looked like her piano in the photograph and began playing an imaginary keyboard on her knees with fingers that ached for something productive to do. In her mind she heard the missing notes whispering like ghosts in her ears. When had she last made a decision that would transform her life? Starting with Mikhail, she was accustomed to letting others decide for her. Would it be like this with Bruce? It seemed that all her talent had won her no independence. She played the imaginary piano, adding up her losses as she went, and trying to make those bits of nothing into something she could tuck into herself and hold there: hope or strength or bravery. Her fingers danced across the invisible keys next to her broken son, but the truth was, she didn't feel brave at all.

"Mama, tell me the story," Greg said drowsily. The tapping of her fingers, even against the fabric of her dress, had awakened him. "How Sasha makes the tundra green." It was August in California, but he was still shivering on the couch. His leg ached every moment—he was already growing used to the pain—but his heart ached even more to see her using her lap as a substitute piano, as though she, too, were lost and wandering in some cold, distant place. In the three days since the Blüthner had been taken away, she was constantly wringing her hands, massaging her fingers. Did they want to play as much as he wanted to hear? He needed her to think of something else. "Please, Mama."

"I don't want to tell about Sasha's music," she said. "There's no more music for now."

"Can you call those men and get them to bring the piano back?"

"No, Grisha. I cannot."

"But you need it, Mama."

"No. Well, yes." She stood up carefully so as not to disturb his leg. "But if I bring the piano back, your father will destroy it." She didn't want to say that Mikhail might do something even worse, starting with Grigoriy.

"I won't let him."

"And you'll sacrifice your other leg for this? No, my son. I will find a way for us to be safe. And happy, very happy. But for now we must wait." She didn't dare tell him what they were waiting for.

"Who were those men?"

"Good men, kind men."

"But who?"

"*Chi-chi-chi*. That's not your concern."

"Where did they take it?"

She shook her head. Greg watched as she looked down at her long fingers as though they were not her own. His mother might've trusted those people who took the piano away, but he didn't. Why should he, when even she didn't know where they'd taken it? She wasn't the same without her Blüthner. What if they didn't bring it back? What would happen then?

Greg didn't speak at all. He grunted when Clara hit him in the chest, let out staccato huffs when she slapped his face; he only mildly deflected her blows and mostly seemed to be waiting for her to finish, like somebody who was used to getting beat up. His refusal to fight back further enraged her, but only briefly. Images of her father began flickering into her white-hot thoughts, and she slowed and then stopped, still straddling Greg, whose arm was draped across his face. She brought her fists down on his chest one final time before collapsing onto the dirt next to him, her body curling around the ripping pain in her right hand and the questions in her mind, and now she was sobbing.

Greg pushed himself onto his side slowly—she'd inflicted some pain, for sure—and touched her on the shoulder. "Clara. It's okay."

Lost inside herself, she didn't register either his touch or his voice. She cried into the dirt until she couldn't any longer, and when she stopped his hand was still resting lightly on her shoulder.

She lay for a while on her side, staring through the dark at the ground's polygon shapes from this unusual angle. Did her father die loving someone besides her mother? Her mouth was dry, her lips caked with dust. She could die there, all her bodily fluids leaching out onto this dehydrated scrap of nowhere. And what would it matter? What good had she done with her life thus far anyway? What, except dragging somebody else's piano from her childhood through an insignificant adolescence and into an unremarkable adulthood? That piano, her upright companion with its eighty-eight keys to her locked store of memories. Maybe she'd tried to access those fragile memories of her parents too often, altering them irrevocably each time until, as with some photographs, she could no longer recall the original experiences, only the last time she'd thought of them. Maybe by now all her memories were lies.

"Did you ever meet him?" Clara asked, her face still pressed against the dirt, in the fading hope that Greg had gotten her father confused with someone else.

"Once. Right after the accident. The night he picked up the piano. I was pretty out of it, but I remember one thing: the port-wine stain on his face. He had one, didn't he? I mentioned it to my mother a week or so later, asked her who the man with the birthmark was, and she burst into tears. It was just after your parents had died, and she was heartbroken. She told me everything, actually, not just a little: when they met, that they hadn't meant to fall in love, that it had been innocent for a long time. She was worried that I'd criticize her, but I didn't. My father was a monster even before he broke my leg. I couldn't blame her for wanting someone else. She wouldn't tell me your father's name, though. She said the last time she'd spoken it out loud was when she'd told him she loved him the night before he died, and she refused to ever say it again. That she wanted to keep the music of his name inside her."

The night before her parents died would have been a Thursday. Her father always worked late on Thursdays, didn't he? Why was that? What would her mother have been doing? Standing with one hand on her hip, smoking a cigarette, and looking out the window, her padded shoulders squared off against whatever it was that made her so irritable? It was a forgettable night, one like any other. Clara couldn't remember the weather, or what they'd had for dinner, or if she'd called her best friend on the phone before bedtime, as she usually did. It hadn't seemed necessary that night to retain those mundane, routine details. She hadn't known that it would be the last normal night of her childhood.

"Bruce," she said.

"What?"

"His name was Bruce. Bruce Lundy. He was a tenured professor of Slavic literature at UCLA. He had red hair and brown eyes. And yes, he had a birthmark on his face."

Greg nodded. "I'm sorry, Clara. I feel bad about being the one to tell you this."

Clara pushed herself up and used her lifted shoulder to wipe the dust off her face. Her hand was throbbing, and she wondered if she'd broken it again. "I'm still not sure I believe it." But even as she said this, she felt an encroaching disquiet. She wasn't even twelve when they died. What could she have known about the inner workings of their marriage? What did she know about either of them, really, except for who they were in relation to her? She had no idea about the histories they brought to their marriage, or the secrets it contained. What child ever does?

"Why didn't you say anything to me before?" she asked.

"I never expected to see that piano again. It was a shock, let me tell you. I thought it was gone in the fire that took your parents. But then there it was, and there you were, all feisty and innocent. I didn't want to tell you who I was. Or who *you* were. I just wanted you to go away."

"Is that why you've been such an ass?"

"Maybe. Mostly, I just *am* an ass." He chortled faintly. "Though my therapist says there's still hope."

For the first time, she considered Greg's perspective. How he might have felt upon connecting her, Clara, to his mother's death. "When did she die?"

"Saturday, September 4th, 1999. A year to the day after your parents died. She made me breakfast. Then she said she had to go run errands. She hugged me for a long time and said to please try to understand if she wasn't back soon, she had a lot of things to do. It was a beautiful Saturday morning and she drove all the way from Los Angeles to Death Valley. She went up to some cliffs . . ." Greg's eyes glistened in the moonlight, but he didn't cry again. "There were witnesses. The policemen who came to the house needed someone to identify her, and my father wouldn't go, so I did." He took a deep breath, closed his eyes. "They gave me the keys to her car. Under the seat, she'd left a letter and the Polaroids I showed you. She wrote that she'd given it four seasons to see if she could survive him. She begged me to forgive her." He pinched the bridge of his nose and sniffed hard. "I've been trying to for thirteen years."

Clara studied Greg, his profile angled toward the ground, his lame leg stretched out. His mother had chosen death over him, because—if it was true—she'd already chosen Clara's father. "I'm sorry," she said.

"It's not your fault. Not your father's, either. Anyway, I took off for New York right then, didn't even stop at home to pack a bag or say good-bye. I just left and didn't look back. I haven't spoken to my father once in all these years. Never will. I don't even know if he's still alive. This is the first time I've been back in southern California since she died."

The cool wind picked up, and they felt a few raindrops. "Come on," Greg said. He heaved himself up into the truck bed, then held out his hand to help Clara up. She climbed inside, and they stood facing each other in front of the open door as though on some precipice. He didn't release her hand. She could see beneath his rigid exterior a hint of warmth, an assurance of mutual understanding. He seemed to be conveying his commiseration, and from the depths of a long perspective.

"How did you break free from it? From losing her?" she asked, searching his face for answers. "How?"

"I haven't. Can't you see? That's why I'm here. I haven't broken free."

"Then what hope is there for me?" She looked beyond him into the darkness, at the landscape stretching out in all directions, the rainfall heavy enough that the moon appeared blurry behind it.

He answered by leaning in and brushing his lips against hers, tentatively, as though to be careful she wouldn't move away. She didn't. The chasm inside her opened up.

He threaded his fingers up the nape of her neck and into her hair—the intimacy of it was stunning—and kissed her and kissed her. And because he was the only person alive who could understand her particular sense of loss, she wanted to do the same, to touch his neck and his ears, parts of him that he couldn't control, and she resented that her cast limited the use of her fingers. Instead, she reached around and pulled him toward her. She had yanked flat tires off axle shafts with more finesse, but he didn't seem to mind. He let go of her hand and held her face, breaking the kiss to look at her, and she saw something beyond lust in his expression, as if he was trying to transmit a silent message, a promise or a plea, and when she smiled, just barely, he kissed her again, and she had the feeling that she could be swallowed whole and indeed wanted to be.

Greg finally said, with his lips still on hers, "Can we . . . ?" She breathed the word *yes* into his mouth, and after a moment he stepped back and threw the moving blankets down one after another, spreading them as well as he could without wasting time. It looked to Clara like a nest, and he led her to it and they lay down so their heads were at the elevated side of the truck, above the tires that were still inflated.

"Are you okay?"

"Yes. Are you?"

"I am."

Then, amid their heat, there was an intrusive image: the morning they first met, Greg standing at her car holding that coffee. She'd thought he was an assailant poised to attack her where she slept. He'd offered her sugar and creamers that he'd pulled out of his pocket, then told her to go home. He'd given her a room at the hotel and mostly ignored her for days afterward. He'd invited her to the middle of nowhere and left her amid the sailing rocks, and all along had let her continue her misunderstanding of the Blüthner's history. Like that last piano piece he'd played, in which he'd alternated his tempos and mixed his tones, he'd pushed and pulled and pushed and now he pulled her with his unexpected music and his sadness and his full, needy lips. Still, her anger about how he'd been the one in control the whole time resurfaced, and she kissed him hard enough to feel it in her teeth. She wanted to strip him of his power, to meet him on an equal level, so with uncharacteristic aggression she said, "Take off your clothes."

He did, and when he reached out to help her with hers, she pushed him away with her good hand. "Get a condom." From his pants pocket, he withdrew two—wait, had he planned this all along?—then tossed the pants away and waited for her to undress. She took off her jeans and her underwear, but left her sweatshirt on. Out of principle, she wanted to withhold something. "Put it on."

While he did, she took inventory of him in the darkness. His skin was very pale, and what hair he had on his chest and arms was dark and fine. His shoulders and arms were tightly muscled, though his midsection was soft and bisected by a thin line of fur that drew her gaze down, where it lingered for a moment before continuing to the raised scar that crossed his knee and fissured up his thigh like the crusted edges of the playa's polygons. The tissue beneath it looked fragile, as if his leg were a piece of china that had been broken and clumsily repaired. Her anger eased as she traced the outline with her finger; that kind of ruin must have come at a great cost. She leaned in with her hands on his chest. How had he compensated for that all these years?

His eyes glazed with animal desire as he kissed her mouth and tipped her head back to kiss her throat, neck, breasts. *Oh,* she thought, or said, she didn't know; they were both panting by now, their bodies having overtaken their minds. She held on to the hem of an idea—that she wanted to be the one making all the decisions—but then, after sliding down onto him, she no longer cared who was because it felt so good to be touched. Ryan had stopped touching her long before she'd moved out, and she wanted, suddenly, to feel her heart beat against another human being's, so she pulled off her sweatshirt after all and pressed herself against him, and they found an intense rhythm, her knees grinding into the rough blanket. Greg fixed her with a desperate stare until he closed his eyes and opened his mouth, and she, feeling the rawness of her power over him, around him, was close too, so close, and she watched his jaw moving as he crested the apex of sensation and went over it like he was falling off a cliff.

And she closed her eyes and what she saw was Peter, threading the cable behind her television set; Peter, holding out a container of *avgolemono;* Peter, sitting next to her at the racetrack. In spite of this she came right after Greg, so hard that she trembled for many seconds afterward. Pushing Peter's image away, she let herself collapse on Greg's chest and tried to catch her breath inside his meager, gasping embrace.

After taking Clara to her friend's house, Bruce dropped his car keys on the kitchen counter with a clatter. His *Rachmaninoff Plays Rachmaninoff* CD was blaring from the other room. How appropriate. Alice certainly did have a morbid sense of humor. Well, at least she knew what was coming. That might make it a little bit easier. He poured two fingers of bourbon into a glass and drank it. Then he poured another two fingers each into his and another and carried them into the living room.

Alice was waiting on the couch, her legs and arms crossed, her shoulders back, a cigarette in her hand. He turned the music off, set the bourbon in front of her, clinked her glass with his own, and sat down on the other end of the couch. Her ashtray, the one Clara had made a few years before at camp, was between them on the cushion.

"Alice," he said.

"I told you to end it, Bruce," Alice said. "I ended mine. Wasn't that the deal?"

"Alice."

"Don't look at me like that, with that sad-puppy face. You don't get to pretend to feel guilty now. What'd you do with that hideous piano, by the way? I hope you gave it back to her. I don't know what the fuck you were thinking, bringing it here. The nerve." She flicked her ash into the tray.

"It's more serious than that."

"Oh? I suppose you want a divorce, is that it? So you can run off with your little Russian princess?"

"Actually, yes."

She blew a mouthful of smoke at him. "Of course you do."

He closed his eyes until the smoke dissipated; he hated it that she smoked, but now was hardly the time to criticize her.

"And how long have you been plotting your escape this time?"

"Look, Alice, I really did try to end it, like we agreed. I told her that you and I were going to work things out, and we didn't see each other for four or five months. But then, I'll be honest—why *not* be honest now—after a while it seemed obvious you were never going to forgive me, and, well, I was lonesome." He shrugged. "And I called her."

"Lonesome! That's rich. That's really rich, Bruce." She took a sip, lit another cigarette.

"Are you telling me that you never thought about what's-his-name again? You didn't ever consider picking up the phone?"

"Of course I did! I was lonely, too. But I took you at your word that we were going to get past it. These things take time, Bruce. You couldn't really have expected a honeymoon again after everything that happened. Not at first. Not even after four or five months. But no, I haven't talked to him since the day after you saw us at the bistro, because I told you I wouldn't."

"I'm sorry."

"Yes, you most certainly are."

They hadn't spoken this many words to each other in months. Except for the cigarette, she looked almost vulnerable.

"Would you like another drink?"

"Sure," she said, and drained her glass before giving it to him.

This time he put the drink into her hand, and their fingers touched. They hadn't touched each other in months, either. She pulled away, as if she'd been given a shock.

"You realize this will break Clara's heart, don't you?" she asked while looking at the ashtray.

"Yes. But I also think that you and I deserve a chance at happiness. That has to count for something."

"Thank you for your generosity, including me in this grand existential plan. Did you hazard to think that this might break my heart, too? You and Tatiana living happily ever after together while I'm left picking up the shreds of Clara's and my life?"

"It's Katya. Not Tatiana."

"Oh, I'm so glad we've got that straightened out. Your order of priorities is quite impressive, Bruce. You've just announced the end of our fifteen-year marriage, but the most important point of clarification is your mail-order bride's name. *Katya*. There. Did I pronounce it correctly?" She ground out her half-smoked cigarette and lit another.

"I don't suppose it means anything for me to say I didn't intend for this to happen."

"It's not meaningless to say it. It's undignified." She blew a lungful of smoke at him. "Not to mention insulting."

"Well, I didn't."

"Of course you did, silly. It's a consequence of fucking someone other than your wife."

He put down his drink and went to open the window. "You should quit smoking, Alice. It's a disgusting habit."

"Close the window. Do you really want the neighbors to hear about your little tryst firsthand? I'm serious—close it. I hope you've been discreet, at least. Then I might escape this misery with a bit of dignity. Clara, too. Do you want her to know that the reason her parents divorced was because her father couldn't keep his dick in his pants? If you're really going to insist on breaking up our family, then I'd appreciate it if you would refrain from trotting your tsarina out in public until an appropriate amount of time has passed. Try to appear somewhat mournful—if not for my sake, then for our daughter's. She doesn't need to know what a selfish schmuck you turned out to be."

He took a step toward her. "Would it make you feel better if you punched me?"

"Don't be ridiculous. It would make *you* feel better, and I'm not in a very charitable mood."

She was right, of course. He *was* selfish. Instead of rebuilding their family for the past year, when he'd had a second chance to do so, he had been slowly destroying it. He'd chosen the easiest paths for himself, those that led to the surest satisfactions. He hadn't been a very good husband to Alice. Why did he imagine he could be a better one to Katya? Well, he hoped he would. And maybe he could figure out how to be a better father, too.

"I love her, Alice. It's that simple."

Alice nodded. She drained her glass, then took a long drag from her cigarette and set it down in the notch Clara had dug out of the side of the clay. Then she stood, looking Bruce in the eye for long enough that he became uneasy, and even, unexpectedly, amazingly, a little bit aroused. It reminded him of when they stood facing each other in front of the preacher and a small gathering of family and friends, on the dividing line between two distinct phases of life, that exhilarating fear as they waited for the ritual to end and the preacher to pronounce their official new beginning. Alice looked sterner now than she had back then, and angrier, but when she stepped forward to kiss him on the lips Bruce didn't pull away. Except for the taste of cigarettes, it was nice. Not necessarily romantic, but intimate in a comfortable, familiar sense. She ended the kiss slowly and leaned away from him.

"You used to love me, too," she said. Then she reared back and punched him, hard, in the stomach.

He doubled over, his arm clasped over his heaving belly. "Shit," he said, drawing out the word.

"Well, what do you know? That *did* make me feel better," Alice said. "And now I think I'll have another drink. Or six. How about you?"

He nodded, still gasping, and sank down onto the couch. Alice went to the kitchen for the bourbon, and coming back into the living room she turned the Rachmaninoff CD back on, then filled their glasses to the tops.

"Cheers," she said.

"Cheers."

They drank and Alice smoked in silence, staring at nothing, until the bottle was empty and the music had long stopped playing, saying only the word "Cheers" when they refilled their glasses, until they were too drunk even for that. Then Bruce said, slurring, that it was time for bed, and Alice nodded. She stubbed her cigarette and they staggered together down the hall to the bedrooms.

"I'll sleep in Clara's room tonight," Bruce said. "We'll figure the rest out tomorrow."

Alice braced herself upright against the wall and stuck out her hand, and he shook it. "G'night. Sleep tight. Don't let the bedbugs bite," she said. It was what they liked to say to Clara just before switching off the lights.

He nodded, and they went into their separate rooms and closed the doors.

The cigarette that Alice had sloppily put out had fallen off the lip of the ashtray when they stood up from the couch, and it lay there against the woven upholstery, gathering heat on the fabric; that heat mixed with the circulating air and ignited into the tiniest of fires, which burned a dime-sized hole in the cushion, curling the threads into a hard black ring, into which the cigarette eventually fell.

It then came into contact with the polyester fiberfill stuffing and triggered a slow growth of fire in the foundation materials, spreading deeper and broader until enough heat was released to engulf the entire couch, a vintage mid-century model, which Bruce and Alice had purchased shortly after Clara was born.

As they slept off their profound drunkenness in their rooms down the hallway, the fire reached from the couch to the rug and the two wingback chairs and pedestal table that had been briefly displaced to accommodate the Blüthner and then soon returned to their original positions. The fire's boiling black smoke collected and swirled at the ceiling, where the untended smoke alarm remained silent, its battery having been removed long ago and its replacement forgotten. Once it had filled the living room, the smoke crawled into the other rooms, devouring the oxygen it needed to burn, until it reached its ghostly fingers into the lungs of Bruce and Alice, stopping their heartbeats before they realized their air had been stolen, that everything around them was turning to ash.

Clara could feel the rising sunlight even before she opened her eyes, as if the morning was knocking at her temples. Squeezing her lids shut only made it worse, so she covered her face with an arm to block out the light as she inventoried and reconciled her memories of the previous night. *Oh no,* she thought, as the events reassembled themselves in chronological order. She fell into relationships fairly quickly, but rarely did she fall so quickly into someone's bed.

Holding still, she listened for the sound of Greg's breathing. He was a heavy sleeper, snoring with his mouth open, and she'd been awakened several times; once, she'd watched his fingers flutter over what might have been an imaginary keyboard. But now the inside of the truck was quiet. Tentatively, she slid her unbroken hand across the blankets, feeling for a body. Finding none, she opened her eyes, recoiling from the pinkish early light, and sat up with a blanket clutched to her chest. She checked for pain in her broken hand and was relieved that it didn't ache as much as it had after she'd finally stopped hitting him with it. Everything else hurt instead: her head, her back, her joints. She cringed at the memory of her uninhibited dominance, the urgent grinding her knees had endured. She lay back and pulled the blanket over her head, pretending as a child does that if she can't see anyone, then no one can see her, either.

The need to relieve herself finally forced Clara to stand and dress and finger-comb her hair and smack away the sour taste of her wine-infused breath. She closed the lid over the piano keys, though it was she who felt exposed.

She poked her head out of the bay door and looked right and left. Greg was fifty yards away, watching the sunrise with his hands in his pockets. She crept out of the truck and went around behind it, on the road side, to do her business. Then she picked up a water jug and took several long swallows, gargled and spit, and splashed some water on her face. Greg had sounded confident about the guys returning early, so she didn't worry about conserving water. She found some gum in her pack and was grateful for her foresight in matters related to travel and comfort, if not in alcohol and men. Then, when she felt like she could avoid it no longer, she walked out onto the playa toward Greg.

"Good morning," he said. He smiled, stopped, and smiled again as though testing whether the intimacy between them had held through the night.

"Morning." Whatever expression she offered must have granted him permission, for he leaned in and kissed her, then turned her toward the rising sun, wrapped his arms around her from behind, and rested his chin on her shoulder. Last night's rainstorm had been intense and brief. Now the sky was clear and the ground already dry.

"Think you and I could get the piano safely out of the truck? This light is perfect. I had an idea of bringing it out here onto the ground and laying it down on its side on top of some blankets. What do you think?" He squeezed her, kissed her on the neck.

"Symbolic."

"Exactly."

"Listen, Greg—"

"Clara, listen—"

"You go."

"No, you."

Clara sighed. "I was going to say that I'm sorry about last night. I drank too much and got a little overemotional. I wasn't myself. I don't know what got into me."

"Apparently I did," he said, turning her around. He winked at her, then kissed her again, more quickly this time, and said, "Don't be sorry. I'm not."

She pulled away, but not abruptly; she didn't want to seem rude. "I don't typically sleep with someone I hardly know," she said.

"I wouldn't have thought so," he said. "That's what makes it all the more important." He took her by the hands, being extra careful with the broken one, cradling it in his open palm. She looked down; her cast was getting dirty, especially around the gauzy edges.

"Greg, I'm not sure . . . I mean, it was great—really great—but I'm not sure *important* is the right word."

His own expression changed, a subtle lifting of the dark eyebrows, his pale stare belonging to someone bent on persuasion. "Actually, it's exactly the right word. Hear me out, Clara. I know I wasn't very welcoming when you showed up here. I couldn't imagine what compelled you to drive all this way and then insist on staying. It was a little crazy, you have to admit."

"I didn't know you. I didn't know if I could trust you."

"Of course not. You couldn't have known that we'd have anything in common, or that I loved your piano as much as you do. Or that we'd have a night like this." His exaggerated leer made her smile. "I'm so glad we did. Aren't you?"

She was, in fact, deeply uncertain about it—so sudden, so unexpected, so rough. But maybe that wasn't a bad thing; she didn't know. Certainly it had been a comfort. A release, at the least. She nodded.

"Good." He took a breath. "But there's something I need to tell you," he said gravely. "Well, maybe I don't need to, but I want to be honest with you."

"Okay," she said, mentally flipping through a catalog of concerns: he was married, he was a criminal, he had a sexually transmitted disease. They had used a condom, right?

"I was going to destroy the piano at the end of this trip. For the last photograph, I was going to push it off a cliff and shoot it as it was falling."

He might as well have said he was planning to do the same to her. She swiveled toward him, ready to—what, hit him again? Before she could say or do anything, he lifted a hand in benediction. "Wait. Please. I didn't know you then. I didn't know about your attachment to the Blüthner. I tried to buy it first, remember? And of course I thought this one had already burned up. I was looking for a replica."

"But why?" Her heart was pounding, visions of her Blüthner falling down the staircase returning to her, along with the same feeling of panic and imagined loss. "Why would you want to do that?"

"I'm not going to, not now. I promise you, Clara. Don't worry; I have something even better in mind." He put his hand on her wrist, over the cast. "Before you showed up, I thought I wanted the last picture to show how my mother's story really ended. But now"—he squeezed her arm—"you're here. That changes everything. You brought my mother back to me."

"I have no idea what you're talking about, Greg. Bringing your mother back?" She stepped away. "This is all too weird."

"Don't, please. It's not weird. Okay, maybe it is." He sighed. "I've been angry for a really long time. Abandonment issues. That's what my therapist calls them, anyway. When he found out about my mother's suicide, he didn't waste any time in diagnosing me with an 'unhealthy coping style.' It was actually his idea for me to do something creative to help me process her death. Something symbolic. So that's why I thought of this, of retaking the photos from our Death Valley trip, but with the Blüthner in them. All alone, nobody playing it, no music to melt the ice. Just like in the story. Don't you see?" he said, his voice going soft. "The piano is my mother. I wanted to show how it felt to me when she died. What it looked like when the music stopped."

"So you were going to push it off a cliff? What's the point of that? It wouldn't bring her back. It wouldn't change anything."

"I know that now, thanks to you," he said. "I woke up thinking about an entirely different interpretation of the whole project. Putting the piano in the pictures doesn't have to represent the *end* of the music. It can symbolize the *potential* for music. You know, like at any moment someone's going to walk into the setting from outside the frame. Like the music's still there, somewhere, even if the musician isn't. It just has to be perceived differently. So now I don't want to illustrate her death by imitating it. I probably wouldn't have felt any better afterward. I might have felt even worse. Just thinking about it now makes me a little sick." He closed his eyes, shook his head.

She looked at him carefully as her heart settled down to a normal pace. His passion was compelling; it was probably the first thing that had drawn her to him. "I like that idea," she said, "illustrating the potential instead of the actual."

Her head was still pounding, from the adrenaline, the hangover, the already too-bright sun. But she was also moved by how he was smiling at her, his straight white teeth like the keys on her piano, and when he reached for her hand she let him take it.

"Think about this. If you hadn't listed the Blüthner for sale when you did, I never would've discovered that it had survived. I maybe could have found another one, and done the essay as I'd originally planned. And we never would have met. It might sound crazy to say so, but it feels a little bit like fate, doesn't it? Or kismet or serendipity or whatever else people call it."

"It is pretty strange," she admitted. What were the chances they would ever find themselves out here, with the piano, in the middle of the desert? All her adult life she'd been prone to inertia, not impulse. Yet here she was. She remembered what Peter had said when she was notified that the piano had been purchased: *I know how much you like signs. You should take that as one.*

They could see Greg's rental SUV approaching, the morning sun lighting up the dust that sprayed up behind it and lingered in the air like the contrail behind a jet. Clara and Greg walked back across the playa to the cooler, the truck, the piano. She looked around with new embarrassment at the tableau: an empty wine bottle lying in the dirt, having spilled out of the cab when she'd heard Greg playing, not far from her thermal blanket, crumpled and wet from the rain. Remembering the makeshift pallet in the truck bed, she climbed inside to tidy up the evidence of their lovemaking while Greg began picking up the mess outside. A torn-open condom wrapper fell from the blankets when she shook them out, but where was the condom itself? She pocketed the wrapper and searched for its contents.

Hopefully Greg had somehow disposed of it. She pushed away the unpleasant image of the movers, having found the condom, disapproving of her.

The truck bed was silent. If at that moment she were asked to hum any part of the Scriabin's prelude, she couldn't have managed to. Gone, too, was the tactile memory of Greg's hands: on the piano, on her skin.

She was grateful to hear the slam of doors and the low Hispanic voices. She jumped out of the truck and watched Juan and Beto haul two new ten-ply tires out of the SUV.

"*Buenos*" Juan said after they'd rested the tires by the truck. "We have food."

Clara was struck by the consistency of basic human needs, even during crises. It seemed a rude paradox that one could feel hunger and confusion simultaneously. Or lust and anger.

"Thank you," she said.

They gathered around the open hatch, and Greg passed out coffee and foil-wrapped burritos and asked questions in a businesslike clip: where did they get the tires (the garage in Beatty they'd passed driving into Death Valley, which was open twenty-four hours), where they spent the night (the Death Valley Inn), did they pick up more water (*si*). After they ate, Greg told the guys to move the piano out onto the playa so he could photograph it while they changed the tires. Against this familiar routine—Juan and Beto unloading and pushing and positioning the piano, Greg setting up his equipment and barking orders—for a moment Clara found it possible to pretend that the revelations and events of the previous night had been nothing but a dream.

She lingered by the truck, wanting to pitch in while knowing that she wouldn't be able to loosen the lug nuts or jack up the truck with only one usable hand. She'd changed thousands of tires since her uncle had taught her how to do it, both in and outside of the garages where she'd worked. It was a small point of pride that whenever she drove past a stranded female, she stopped to offer aid. Protecting other women from the dangers of the road made her feel like a minor hero. Twice she'd stopped to help out male drivers. The first, a young professional in an uncomfortable-looking suit who was trying a little too hard to promote an image of power, hissed that he didn't need any help, that an emergency roadside service had already been summoned. The second, a heavyset retiree sweating in his golf shirt, had accepted her offer with a lascivious smile and pushed his thin white hair off his forehead. While she was bent over, setting the jack under his car's frame, he placed his hand on her rear end. She spun around to see that the other was down his pants. She only stopped for women after that.

She had gotten as far as positioning the jack beneath the truck's rear axle when Juan returned from setting up the piano and took the tire tool from her. "You sleeping okay last night?" he asked, sounding genuinely concerned. He began loosening the lug nuts on the truck's rear tire with an ease that made Clara jealous.

She nodded. "I'm good." She looked away so he wouldn't see the heat coloring her face. What portion of her shame was due to her inability to change a goddamn tire and what was due to how she'd passed the small hours inside the truck, she couldn't say.

Under the bright sunlight, the polygon shapes of the playa blended together once more into an almost seamless plane. Greg moved around the piano, which was lying on its back atop the moving blankets, just as he'd suggested to her earlier, its fallboard open to the sky like a gaping mouth. She wasn't worried for its safety; they'd been careful positioning it, far more so than she'd been with Greg the night before. He photographed it from various angles, then lay down on his stomach in front of it to shoot it from there. She couldn't see his face at this distance, but the felicity of his movements made her wonder what he was thinking as he lay there next to the piano. About his mother or her? If his mother and her father had lived, had married, then she and Greg would be step-siblings. She considered this idea numbly.

When he finally stood up, with some difficulty, his clothing was covered with light-colored clay dust. She looked down at her own rumpled front. What she wouldn't give for a shower. She found three aspirins in her bag and chased them with water from the plastic jug.

Minutes later, when Greg raised his hand and gave the circling motion with his finger, Clara said to Juan, "I think he's finished," and slipped one octave deeper into a sort of melancholy. Confused, broken, aching, dirty, watching everyone else fulfill some purpose either intrinsic or imposed.

Having replaced both tires, Juan and Beto walked out to fetch the piano. She wandered after them, thinking she could at least help Greg with his equipment. When she held out her good hand in a wordless offer, he gave her the tripod, then kissed her. She didn't quite kiss him back, but instead looked over his shoulder in case the movers were watching, and was relieved that they weren't.

G reg had hardly left the couch in the ten days since the accident, refusing the privacy of his own bedroom so he could keep an eye on his mother. Each time his father passed through the room, Greg glared at him but said nothing. Katya had started sleeping in his bed, anticipating the time when she could leave Mikhail and begin a new life with Bruce, reunited once more with her Blüthner.

She carried a lunch tray to Greg and put it down on the table. He stared blankly at the television, where a newscaster was reporting from the scene of a fatal house fire. "Grisha, why are you watching this? So depressing." She picked up the remote but hesitated as the camera panned to the hollowed-out house. "Two people confirmed dead," the woman was saying. "Total loss of property."

"So terrible," Katya said, switching it off. It was hard enough to manage her own sadness; she couldn't contemplate someone else's. She thought of Bruce and wondered if he'd asked Alice for a divorce the night before, if he'd carried his promise through, how she had reacted, and when they would tell their daughter? Katya looked at the telephone in its charging base. Surely he would call her soon, tomorrow if not today.

By Monday, she still hadn't heard from him. She didn't want to call him at home—she never did that—so she tried his office number at the university. It rang and rang, then went to voice mail—an automatic recording, not even his voice—and she remembered that he'd be teaching a class right then. She didn't leave a message.

*

On Tuesday, she dialed his home number. If Alice answered, she would hang up; if Clara did, she'd ask to speak with her father. But no one picked up.

Wednesday morning, she was wrecked. It had been six days since they'd spoken. They couldn't meet at the bungalow because Katya refused to leave her son, but Bruce had called to say he loved her, that Clara's sleepover had been arranged, that he was moving forward with his plan. Why hadn't he called since then? Maybe he was sick. Still, she needed to see him to put her mind at ease, so she decided to drive to his house. If his car was there but not his wife's, perhaps she would be bold enough to ring the bell. Or perhaps she'd just pass by; she was desperate enough for that. What if he'd changed his mind? Or if when he'd asked, Alice had convinced him to stay, maybe just for the girl? That's what had happened the last time, after Alice had discovered them.

Her heart beginning to pound, Katya turned onto his street, hoping she was about to fall into his open arms. *I was so worried,* she would say. *I'm sorry, I'm sorry,* he would say. *I've had the flu, but everything's fine, I told Alice, soon we'll be together.* The idea of losing Bruce now was untenable. She loved him, and she needed him. She couldn't imagine staying married to Mikhail but didn't believe she could leave him on her own.

When she saw the burned-down ruins where his house was supposed to be, she sucked in her breath and slowed to a stop. There were only blackened remnants, mounds of unidentifiable rubble inside and on the lawn, a bright yellow DO NOT CROSS tape encircling the entire mess. Her panic turned to relief: she had taken the wrong street. Yes, in her confusion, she hadn't been paying close attention. This must be that awful fire that had been on the news. How unbearably sad.

Katya continued down the block and rounded the corner, checking the street signs. No, no, no. He lived on Twenty-third Street, didn't he? Maybe she'd remembered the address wrong. She circled the block, wanting it not to be familiar. She wasn't wrong. Her heart beat into her temples; she was suffocating.

At his house once again, she flung open her car door and ran to the edge of the devastation. No, no, no. She called his name, though no sound escaped her. The news had said *fatal house fire, two dead, property destroyed.* Her mind went blank. She stepped over the yellow tape into the debris of what had been the living room. She remembered that it had faced the street, with sunlight pouring through the picture window.

Bruce was dead? That couldn't be possible. He couldn't be dead. She couldn't make herself believe that her love was gone, so she thought instead of her piano. It would've been right where she was standing. Yes? The house was small enough that this was the only place he could've put it.

"Bruce!" she called out loud, yet her voice, trapped in the back of her throat, sounded strangled. "Bruce!"

She sank to her knees in the middle of the ruined room, the traitorous sunlight on her head and neck. She ran her hands through the gray, powdery ash, digging for evidence. There must be something there. Where had Bruce and Alice been? Where was his body? Frantic, she clawed at the cinders; underneath it was still warm, damp in places, bone-dry in others. "Bruce!" Ashes covered her clothes, floating up and coating her arms, face, and hair, while she dug, desperately searching for something—teeth, piano keys—or anything at all.

"Hey there!"

Katya jerked her head up.

"Bruce?"

"Lady, stop. You're not supposed to be in there." A policeman walked toward her, another officer trailing behind him.

She crawled on her hands and knees, still sifting, picking up any hard object she felt, trying to identify it as meaningful. *Bruce.*

The female officer crouched a few feet away from her. "Ma'am, I need you to stop. It's not safe. You can't be here."

Katya looked up at her but couldn't begin to understand what she was saying. She became aware of a tightness in her chest so intense that it seemed to go beyond pain and into an absence of sensation.

"Do want me to call someone for you?"

Where was he? Where was his body? She clutched a handful of ashes and looked down at it. Was *that* him? Was that all that was left? The officer stood and took Katya's arm. "Come on, let's get you out of here."

But Katya sank down harder and began filling her pockets with fistfuls of it, as much as she could grab, before the other officer stepped in to take her by the other arm and lift her up.

She stopped resisting then.

"Don't cuff her," the female officer said. "I just want to sit over here with her for a minute."

Katya allowed herself to be led onto the sidewalk and seated on the curb, facing away from Bruce's house. The officer was talking to her, but it sounded faint and unimportant, just ambient noise from far away. She sat there staring at nothing and chanting his name over and over in her mind. A gentle breeze came through, blowing some of the ashes off her and raising goose bumps on her skin. Even with the relentless California sun beating down, she felt as cold as ice.

G reg chatted throughout the slow, shuddering, three-hour drive back to their hotel. He told her about his mother, who went by Katya, his demonic father, his childhood in Los Angeles. He asked her about her parents, her hobbies, her friends when she was young. He was amazed that they'd grown up only a few miles apart. He talked about his photography and asked her what it was like living in Bakersfield. Although flattered by his curiosity and what seemed a genuine interested in the details of her life, she couldn't stop thinking about her parents.

Her mother was home from a long day spent teaching polit-ical science to her undergraduates at UCLA. Clara sat at the table doing homework while her mother listened to NPR on the small radio in the kitchen, occasionally taking a break from peeling carrots and potatoes to take a long drag from her ciga-rette and flick the ashes into the sink. She'd removed her blazer but not her shoes; it was warmer than usual for August in Santa Monica, and on her silk blouse, there were small sweat stains under the armpits.

Alice closed the oven door and set the timer. "It's almost six. Your father's late, as usual," she said, inhaling sharply through her thin nose. Clara felt a sting of guilt, as though this were somehow her fault. But of course it wasn't; she had no idea where her father was.

When he did come home that night, long after the stew had

been eaten and the leftovers put away, Clara was in the bathroom brushing her teeth and getting ready for bed. She heard the front door bang open and her father say, "Whoa now, careful coming through the door."

She stepped out into the hallway, ready to call out a greeting, but stopped when she saw him and two of his colleagues—all of them professors, soft-looking and vaguely out of shape—come through the front door, panting and struggling under the weight of a huge black piano.

Alice, standing in the doorway between her office and the foyer, pushed her reading glasses back on top of her head. "What's this?" she said in her centurion voice.

Clara froze, the toothbrush still in her mouth. Even as the men jostled inside, she felt a grave stillness descending. Alice's padded shoulders were squared above her crossed arms, and she looked both angry and frightened.

"What are you doing with that piano, Bruce?"

Her father's back was turned, and he glanced over at her with a tentative expression that Clara didn't recognize. But Alice must have, because in that instant came a private exchange between them. In all the years since, Clara had tried to translate that silent conversation into something she could understand. But all she could remember was how her mother held her breath for a moment too long, her body going oddly rigid until she finally exhaled in a slow, measured way that seemed to empty her of both her breath and her fight, as if whatever battle might lie ahead had already been lost.

"It's for Clara," he said. Then, with too much enthusiasm: "An early birthday present."

"Her birthday isn't for another six weeks," she said, in a slow and menacing tone. Bruce's helpers seemed to be trying to hide behind the narrow width of the piano as they took small, shuffling steps forward.

Bruce didn't meet her eyes. "Like I said, an *early* birthday present." The piano shifted slightly and one of the men grunted. "Oh," her father said, "you remember Paul, don't you? From the English department?"

Paul leaned his head out from behind the piano. "Nice to see you, Alice." His cheeks were red.

Bruce continued, "And of course you know Ben."

"Hel-lo," Ben said in a tight singsong from behind the piano.

"Hello," Alice said, making it sound more like *good-bye*. Then she leaned sideways and rested against the doorway with a simulated forbearance, as she watched them wrestle the massive piano into her foyer, wet spots blooming under their armpits, too.

"Where do you want to put it?" Ben asked.

"Here, let's just set it down for a second." They did, and Bruce wiped his forehead with the wad of shirtsleeve rolled up to his elbow. "This thing weighs a ton." He flexed his hands, then rested the backs of his wrists against his hips, elbows akimbo, and looked around. "I don't know, actually. Maybe the living room. That makes the most sense. We could move the armoire and put it there, or maybe in front of the window—though it's pretty tall. It would block out some of the light. Or Clara's room? I don't know, is there enough room in there, honey?" He offered Alice an awkward smile.

"Really?" she said, cocking her head like she did when she checked Clara's homework and found a careless mistake. "You're actually asking me that?"

"Well, I just thought, you know, that you'd have an opinion, since you usually do." They stared at each other for a long moment while Bruce's friends found other things to look at: the abstract painting on the wall, the grain of the wood floor. Clara couldn't seem to move at all.

"I don't think I need to tell you where to put it, Bruce," Alice finally said. Then, using her shoulder for leverage, she pushed herself off the doorjamb and went into her office. Clara could feel the slam of the door in her chest like a thud.

He ran a hand over his graying red hair, squeezing his scalp at the top. "Oh, well then," he said, shrugging his eyebrows at his colleagues. "I guess it's up to me."

Clara slipped back into the bathroom and closed the door carefully so it wouldn't make a sound. Her mouth, she realized, was full of toothpaste and saliva. She spit it out and turned the water on full blast, so that anyone who might be listening would know that she was in there, then sat down on the edge of the bathtub. She looked at her feet and moved them up and down, pointing and flexing. Her toenails needed to be trimmed. She could hear her father and his friends murmuring and moving furniture around. He'd decided on the living room after all, and she was glad because there wasn't any extra space in her room. She already had her bed, her bookshelf, and the desk and chest of drawers that had been her grandmother's, making the rug in the center the only place to lie down and do her homework or play board games with Tabitha, her best friend. There wasn't room for any piano. And why did he think she wanted one, anyway?

She heard her dad thank his friends, then all of them saying their good-byes, the front door opening and closing. Finally, she stood up. She flushed the toilet and ran the sink water, trying to camouflage the fact that she'd been hiding. After opening the door, she walked down the hall and pretended to be surprised when she saw her father struggling to push the dark, hulking piano closer to the living room wall where her mother's sitting area had been, the two wing chairs and the pedestal table now huddled in the middle of the room.

"Hi, Daddy," she said.

"Hello, sweet," he said.

She walked over and threaded her arms around his waist, rested her ear against his chest, listening to his heart for a few beats until he took a step back.

"I have something for you," he said, filling his low voice with mystery. He turned her toward the piano.

"Oh," she said. "Wow."

"What, you don't like it?"

"I guess so. But I don't know how to play."

"Not yet." He put a hand against her back and guided her forward. "Try it out." He wiggled his fingers over a few random keys.

She stepped up and pressed down on a key at the near end.

"Sounds great, doesn't it? Well, maybe a little out of tune, but that can be fixed. Also these gouges here on the case." He ran his hand over the top, and it struck her even then how gently he caressed the damaged wood. "And we'll get you lessons, of course. Hey, maybe I'll even try some, too. I can't play at all, but I'd love to be able to. Wouldn't that be fun?"

She nodded, pleased but a little embarrassed by his sudden interest in her. Maybe it would be fun, she thought. She didn't get to spend much time with her dad, and if taking piano lessons was her only chance, she'd do it. "What about Mom?"

He shrugged his hands into his pants pockets. "What do you mean?"

This amplified tension between her parents, so dense and sticky, always came and went, and now it was there again, like a spider web that had been spun in the night. She pushed down on another key, harder this time. It didn't sound any better, just louder. "She seems mad."

"Mom's just readjusting to teaching again after the summer break is all. We both are. Lots of new students, all these papers to grade. We're a little out of sorts, but everything's fine. Don't you worry." He tipped her chin up with his finger and smiled until fine lines fanned out from the corners of his eyes.

Why shouldn't she believe him? Her mother was always prickly for the first few weeks of a new semester. He was, too. That's probably all it was. Clara played a few more keys, both hard and soft, and liked the sounds it made. Then she dragged one finger down the length of the keyboard, producing noises from very low to really high, and her father smiled. "A virtuoso already," he said. "Soon you'll be able to play Scriabin's Prelude no. 14 in E-flat Minor for me."

"What's that?"

"Oh you've heard it, I'm sure. It's poetry and color and imagination. In any of the languages I know, I can't find the right words for it. I'll play it for you tomorrow on the stereo. You'll love it."

She thanked him for the gift, and he shooed her off to her room. In the hall, she knocked softly on her mother's office door. There was no answer.

Sharp voices from her parents' room awakened her that night, and she crept out of her own room to listen. A few harsh phrases were loud enough to make out—*under my goddamn nose* and *think I wouldn't know* and *don't want to see that thing back here ever again*—followed by her father's responses in an equally angry but lower register that she couldn't hear as well. Sometime the following day, while she was in school, the piano was taken away.

Remembered again through the nuance of all the new information, the fragments of fighting she'd heard through their closed door took on a different meaning, but back then she'd been too young to infer that there was more to their argument than the piano's unexpected arrival. The living room had been restored to its long-standing arrangement, but the household had not. At the dinner table the next evening, she cautiously asked where the piano was and noted how her mother drew her shoulders back and raised an eyebrow at her father, who lowered the newspaper he was reading and said, "It was terribly out of tune. I had it moved to a dealer nearby so they could fix it up for you."

Years later, she learned that pianos go out of tune each time they're moved and that tuners go to the piano, not vice versa. But she'd never, until now, questioned her father's explanation, because after he was gone she was grateful that he'd sent it away. A week or so after she went to live with her aunt and uncle, Jack received a phone call from the technician. "Do you know anything about a piano?" Jack asked her after hanging up, and she told him it had been an early birthday gift. In the painful aftermath of her parents' deaths, she'd forgotten all about it—not having had it long enough to feel like it was hers, hadn't wanted it to begin with—but she sobbed with relief when her uncle said, "Well then, let's go get it."

Then it seemed miraculous to have something that had been theirs, even if only for a day, when everything else was lost: her white wicker furniture, the yellow bedspread with white and pink flowers that her grandmother had made; the posters of Aerosmith, Ace of Base, and Boyz II Men; the photos of her and Tabitha from camp, Halloween, and school; her favorite pair of green corduroys, which fit her better than anything else, and the new sweater she'd saved three months' allowance money to buy; the book she'd been reading about an eleven-year-old girl in foster care who was sent to live with relatives in another state, which in retrospect seemed so prophetic that she rarely read fiction again after she moved to her aunt and uncle's home; her diary, which contained only a few entries, one of them a thorough reenactment of the time a boy named Jamie, the first to ever make her feel a little dizzy, said hello to her in the sixth-grade hall; the Mickey Mouse ears from the trip to Disneyland for her fifth birthday; her drawing of an owl that won third place in her fourth-grade art show; her entire home; her parents; her childhood.

The Blüthner was the only thing she had left.

She hit the button on the dash to turn off the music, and pivoted sharply to Greg. "You're not going to try to take the piano back, are you?"

"What? Why would I do that?"

"Is that what last night was about? Did you seduce me so I'd give you the piano?"

"No! Of course not. Why would you think that?"

"Because you said you had no desire to sleep with me, remember? At the hotel?"

"You said it to me first—quite loudly, I might add. 'You're dreaming if you think I'm going to sleep with you.' I think every single guest heard you. It was embarrassing."

She considered that. "Sorry."

"It's all right. I'm really glad you changed your mind." He reached over and stroked her arm above her cast. "And no, I'm not trying to take the piano away from you. It's yours now. It has been for fourteen years."

"Okay," she said. "Thank you."

A moment later, he looked at her and smiled. "Though you know there's always a chance that we'll all end up together someday. You, me, and the piano."

"Oh?"

He looked hurt. "Wait. Was that a one-night thing?"

She gazed out the windshield—not away from him, but not at him, either. "I don't know. I haven't really thought about it. Everything's happening so fast. Five days ago, you couldn't wait to get rid of me."

"What can I say? You were quite a surprise."

Wasn't every romance a surprise in the beginning? She recalled how she'd been drawn to Ryan's mysterious benevolence in that grocery store, then dazed when he left with a bag of produce after agreeing to take her on a private flight. "I live in California. You live in New York."

"Two states connected by phone, text, and airplanes. Have you ever been to New York?"

She huffed. "I haven't been east of Nevada."

"Ever?"

"Nope." Travel was something she had on a vague future

to-do list, along with: learn to play the piano, get a college degree, learn at least one of the foreign languages her father knew, pay attention to world politics like her mother had, and several other seemingly impossible goals.

"Well, we have to fix that. You'll love New York—and not just that. We could go anywhere in the world. I've never been back to Russia. We could go to St. Petersburg, where I was born, and hear the orchestra there. Or Zagorsk, where my mother grew up. Moscow. Maybe we'd stop over in Paris or Amsterdam. Amsterdam's amazing. I once saw a guy Rollerblading half-naked along the Schinkel River in the dead of winter."

She felt a dozen car engines revving in her chest, and it wasn't a good feeling. "Greg. Tap the brakes a little bit?"

He glanced at her, obviously noticing that she'd shifted away from him in her seat, then nodded at the road stretching out ahead of them. "You're right. It's hard not to get a little carried away, though. You asked me before if I had a lover or a spouse, but the truth is I haven't cared about anyone in a long time. I haven't met anybody else who understands what's really important to me, you know? And out of the blue you show up, and I think you might be the one who does. You get it. Now here we are, and with the piano . . . it all fits."

She examined his pale face in profile, his severe grip on the wheel, his dust-covered magician's clothing. He'd worn only black since they met, like he was in perpetual mourning. Or was that the uniform of artists and New Yorkers? She thought of the sturdy, navy-blue work pants she and the guys wore at the garage, their comfortable utility. She liked it when the uniform company picked up the bag with a week's worth of grease-covered pants, hers and theirs mixed together, and brought them all back clean, folded, and stacked. She liked finding the S's amid the L's and XL's and putting them on at the beginning of a workday, the stiff cloth relaxing as she went along. That satisfaction of belonging.

"This all feels a little . . . sudden."

"Look, I know it's fast. But I like you, Clara. I'm not asking you to marry me. I just want to see where this thing between us might go. What do you say?"

She didn't answer right away. His interest was flattering, and his reasoning mostly logical. Because of their parents, they shared a history that nobody else could understand. Somehow she was comforted by the fact that he'd met her father, even if only once—that Greg knew what he looked like. He was intimately connected to her past. And unlike Ryan and the others, at least Greg would never underestimate the importance of the Blüthner. He'd never suggest that she sell it or store it or let it get buried under the detritus of life: mail, keys, jackets, books. What did she have, really, that kept her in Bakersfield? Her crappy apartment? Her job? She could find one in a garage anywhere, even in New York if they made it that far.

The road evened out and Greg picked up speed. Clara checked the side mirror; the truck kept pace behind them, but she couldn't see the guys' faces behind the thin cloud of dust between the two vehicles. She leaned her temple against the window. There was nothing but empty cornflower sky.

Maybe, if they actually did become a couple, it would be like an arranged marriage between virtual strangers, a practical union at first. Love, if it came at all, might come later. Meanwhile, she would at least have the Blüthner.

When she turned to him, he met her eyes, and she smiled.

"Yeah?" he said, raising his eyebrows hopefully.

She nodded. He did too, smiling, and held her broken hand for the rest of the drive.

Katya was up early on Saturday morning—if not technically *up,* since she hadn't gone down the night before. She hadn't even tried. The past year had been the worst of all the many awful ones she had to choose from. The voice of the lost music spoke to her in dark whispers almost constantly. She was unable or unwilling to get out of bed on some days, and on those she could she would wander aimlessly through them. She had largely stopped cooking because she no longer enjoyed any of the flavors, so she fed her husband and son American fast food or something that could be delivered to their home, like pizza or Chinese. She staggered through the seasons like she was waiting for something, but she didn't know what it was until the night she found herself driving past a new house that had been erected where her lover died. She imagined that a hopeful young couple, possibly newly married, would soon occupy it; they might spend their whole lives together in that house, if they were lucky. Thinking about this gave her an idea that, in turn, finally provided her with a sense of purpose. She nodded to herself in agreement. It didn't make her happy, but it did give her something to look forward to.

Mikhail came home at five that Saturday morning, after driving a graveyard shift. He thought that what he'd done to their son the year before had taught her a lesson, and since then he'd left her mostly alone. He had no idea that her grief was far deeper and wasn't simply about that outrage. When she saw his headlights' beams slash through the living room window, she went to the sofa and pretended to be asleep. But once she heard his heavy, mouth-open snore from their bedroom, she returned to the score she had spent all night composing longhand at the kitchen table. Just about the time the treetops began to glow yellow-orange and the mockingbirds commenced their daily repertoire, she decided it was finished.

The breakfast she'd planned was excessive, she knew, but she felt very clear-headed and determined about it, now that the day was here. She hadn't cooked for Grigoriy in so long that she wasn't about to be stingy with the menu this morning. She remembered the decades of food shortages in Russia, of how often they'd broken their starving fasts with only dry bread and coffee. Katya hadn't learned many of the traditional recipes until after they immigrated to the United States, because back home they never had enough money to buy all of the ingredients, even if they could be found in the shops. She thought of her mother, hoping that she, too, by the end of her life, had been able to enjoy a meal such as the one Katya was about to prepare. She would've liked to have been there to ask her.

She started with cottage-cheese pancakes, *syrniki,* with caramelized fruit on top, and savory *blini* with a dollop of sour cream and spoonful of red caviar. Usually she used smoked salmon or some other cheaper fish, but today she would not scrimp. Next was *tvorog,* also a kind of cottage cheese, with honey and berries, one of her son's favorite dishes when he was small. And of course *buterbrody,* open-faced sandwiches with black bread, butter, cheese, and sliced *doktorskaya* sausage; this was standard fare, but hearty. Last, she made strong, sweet tea and arranged the feast on the table.

"Grisha," she whispered into his ear, and brushed his hair off his face. "I made breakfast for you." He made a groaning noise in protest and turned over to nestle into the covers. "Please come eat now, before I have to leave."

"Where are you going?" was his muffled reply. When he sat up, she looked at his profile. By now it shouldn't, but it still surprised her to see whiskers on her baby's cheeks.

"Shopping," she said, and the lie caught in her throat. She coughed to clear it. "I have many errands today. I will be gone for a while. Longer than usual, okay?"

"Why?"

"*Chi-chi-chi.* I will explain later. For now, come eat what I've made for you."

Katya sat with him, watching him eat, encouraging him to take second and then third helpings, but of the abundant food she took only a few bites herself.

"Aren't you hungry?" he asked. "Why did you make so much just for me?"

"I tasted it all while I was preparing it. I can't hold any-more." She twirled a piece of her hair, the gray now almost equal to the brown, and hummed the arpeggiated melody from her new composition.

"You seem nervous."

"No, no. Everything is fine." She smiled and poured herself more tea. "Would you like more of the *tvorog*?" she asked, already serving him another heaping spoonful.

"No more, please. I'm stuffed."

She nodded and began to clear the table.

"Mama, are you okay? Is something wrong?"

Katya glanced at him over her shoulder, then turned her attention to the dishes. She wanted everything to be clean and put away before she left. "I told you, Grisha," she said brightly. "Everything's great." What an American thing to say. It sounded strange coming out of her mouth. "I left some money for you in your room. Maybe you want to buy some new films and take pictures today. Or if you'd like to go see the movies. Anything you want. Or go someplace for dinner with your father."

"You won't be home before dinner?"

"Oh, I'm only saying just in case." She cleared her throat again. This was difficult, but her decision had been made. Better now not to think about it too much. "There's plenty of food here, yes? I'll wrap everything. Leftover *buterbrody* is good for dinner."

She could feel his eyes on her back as she worked, but he didn't ask any more questions. He was a good boy, she thought, though he worried about her too much. She hadn't meant to become the kind of mother that made her child worry. He wouldn't even go away to university, he was so afraid to leave her alone. He deserved better than that.

When everything was spotless, she surveyed the room. It was still as white and light-filled as when they'd first moved in but now had more personal items on the countertops and walls. It was a very nice kitchen. She wouldn't miss it.

"*Я люблю тебя, сынок.*"

"I love you too, Mama." He eyed her skeptically. "Are you sure nothing is the matter?"

"Nothing is the matter," she said, and pulled him close to her. "I promise." Then she collected her satchel, where she'd put her new sheet music and purse, and left the house without saying good-bye.

She refused to feel any remorse, or sadness, or second thoughts as she backed out of the driveway. She drove north out of town, toward Lancaster, then northeast on 14, skirting the southern edge of Red Rock Canyon, and due north along the western slope of the Panamint Range. When she reached the turnoff for Death Valley National Park, she had a surge of exhilaration. Here she was again, alone this time, in this desert that to her still looked like the tundra.

She had once shown Bruce the photographs and tried to explain what they meant to her. The lost music, the abandoned girl. Of course in real life, Bruce had been the one to come along and save her from her frozen grief, at least for a while. She could laugh easily by the time she shared the made-up story with him. Upon hearing it he suggested they take their honeymoon in Death Valley, partly because it was interesting, and partly to dispel the myth of sadness. "My father took us there when we were kids," he told her. "My sister, Ila, was terrified of the name. She thought we were going to die the minute we got there. I have a vivid memory of climbing up to this point called Coffin Peak, which was sort of off the beaten path. All the other tourists were walking out to Dante's Peak, since it's pretty well known, but my dad told us the best view was from the point off to the side of it. God, it was beautiful up there. You could look down and see the salt basin and wild desert and canyon scenery, and across the valley there were these snow-covered peaks." He shook his head. "I'd totally forgotten how incredible it was until now."

"I wanted to go there!" she exclaimed, then handed him the picture of her looking up at it from thousands of feet below. How strange to think they'd once been on opposite points of that enormous empty space.

Then he'd taken her hand and kissed it. "I have an even better idea. Let's get married there. It's a morbid name, Coffin Peak, but I bet nobody else has ever done it. It can be all ours. What do you think?"

It was nearly three o'clock when she got to the spur off CA 190 that led to Dante's View, the car groaning as it climbed up the sharp incline. She knew nothing about cars—her friend Ella had patiently taught her how to drive, since Mikhail didn't care if she could, but she'd never liked it much. When she'd stopped for gas, the attendant had topped off her engine with coolant and insisted she bring extra water along in case it—or she—overheated in the park. It was hot, nearly a hundred degrees, but she wasn't worried. She'd been told it would be twenty degrees cooler at the peak. If her old Accord gave up before then, she could simply walk the rest of the way.

There was a pullout on the road leading up to the vehicle parking lot where buses had to turn around because the rest of the climb was too steep. She turned into one of the few parking spaces by a public restroom. The cars that had been ahead of her continued without stopping, as did the few that followed. Apparently, Bruce's father had been right: everyone else seemed to be going to Dante's Peak.

With another mile still to go on foot, she didn't waste any time. From her satchel she withdrew the old Polaroids, wrapped in the linen tea towel, and a sealed envelope with her son's name written on the front. Inside was a letter. It was shorter than she'd intended, because she hadn't been able to find the right words. In the end she'd realized those didn't exist, so she'd explained as best she could and then begged him to forgive her. She slipped the letter and keys beneath the driver's seat, then emptied the contents of her purse onto the passenger seat—her wallet with only a few dollars in it, a pen, lip balm, a hairbrush, those useful damn sunglasses Ella had given her sixteen years before. She was holding the composition she'd finished earlier that morning in her hand, and left the satchel and her purse, both empty now, on the seat. That felt right. Let someone else have them. She didn't need any of it anymore.

She followed the path eastward over a grassy hillside strewn with sparkling crystals and scrubby shrubs, and climbed over two false summits separated by ravines before reaching her destination. It wasn't a difficult walk, though once she got there she was sweating and tired. She rested for a moment, then moved carefully through some loose rocks to the very top and stood on the edge of the rugged south face. Oh, it was indeed beautiful, so still and serene. The basin below was an endless expanse of salt and sand that looked like a snow-covered valley. That was where she had stood once before, at the lowest point in the continental United States. On the other side, far in the western distance, she could see Mount Whitney, which was the highest. It seemed entirely appropriate, especially today, that she could see both from her unique position.

A breeze bristled the nearly invisible hairs on her arms, and she lifted her face toward it. "Hello, my love," she said. Her voice was swept away by the wind, but she knew he could hear her. "It was exactly one year ago that you had to leave me."

She closed her eyes. Standing at the edge of Coffin Peak was much better than visiting an empty grave. Though they'd never made it to Death Valley together, she knew he would come for her here. He was now all around her, and she could hear his voice and feel his embrace on the wind. She opened her eyes and gazed out from their would-be wedding altar at the empty space between earth and sky. If such a thing were possible, she would like to catch a small, shimmering cloud and carry it for a bouquet.

"When I used to play my piano," she said, "this is the kind of place where the music wanted to go. Up high, far above the silliness of the world, and filling the quiet with beauty." She hummed a little melody and checked to see if the birds nearby might be dancing instead of flying. "I like to think that you and my piano are together now, yes? Perhaps during the passage you were given a thousand lessons at once and now, on the other side, you can play even more beautifully than I ever could."

The sky was changing, the light lower and gilding the mountain faces. They had talked about being married at sunset. She unfolded the score of her new composition, which was only two pages long.

"I have written the story of my life," she said, and began humming again. "It is structured in two sections, and each one crescendos all the way through to the conclusion. Of course you have my Blüthner with you now, so I can only pretend to play it for you. But please listen anyway." She hummed some more, her fingers moving, her expression changing as the music evolved from simple to complex, from curious to grieving. While there were moments of joy, too, they were small, like fireworks displayed only once every year. The pause in the middle was just long enough to qualify it as a crossroads.

"I'm calling it 'Die Reise,'" she said. "It means 'The Journey.' My piano was made in Germany, of course, so I think it's a good choice for a title, don't you?"

The wind whistled past her and she tilted her head. "Is that right?" She nodded. "Yes, naturally. How did I not see that before? The parallels are very clear." She laughed out loud, and to her sad ears it sounded as rich and colorful as the setting sun, as the music she'd lost and missed terribly. "Then it will be the journey of both our lives, mine and my piano's. Thank you, my love. Thank you for keeping my Blüthner safe with you." She nodded once more. "Yes, I like the ending, too. It feels exactly right."

She tore the two pages in half, smiling, then folded them up and tore them over and over again until her life was too thick to rip further apart. The sun hovered at the horizon.

"I love you," she said. Then she flung the scraps of paper into the air, and the wind scattered them into moments, the notes now separate and meaningless. "I love you!" she called out as loudly as she could. "I love you!" And then she stepped off the crumbling edge of the rock and followed the music into Bruce's waiting arms.

It was close to noon when they pulled into the gas station across from the hotel. They got out and stretched, and as Greg unscrewed the cap he said, "I'm hungry. You?"

"Famished. But I need to take a shower first. Do you think they've given away our rooms?"

"They're ours as long as we want them," he said. "Oh, and if you'd like to move in with me, I won't object."

She smiled. "I'll meet you at the restaurant in twenty minutes, okay?" she said, collecting her bags from the back. "But I wish I had some clean clothes."

"Here," he said, "take this." He pulled a T-shirt from his camera case, like a black rabbit from a hat. "I always carry an extra in case I need a change of clothes or to wrap up my equipment. Or share it." He winked at her. "It's clean."

She jogged across the road, even though it was empty of traffic, and let herself into her room in a rush, relieved to be alone. The shower, too, was a relief. Washing away the clay dust and dried sweat from her skin, the oil from her hair, the night from between her legs. Holding her cast outside the shower curtain, she stood under the hottest water she could bear for far longer than the two-minute limit suggested by the admonishing little plaque on the wall.

Greg's T-shirt carried an unfamiliar, if not unpleasant, scent—metallic with a hint of floral laundry soap. What did his apartment smell like? Did he cook his own meals, wash his own clothes? Putting on his shirt, letting her wet hair dampen the back, felt prematurely intimate. She still could remember the first time she'd spent an entire night with Ryan, a month after they'd first started dating, and how strange and wonderful it had been to use his shampoo and shaving lotion the next morning, to dry off with his towel, to sip coffee wearing his Golden State Warriors boxer shorts. More than their weeks of sexual intimacy, wearing his favorite underwear seemed to mark the beginning of their coupledom. Taking off a sexual partner's clothes was more straightforward, like stripping off a layer from the armor of identity. Nudity could be neutral, even though people did reveal something of themselves at the skin level, evidence of things often beyond their control—*here are my moles and freckles, here is where I'm ticklish, here are my scars*. But people communicated a great deal more by how they chose to cover their nakedness, whether with their own clothes or that of others. Clara looked down at Greg's T-shirt, which was too big, and realized that in wearing it a choice was being made.

She finished dressing, gathered her hair into a ponytail as best she could, and brushed her teeth. She practiced a smile in the mirror, but noticed that it didn't reach as far up as her eyes. Sighing, she stepped out into the glaring sunlight and walked toward the restaurant, where Greg would be waiting.

A couple she'd already seen a few times, both of them wearing serious hats and vests and carrying tripods, waved to her as she passed. There seemed to be a camaraderie among visitors here in the desert, perhaps because in spite of the few pockets of civilization they were just barely removed from the threats of the elements, of isolation. On the walls of her hotel room, there were framed pages from books—*Plant Ecology of Death Valley, Desert Recreation and Survival, Struck for Gold*—that highlighted the place's precariousness. Maybe being friendly was just another means of increasing your chances of making it out of Death Valley alive.

Her gaze was on the Grapevine Mountain Range as she approached the open-air courtyard; she was imagining the difficulties faced by the gold-rush pioneers who'd journeyed westward across it almost two hundred years before when she noticed someone standing near the front office. He was a hundred feet away, with his broad, unmistakable back to her and his hands shoved in his pockets. A restlessness in the bend of his body suggested that he wasn't much interested in whatever he could see in the gift shop's window, that he was just passing time, waiting for something. She knew he was waiting for her.

Tingling with recognition and relief, she broke into a run even before she realized it, sprinting across the desert compound as if toward a mirage. "Peter!" she called.

When he turned, she saw the mix of surprise and pleasure on his face and came to a stop against him, wrapping her arms around his sturdy midsection and pressing her cheek against his chest. He staggered a moment from the impact but recovered by taking her into an embrace that cocooned her from the outside world. Even in the apparently limitless desert, he occupied an impressive amount of space.

"Clara," he said, his deep voice seeming to travel not from his mouth but from the depths of his insides, trembling from his heart directly into her ear, the rawness of it both warming and unnerving her until she recognized this moment as a mistake, that there was a reason they'd hardly touched each other since the night they'd spent together. She abruptly pulled away.

"What are you doing here? How'd you know where I was?"

He tensed at her release and returned to a more platonic stance, arms hanging empty at his sides. "I tried calling you but it kept going to voice mail. So I looked up where to stay in Death Valley to call you there, which wasn't hard because there's only two hotels in the whole park. But you weren't registered at either one and that bothered me, you being out here all this time. Then I wondered where the hell you could be for days on end if you didn't have a hotel room, so I just decided to come. I happened to try this place first, and I saw your car—"

"But we talked yesterday. I told you I was fine."

"I know, but after we hung up I couldn't stop thinking about how this just wasn't like you, taking off like that without any real plan. You've been gone almost a week. I was worried about you. I thought about your car breaking down, or you having a flat, and with your hand and everything . . ." He tried to hide his embarrassment by quickly running his eyes over her to assess any possible damage. "How is it, your hand?"

She looked at it. The aspirins she'd taken earlier had helped, but it still ached. Her mind flashed to the fisticuffs with Greg, how she'd flung herself at him, knocking him over, and pounded him with her fists. *Greg.* She thought of the playa, the Scriabin, the sex, and was immediately ashamed. "It's okay, I guess."

"But are *you* all right, Clara?"

"Yeah, sure. I'm okay."

"And everything's okay with your piano? That was what you were worried about, right?" Peter shoved his hands into his pockets and hunched forward. "That's why you stayed?" The hopefulness in his voice made her cringe. He looked directly at her, his eyes pleading and loyal. Unlike Greg, whose expression could be as opaque as the surface of a frozen lake, Peter's betrayed everything inside him. It was almost unbearable seeing this display of emotion, this struggle with restraint. She lowered her gaze from his face to his chest and mimicked his posture by putting her hands—as much as she could with the cast—into her own front pockets. They did this whenever they got too close to touching. A handcuffing against some unspoken point of no return. She pushed her good hand deeper into her pocket and touched something she'd forgotten was there. Then she remembered: the condom wrapper. She turned away, unable to look at him at all.

"Is that why you're still here?"

"Yes," she said, finally. There was a trash receptacle a few feet away, and she thrust the evidence into it.

"How much longer are you going to stay?"

"I don't know."

"I could stay with you. I mean, if you wanted some company." He glanced around at the low, rustic hotel buildings and, across the street, the general store, the gas station, and the RV park and campground next to it that was full but as lifeless as a cemetery, with the campers lined up like headstones. "Seems like it would get pretty lonesome out here."

Clara didn't trust herself to speak. She thought again of when she'd first started seeing Ryan and had mentioned it to Peter, deliberately casual, while they were disassembling the alternator on a vintage Porsche 928. How his concentration had seemed to narrow as he'd marked the alternator's case with a piece of chalk where it had split at the seam so he could put it back together correctly. How the slot screwdriver had slipped as he was trying to pry the case apart. "It's not serious," she'd told him. "It probably won't last the weekend." He hadn't said anything, only nodded. When she'd told him a few months later that she was moving in with Ryan, Peter had helped her carry the boxes.

She closed her eyes, suddenly weary of her small life, and when she opened them Greg and the movers were approaching from across the lot. Greg said something to Juan, who nodded and went with Beto into the restaurant. She regarded Greg much as Peter probably might: his cool stare absorbing the scene, his awkward gait. Step, *thump,* step, *thump,* step, *thump.* A knot formed in her chest. She hadn't had enough time to make sense of the situation with Greg in her own mind, much less justify it to Peter.

"Greetings and salutations," Greg said, looking from Peter to her, clearly wondering who this guy was. Whether he was just another guest at the hotel, or a potential rival, or both. That Greg might be the jealous type did not surprise her.

"Peter, this is Greg, the photographer." Clara turned.

"Greg, this is my friend Peter." She stood back, as if she'd just tossed a match onto gas-soaked kindling, and watched as they shook hands and appraised each other.

"The not-boyfriend friend?" Greg asked.

"The what?" Peter dropped his hand.

"Clara was talking to somebody on the phone a day or two ago but was quick to say afterward that it was just a friend. Not a boyfriend. Right, Clara?" He winked at her. Peter looked at her, stricken, although certainly what Greg had said was true. No, it was the arrogance of his tone. Clara looked down.

"Right," she said.

"Anyway, Peter, what brings you all the way here?" Greg said, like a host, forcing cordiality on an unwelcome guest. "Did you come to join our merry band of travelers? Come to lend a hand moving our piano?" *Our* piano.

"I came to make sure Clara was okay."

"Oh, she's more than okay. Isn't that right?" He moved to stand behind her—step, *thump*—and wrapped his arms around her waist. He kissed her lightly on the neck and kept his eyes on Peter as he whispered in her ear, "Nice shirt." Then he let her go and said, brightly, "Join us for lunch if you'd like, Peter. But we need to get moving if we're going to get the sunset shot I've got in mind. The light changes fast out here."

Nobody moved.

Greg leaned in and kissed Clara once more, quickly this time, on her cheek. "Up to you," he said, though to which one of them she wasn't sure. "I'll meet you inside."

They watched him limp up the sidewalk and the steps then go into the restaurant.

Peter had gone rigid. "It's not just the light that changes fast," he said, so quietly she probably wouldn't have heard it if she hadn't been standing right next to him.

She sighed, but it did nothing to relieve the pressure. "It wasn't what I was expecting when I drove out here."

"No?"

"No, it sure wasn't."

Peter turned back to the gift-shop window and studied the display of rocks, crystals, Native American crafts, then rested his forehead against the glass. "Do you even like this guy?"

She sat down on the low wall bordering the covered walkway and kicked the pebbles on the concrete. She thought back over the past few days, trying to summarize the strange, accelerated evolution of her relationship with Greg. Even she found it difficult to understand how they'd gone from antagonists to lovers so quickly. *Were* they lovers? "I don't know. I'm not sure. Maybe."

"You could've at least mentioned your little tryst on the phone yesterday. It would've saved me the drive."

"I didn't ask you to come."

He spun around to face her, the physical embodiment of a roar. "Damn it, Clara! Why do you do this? Why do you just go from one half-assed relationship to another? You know, all this time I've been trying to put together a pattern, but there isn't one. You don't even have a *type*. The only thing these assholes you end up with have in common is that you don't really care about any of them. You're the car, they're the driver. You don't even give a shit where they're going. You just let them drive you around until they feel like parking somewhere, then you freak out and leave." He shook his head and set his jaw as firmly, as if he was trying to stifle a howl. "You know what your problem is? You don't want to be alone, but you don't want a relationship that means anything. You're too goddamn afraid of real intimacy. You'll let someone have your body but not your heart. What a fucking waste."

He'd never spoken to her like this, but that wasn't what burned her cheeks and made her turn away; it was the shock and shame of knowing he was right.

"So is this guy any different, or just your next distraction?"

"Fuck you," she said, her back still turned.

He opened his mouth to say something, closed it again. There was so little for them to hold on to out there, just little gasps of air.

The door to the restaurant swung open, and Greg stuck his head into the sunlight. "Clara, please come on," he called out. "You too, Peter, if you're staying. We'll lose our shot if you don't hurry up."

She raised an index finger, and Greg lifted his chin once in response and watched her and Peter for a moment before disappearing back inside.

Clara turned back to Peter, who looked down at his feet. There was a sort of grief pulsating between them in the dry desert air that she had never felt before. A sense of finality that she forced herself to acknowledge. If she went off in this unanticipated direction with Greg, if they did end up together, maybe in New York, maybe somewhere else, it wouldn't only mean leaving Bakersfield and her job at the garage. It would mean leaving Peter.

Would they stay in touch if she left? Would they ever see each other again? She imagined herself in a distant future, sorting through the mail in an apartment lobby or a foyer somewhere and finding a holiday card from Kappas Xpress Lube. Every November, Anna made everyone pose inside the open bay door for a photo and had cards printed up—with their signatures—which she sent to all their customers, even ones who hadn't been to the shop in years. In all the photos taken since Clara had started working there, Peter had made sure he was standing next to her. What would it be like to open a card next month or next year, or every year for the rest of her life, and see that empty place where she used to be?

"Greg's a direct connection to my childhood," she said. "I don't expect you to understand, but—"

"Stop. *Please*."

She took a sharp breath, blew it out slowly. Kicked a small rock. "Do you want to stay? For lunch, I mean?"

He shook his head without looking at her. "I don't think so. I'm going to head on back." The sadness in his voice was terrible. He straightened up, stretching his slumped shoulders until he reached his full, abundant height, then walked over to his car. He withdrew a bag from the trunk and handed it to her.

"I figured you didn't have many clean clothes with you, so I brought you some. Pants and a couple shirts from the shop. There's some cookies in there, too. My mom made them. Your favorites."

She closed her eyes and nodded. "Thank you," she whispered.

"Take care of yourself, Clara."

"I will."

"Clara!" Greg was standing at the door again. "Come on!"

"I'm coming!" she shouted. Then to Peter: "I'm sorry."

"Don't be. It's your life. You have to do whatever'll make you happy." He turned to go and then stopped. "It's a little embarrassing, though. Here I thought I was coming to rescue you from something and take you home."

Home. The word echoed in her mind. Where was that, anyway? A promised land that existed on the periphery of her existence, something she'd felt denied of ever since her parents died. Or that maybe she'd been denying herself. For half her life, she'd sort of assumed without thinking too much about it that home was wherever she had her piano.

Before she could figure out something to say, Peter got into his car, turned on the ignition, and pulled away. Dirt whirled up, clouding the air between them, and by the time she lifted her hand to wave he was already out of sight.

The piano felt itself being pushed up the rocky dirt foot-path that cut across a jagged mountain summit. The wind blew, hard and bitter, seeping through the slivers of space above the plinth and under the key bed and into the recesses of its case, chilling its pinblock and hammer rail and bridge. Its soundboard, already so heavy with remembered tunes, suffered several thin cracks from the dryness, enough of them to have a musical consequence. The thick steel wires conducted the cold and strained at their pins, compromising their unison. The felt on the hammers compacted so densely that if someone were to play the piano then, the sound would be as harsh as the wind.

Yet inside it vibrated with the recent memory of the piece that had been played on its lonesome keys a few nights before: Scriabin's Prelude no. 14 in E-flat Minor. Could anyone still hear it? And it had been so long since the hammers had struck its strings in that specific, energetic combination. Oh, how hard it had tried to produce the right sounds, grateful as it was to finally have been asked to once again, but it had been jostled badly out of tune and already sagged beneath the weight of more than a hundred years.

The Blüthner carried the memory of every note it had ever created. Every chord, every scale. It held on to the emotion of every prelude and sonata. It had absorbed all the grief and longing and joy and exultation expressed through its action, the impression of every touch and every tear shed at its keyboard. And it remained partially wounded, even after the passage of time, by various scratches and dents and occasional episodes of careless, angry banging.

It felt as though it were twice its actual size, a burden to itself and to others. When the wind blew at it now, it could feel its insides shifting. Instead of music it produced only small, inaudible creaks and groans. It was like a very old woman, an ancient and childless *babushka* with little left to offer.

The hands that pressed against it weren't there to play, only to push. After yet another uncomfortable and bumpy ride, it was wrestled off the dolly and positioned at the precarious rim of a cliff. *Right there,* someone yelled, *as close to the edge as you can!* Someone unwrapped it from its blankets, ran a soft cloth over its ebony case to erase the dust and fingerprints. But its brass pedals were neglected. Once gleaming and fleet, they were now as dirty as the bare feet of a prisoner being dragged to the gallows. The hands let go and stood back away from it, without anyone even noticing that the bottom beam on the bass end wasn't touching anything. All five hundred and sixty pounds—plus the invisible emotional and musical heft—was imperfectly balanced several thousand feet above the ground below. *I know how you can be free.*

More hands on its case. Its fallboard was lifted to expose the keys, and the low-angled sunlight glinted on the ivory. *Come stand here with me.* Someone touched its keys, a stroke from the bass to treble end, then a plinking of notes one after another, not music. That's not music. Let me go. There was a moment of stillness, bodies pressing close to its treble end: an arm draped on the top, a leg next to the truss. Can anyone hear me playing? Music of its own making, a record of its journey, pulsed and swirled silently inside.

Then there was movement, quick and explicit. Was it the music? The light? Then there was nobody standing close by, with only cold air pushing and voices shouting across the empty air.

I'm sorry.

The breeze collected some dust from the mountain and flung it all over. The music stopped; now there was debris inside the keyboard. The Blüthner wavered, paused, then wobbled harder when another gust pushed it off its dangerous balance.

What would it feel like to fly? To leave the summit and fall into the great void?

This is what it would feel like. Its lid and fallboard would lift at their hinges and sail away. The key sticks would rattle out of their octaves, come apart from the action, and all eighty-eight of them would float into the blue. The strings would unwind from their pins, sighing at the loosening of tension. The back-stays and untended pedals would come loose from the rod, and the bridges and frame would break the case apart. The trusses would quit the key block and plinth, and the only thing the hammers would ever strike again would be the hard, salty surface of the earth. When the soundboard finally collapsed into splinters, all the accumulated notes would finally be released, and the piano once again as weightless and pure as it had been so long ago, when it was nothing more than a melodious idea contained inside a very tall spruce tree in the mountains. *Good-bye, good-bye.*

G reg made no further mention of Peter. When she sat down at the table, he said, "The not-boyfriend won't be joining us, then?" She shook her head, to which he nodded, and that was that. It was clear that he hadn't expected Peter to stay, having already ordered and paid for just two matching meals—fried chicken strips, vodka martinis—and now he urged her to finish hers quickly so they could get on the road. She took a few bites, then slid her glass across the table to him, her appetite gone. He gulped the martini down and said, "Let's go." He drove fast, apparently trying to make up for the delay.

He put on a CD—a collection of Scriabin's études, preludes, and mazurkas—and pursed his lips as though to blow her a kiss. "Fate," he said. They passed stark-white sand dunes teeming with tourists and photographers. "Who knew a place called Death Valley would be so popular amongst the living?" he said. Clara could see a little boy sliding down a dune near the road on a flattened cardboard box, laughing while his father took his picture. She wondered if someday that photograph would replace the memory it was meant to memorialize.

A few years ago, a long-time Kappas customer became the accidental owner of a 1966 Triumph Bonneville when he successfully bid on an abandoned storage unit. The guy had never ridden a motorcycle before but wanted to, so he brought it to the shop to get it tuned up and said they were welcome to take it out if they felt like it. A beautiful machine, it was ported and polished, with high-compression pistons and rings, a welded crank, and a racing clutch. Peter and Clara opened it up on their lunch break, taking turns in front. On a straight stretch of highway heading east out of town, toward the mountains, Clara had gotten it up to 110 miles per hour with Peter holding on around her rib cage—gently, not clutching, trusting her—when they saw a police cruiser parked on the shoulder in the distance. What a rush of adrenaline! She knew that even if the cop wanted to stop them, by the time he got up to speed they'd already be miles down the road, and at exactly the same moment she decided not to slow down Peter shouted above the rushing wind into her ear, "Keep going!" like he was reading her mind. If that bike had wings, they would've been flying. They leaned forward together, shouting and laughing as they passed the policeman.

How close to home would Peter be by now? She leaned her head against the glass, pretending to nap so she wouldn't have to share her thoughts with Greg.

That evening Clara begged out of dinner, claiming she didn't feel well. And she didn't—not having had enough sleep the night before on the playa, having spent far too many hours on jarring roads and in the car in general—but mostly she wanted to be alone. Also, it had been strange at lunch, Greg ordering her food and the movers watching them with dawning awareness, then trying not to look at them at all. She didn't want to repeat that experience, at least not yet. Instead, after letting him kiss her good night, she showered and fell right asleep so she wouldn't have to think about anything at all.

Nor did she go back out with them on the following day's shoot. Greg woke her with a knock on her door. He put the coffee and muffin he'd brought her down on the nightstand, then pulled her back into bed. "I still don't feel great," she said, heading off any question of intimacy.

"Let's just lie here for a minute, then." Fully clothed, he spooned himself behind her, his breath slow and hot on her neck. After a moment she could feel him getting hard, and he wriggled closer. "Feeling any better?" he whispered.

"Maybe later," she said, and lay rigid, like she was playing dead.

Finally he sighed and pushed himself off the bed. "Well, I hate to leave you here all alone."

"I'll be fine. I just really need some more rest."

He came around to her side of the bed and kissed her. "I'll come back later to pick you up, okay? I'm going to do a couple shots nearby, and then there's only one left, the last one of the series. It'll be incredible, but it won't work if you're not there. Think you can make it to that one?"

She nodded.

"Wear that shirt I gave you, okay? I'll meet you out front at three." He kissed her again.

She lay there for a long time after he left. The coffee he'd brought her went cold, then stale.

"This is going to be great," Greg said. "Remember I said I had something better in mind for the last photo? Instead of capturing the end of my mother's life, I want to capture the beginning of ours." He ushered her into the parking lot without waiting for a response. It seemed she had been appended to Greg's vision of his future, even without a hint of her approval.

They drove along the eastern side of the valley, with sunbeams lighting the pale hair on Clara's arms and crawling into her lap through the glass. For half an hour, Greg didn't stop talking as the road gradually wound up into the mountains, cutting through low hills speckled with shrubs that looked like fat, grazing sheep. She watched the moving truck in the side mirror, noting the lack of expression on Juan and Beto's faces.

"Almost there," Greg said as they approached a turnaround where a few campers and trailers were parked. A LIMITED ACCESS sign warned visitors in a vehicle longer than twenty-five feet not to risk driving the last few steep miles to the summit. Clara could hear the truck downshift behind them as they kept going up the fifteen-degree incline and around the tight, blind hairpin turns, with only low guardrails to prevent them from falling over the edge.

On car trips, her father used to indicate on the steering wheel how far away from their destination they were. The starting point was at the nine o'clock position, the destination at the three. Asked how much farther it was, he'd point somewhere on that top semicircle—her first lesson in percentages—and she would settle back into her seat, her expectations recalibrated. Greg, incessantly tapping on the steering wheel with either thumb, probably to a tune sheltering in his head, offered no such comfort, and to her it felt unsettling, as if they were going backward.

But wasn't that what she was doing with Greg? Going backward into the past?

"Come on, come on," Greg said, urging the car to giddyup. As they neared the parking lot where the road ended, the mountains released them into a panorama of light and sky. Only two other cars were there, passengers strolling along the perimeter with their jackets flapping and their hands roofing their eyes, taking in the view.

It was at least twenty degrees colder than at the hotel, and Clara held her arms wrapped around herself, shivering inside the flimsy T-shirt as she surveyed the vista. Juan and Beto wandered over, stretching, and Greg pointed at the ridge extending off to the southeast and along the dirt footpath cutting across it that led to the actual summit of Dante's Peak. "Let's get it out there, on top of that knob." Juan cocked his head, as though calculating the possibility, and Greg said, "It's fine. Just take it easy."

According to the information plaque, they were at an elevation of 5,475 feet and directly above the white salt flats of Badwater Basin, where they'd been on Tuesday. Unencumbered views of the mountain ranges rose up all around before fading into the distance. The Funeral Mountains to the north, Coffin Peak to the southeast. With the exception of the wind and a couple trying to take their own picture—the woman holding her hat down, the man holding the camera out, both of them smiling into the sun with their backs to the valley floor below—everything was still. It looked abandoned, as though everything that could possibly happen already had, all its potential having been overtaken by the actual.

A deep sadness welled in her while she watched the movers struggle against the muscular wind to keep the piano on the dolly and Greg huddled over his equipment. After gathering what he needed, he leaned into the wind and, limping, led Juan and Beto toward the summit. "You coming, Clara?" he called over his shoulder, but she just stood there, unable to follow him any farther.

Perhaps it was a trick of the air moving so quickly at this high altitude, or maybe it was a reflex of her mind to counter the morbid silence, but Clara thought she could hear music.

She angled her head toward the sound: it was the Scriabin piece, though slow and dirgelike, not at all how she was used to hearing it. But it was so clear she could swear it was coming from the piano, as if both the instrument and the music were trying to tell her something. Yet the Blüthner was wrapped and mute, being simultaneously pushed and pulled up the rocky pass. She thought of her father sitting in his study with his fingers tented at his forehead, listening to his stereo. *We'll get you lessons; you'll learn to play the music in your own head.* If he'd lived, would he have left her mother? Would he have gone to live with Katya, and taken the piano with him? Would she have lived there too, with Greg as her stepbrother? Would she have grown up without the mortal daily fear of being alone?

For fourteen years she'd wondered where her piano had come from, what stories it carried with it when her father and his friends heaved it into her life and left it there. The various dealers and tuners and teachers had all remarked on it: how old, how solid, how moody, how nearly impossible to keep in tune. Whenever anyone played it, even an upbeat piece, it sounded melancholy. Had it also been melancholy for Greg's mother? What if every single thing ever played on her Blüthner left an afterimage, a shadow of emotion deposited somewhere inside the case, on the soundboard or the hammers or the strings? What if—just as a photo album grew thick with memories of holidays, vacations, family, and friends—the piano gained the weight of each owner and his and her music?

She thought again of how it had looked sitting on Racetrack Playa among the sailing stones, all of them in a freezeframe moment of departure with their dried-out trails curving behind them. Maybe they were so still not because they were at the mercy of the ice and wind, but because they were simply too heavy to go any farther. Was there a limit to how much her piano could absorb before it began to disintegrate under its own weight? Then she wondered, with a measure of guilt and grief, how much of her own inadequacy and unhappiness and sorrow had been imposed on it?

Before Clara, it had been Katya's. And before that, whose? A long, fanciful history unspooled in her mind as Greg and the movers slogged along the ridge to Dante's View, of the owner or series of owners and players and teachers and tuners before them. The piano's maker. The person who sounded it for the first time. The people who carved the wood and assembled the innards. The person whose imagination conceived it and held it as a thought before it came into being, ready to make the music it was destined or fated to. She pictured them as ghostly revenants, with their individual claims, trapped inside the ebony case. She, too, had been a ghost of sorts. But she didn't have to remain one.

Greg pointed at the precipice and shouted, "Right there, as close to the edge as you can!"

They maneuvered it off the dolly and unwrapped it, the shine of its thick, black finish like an aura in the low slant of light. Clara's breath caught in her throat; Scriabin's ghost prelude banged inside her temples. Her head and chest were pounding. She had kept the Blüthner as a talisman, the only souvenir that had survived her childhood, the last gift her father had given her. Yet it hadn't been a gift at all. It had been a cover story.

Death, Funeral, Coffin—it was all right there on the information sign. And she, who was always looking for signs, had failed to notice it until now. She gazed down at the valley floor, then back at the piano, swaying on the dolly, Beto and Juan shouting directions at each other about how to stabilize it. She imagined herself trudging up the difficult ridge with them on their forced march, pushing the Blüthner up and up and up like Sisyphus did to his boulder, always pushing toward something—which might feel like happiness or home—only to have it come back down again. She had suffered from the fear of loss for so long that not until now did she realize how shackled she'd become by it.

She gasped as the spell broke inside her, and she took off running toward Greg as fast as she dared on the unstable path.

He was crouched over, attaching a lens to his camera. "What is it?" he said as he stood up. "You look so happy. I'm glad, because I need you in this one. This, our first portrait together. With the piano, of course."

"I know how you can be free," she told him, panting through a grin. "Both of us, we can just let it go."

He put his hand on her shoulder, then slid it down the length of her arm to intertwine his fingers with hers. "What are you talking about? Let *what* go?"

"The piano."

"Clara, I can't even guess what you're talking about. I told you, we have a chance at a new beginning right now. We have to hurry, though. It's all set up, and I already set the timer, but we only have a little bit of time in this light." He pointed at the sheer outcrop on a ridge beyond the piano. "See that cliff? My mother died there. I want to photograph us standing together next to the piano with the cliff blurred in the background. A triumph over tragedy."

Clara didn't care if her father had loved another woman. It didn't matter. She even felt a surge of affection for him, and for her mother, too. Who knew what burdens they'd borne? What good would it do for her to blame them now for their failures in love?

"No, Greg." She pulled her hand away, but still looked into his eyes. "It's a terrible tragedy that we lost our parents. They lost each other. But we don't have to keep doing this."

"But I want to." He looked hurt, and also scared.

"You don't even know me. And I don't know you."

"We know enough."

She smiled at him. What was he really hoping to accomplish here? Why did he think he could bring anything in Death Valley back to life? Greg was, she realized, just another way the piano would always hold her down. "What I know is that for me this piano was my father. I just didn't realize that until a couple minutes ago. For you it's your mother. But it's not either of them. It's only a piano. An old, out-of-tune, impossibly heavy, sad old piano that we've loved for all the wrong reasons." She stepped toward him and gently held her bare hand to his face. He'd shaved around his goatee, and the skin was smooth and cool. "As wonderful as the other night was, it was for the wrong reasons, too. I can't be with you, Greg. I don't think we'd have a future together as much as a weird reenactment of our parents' past."

"Clara you're being ridiculous," he snapped. "What are the chances we would ever find each other? Doesn't that mean anything to you?"

"It means we have the chance to let go of all of it," she said, swiping at the horizon with her arm. "We're literally where your mother ended her life. In Death fucking Valley. So let's do what you originally planned to and push it off the cliff." Saying it out loud thrilled her, and she had to restrain herself from rushing up and ramming it off the precipice to finally watch it go, its provenance, its music evaporating in the air as it fell. Its infinite heft was tottering already, so it would only take one stiff shove with her good hand.

"No! My God, what's gotten into you?"

She thought of Katya flinging herself off the rocky precipice in the distance. What was her last thought as her feet left the ground? Was it grief that led her there, or perhaps hope? Did she find Clara's father somewhere on the descent? Did they soar away together—lighter than birds, lighter than anything—before her body hit the ground?

"I don't want to be Sisyphus anymore," she said, shrugging a smile. Her own conviction was overwhelming. "You don't have to, either."

"Please, Clara. Come stand here with me. Let me take this one picture and then we'll talk about what's next." He tried guiding her by the shoulders into position next to the treble end, but she resisted. She did, however, want to touch the piano one final time, so she went to it. Misunderstanding her actions as compliance, he said, "Good. Rest your arm on top so your cast'll be in the picture, okay? I just need to set the timer, then I'll come back here and stand on your right side."

She caressed the case, feeling the repaired dents, noticing

the countless scratches. Then she pressed a few keys and listened to the notes. Her meager call, the Blüthner's forlorn response. Then she dragged her index finger down several octaves, starting at the bass end and moving toward the treble. Then she picked out notes one by one, zigzagging down the keyboard between black keys and white. It wasn't musical, just a mechanical progression of sound from heavy to light. Scriabin's prelude, she noted, was gone. Except for that single piece that she could sometimes remember but never could play, there was no music in her head. And there never would be any. It wasn't how she was made.

Then Greg was there, pinning her against the piano. He took her good hand and squeezed. "This is perfect," he said. "Now smile." She saw the red light blinking faster and faster on the camera, which would go off at any second. "Smile!"

"No," Clara said, "I can't. I'm sorry." She wrenched herself out of his clasp and was moving out of the frame just as the shutter opened and closed, failing to capture her as Greg had hoped to. She would be just a blur, a sailing stone on the move. "Get your camera," she told him.

"What?"

"Take it off the tripod." She glanced over her shoulder at the movers. They were standing near enough that they could rush forward and pull her away from the piano. But they just stood there, only mildly interested in what was going on. It might have been her imagination, but it looked like Juan was smiling.

"Why? What are you going to do?" Nevertheless, he did as she asked, and she took this act as a sign of complicity.

She was tired of wearing other people's clothes, guarding other people's histories, being inhabited by other people's ghosts. She wasn't the first person to own the Blüthner, though she did want to be the last. "Ready?" she asked.

"No wait, Clara. Ready for what?"

She answered him by kissing her unbroken hand and placing it on the side of the piano's case, toward the back where most of the weight was. "Good-bye," she whispered. Then, with all the strength she had, she pushed.

The Blüthner went over far easily than she'd expected. It seemed to glide across the gravel beneath its feet and even, improbably, to gain a bit of altitude when it lost contact with the cliff before it began to fall. She saw it suspended briefly then called home by gravity, as she imagined all of them—Katya, her father and mother, her uncle and aunt, even Greg—releasing her. The Blüthner made no music, but it was calling out to her still: *good-bye, good-bye.*

Beside her, Greg released the shutter on his camera again and again as the piano dropped, and even after it hit the ground and bounced up, shooting splintered wood and metal guts and ivory keys out in every direction before falling back down, until it had come utterly and completely apart and lay scattered and still hundreds of feet below.

Then everything was quiet again. Greg stared at the crime scene with his mouth open for what seemed like minutes. Then he turned to Clara. Neither of them spoke, but they gazed at each other for a long moment. She stepped forward and lifted herself on her toes and kissed him softly on the cheek. He nodded, then turned to look down once more at the trail of piano parts beneath them.

Clara backed away from him and the edge of the cliff, each step bringing greater relief, lightening her by octaves. Maybe that was how it worked: the start of knowing what she did want was realizing what she didn't.

"I'm going to go. I can hitch a ride back to the hotel," she told the movers, still walking backward, feeling hopeful and brave for the first time in longer than she could recall. She could steer her own car to anywhere she wanted to go. She would ask the couple taking self-portraits, or one of the other tourists. People were friendly out there in the desert. She waved to Beto, and then to Juan, who tipped his chin and gave her a wry smile.

"Good luck, Greg," she said. But if he heard her, he didn't show any sign of it. "I hope you find what you're looking for."

She turned and started jogging across the lot as effortlessly as if she were bounding across the moon. Then she stopped to pull her cell phone out of her pocket. Still no service, but eventually there would be. She imagined him answering her call, forgiving her, saying her name—*Clara?*—and the hope that might curl it into a question. She thought of his *avgolemono* and the garage, of the Christmas photo Anna would take in a couple of weeks with her standing next to Peter. She thought of riding fast on a motorcycle with his arms wrapped around her, not knowing what was ahead of her, not caring about what was behind, and not being afraid of falling.

Die Reise

2

Acknowledgments

I am deeply grateful to the many people who contributed their expertise, insight, support, encouragement, and enthusiasm to this novel along the way.

When I was first searching for the eponymous piano's make, Larry Fine, publisher of *Acoustic & Digital Piano Buyer,* introduced me to Helga Kasimoff, a charming and expert Blüthner dealer in Los Angeles. It was she who taught me about Julius Blüthner and his "peerless golden tone" and helped me imagine the troubles Katya would encounter when trying to immigrate to the United States with her beloved piano. I can't express enough thanks to Kristina Richards of Julius Blüthner Pianofortefabrik GmbH, who gave copious, careful attention and insight to my many questions about the manufacture of Blüthner pianos and who generously checked a late draft for accuracy. Any errors having to do with this aspect of the book are mine alone. To Joe Taylor of Taylor Pianos in Oxfordshire, England, I thank you for "giving" me this specific piano. Thanks to Maciej Brogiel and Mike Ello for instruction on piano maintenance. I'm grateful to Brian Davis and my dear friend Andrew Lienhard for patiently answering my questions about classical music and piano playing in general. Many thanks to Konner Scott, who perfectly grasped the tone I was after in his composition "Die Reise."

To my beloved *sestrichka,* Irina Orlova, I send endless love and thanks for her ideas and the translations that permeate this book. Thanks to Vladimir Tabakman for sharing information about life as a Russian Jew in both the USSR and America. I owe German Gureev of the Eifman Ballet of St. Petersburg a debt of gratitude for helping me imagine how Katya's piano could be smuggled out of Russia. To Zev Yaroslavsky and Ella Frumkin, public servants and refuseniks themselves, I send endless gratitude for their insight on emigration from the former Soviet Union.

I am grateful to Peter Georgalos and his late mother, Anna Georgalos, of John's Xpress Lube, who directly inspired their fictional counterparts, and to Keith Grode of Bellaire Tire & Automotive for their patient instruction on car maintenance and terminology.

Thanks go to photographer Clayton Austin, whose "Hammers and Strings" collection inspired the Death Valley National Park setting, and also to photographer and friend Andy Biggs, who helped me imagine Greg's itinerary throughout DVNP and the images he would capture there. After I wrote the first draft, I joined John Batdorff and Staci Prince on a four-day photography workshop in DVNP. With their expert assistance, I photographed a miniature piano in all the same locations as Greg and Clara, which enabled me to make important adjustments to the story. Barry McKay told me a story about driving a 1966 Triumph Bonneville, which I incorporated as a joyful memory for Clara. Thank you.

I can remember the exact moment the idea for this book came into existence: after speaking with a book club for my novel *11 Stories,* I overheard Meredith Canada telling a friend that she'd finally found a recipient for the piano her father had given her for her seventh birthday. I was captivated when I learned that he'd died a few months afterward, and that she'd spent the next several decades trying to find a meaningful way to dispose of it. Thank you, Meredith, for granting me permission to explore that idea in what would become this novel.

I am immeasurably grateful to friends and early readers: Holly Wimberley, Summer Shaw, Ellory Pater, Cameron Dezen Hammond, Theresa Paradise, Sabrina Brannen, Caroline Leech, and especially: Charlie Baxter, Tobey Forney, Sarah Blutt, Louise Marburg, Lucy Chambers, Emma Kate Tsai, Heather Montoya, W. Perry Hall, Heidi Creed, Michelle Gradis, Lee Ann Grimes, Mimi Vance, and Jennifer Rosner for their extensive feedback. These pages are alive with your generosity. Many thanks go to Alexander Chee, Alice McDermott, and members of my workshop groups at the 2016 Tin House Summer Workshop and the 2016 Sewanee Writers' Conference for their comments and encouragement.

I am beyond fortunate to have Jesseca Salky as my agent, for her editorial insight and unflagging support. She and her team at Hannigan Salky Getzler (HSG) Agency—especially Ellen Goff and Soumeya Roberts—are wonderful. My deep and humble gratitude goes to my editor, Gary Fisketjon, for the passion he brought to this project. It's been an honor and a joy to work with him.

I can't thank my sister, Sara Huffman, enough for her love and friendship and for reminding me each time I get stuck that the only way out is through. To my parents, Cindy and John Slator, and Larry and Brenda Pullen, thank you for your love and support and for being my first fans. Sasha and Joshua are the bright lights of my life. Finally, I send gratitude and endless love to my husband, Harris, for being always at my side.

ABOUT THE AUTHOR

Chris Cander is the author of two previous novels. She lives with her husband, daughter, and son in Houston, Texas.